risen

COLE GIBSEN

risen

Entangled Publishing, LLC
2614 South Timberline Road
Suite 105, PMB 159
Fort Collins, CO 80525

Entangled Teen is an imprint of Entangled Publishing, LLC.

Visit our website at www.entangledpublishing.com.

Edited by Liz Pelletier and Candace Havens
Cover design by Erin Dameron-Hill
Interior design by Toni Kerr

ISBN: 978-1-63375-893-3
Ebook ISBN: 978-1-63375-894-0

Manufactured in the United States of America

First Edition March 2018

10 9 8 7 6 5 4 3 2 1

an imprint of Entangled Publishing LLC

To Rianne. You're my reason for all of this.

Chapter One

The big baby of a dog is freaking out again.

Jax tilts his head to the side, big ears twitching. He lifts his nose in the air, his body going rigid. After several deep sniffs, he turns to me and whimpers.

Sighing, I trudge up to him. "I swear you worry more than Aunt Rachel. Whatever you're smelling—it's probably just a deer." I stop beside the German Shepherd and search the trees for whatever has him upset. The dirt path we've been hiking is worn from deer, raccoons, and even my own nature walks, so it's far too narrow to make out much. A branch claws my leg—almost as if it's trying to pull me off the path and deeper into the woods. I consider letting it. As reclusive as Aunt Rachel is, living in a cave would feel like a vacation.

Whining, Jax whips his head around and stares at something over his shoulder.

"I thought German Shepherds were supposed to be brave," I tell him. "If Aunt Rachel bribed you with extra cookies to end our walk early, I'm going to be pissed."

He blinks.

Squinting, I follow his line of sight. I'm not surprised when nothing moves. Still, it is strange how quiet the woods are this early in the evening. There are no cicadas humming. No rodents scurrying. And no nocturnal birds flapping through the trees. The phrase *deathly silent* swirls in my head.

I can't fight the tremor of unease that pulses through me as I stand still, waiting for the slightest rustle of leaves or snap of a branch.

Nothing.

"Ugh." I give myself a mental shake. "Look at me, freaking out for no reason. You and Aunt Rachel really are rubbing off on me."

Jax nudges my hand, his eyes trained on something ahead. The cold of his nose seeps through my skin, chilling me. A low growl emits from deep inside his chest.

In the three years since I found Jax, when he was a softball-sized ball of fur in a cardboard box outside a gas station bathroom, I've never heard him growl. I didn't think he knew how. I place my hand on his back, weaving my fingers through the coarse fur to touch his skin, just so I can feel the vibration to be sure the noise is really coming from him.

The heat from his body does nothing to warm me. "Dork," I mutter. "When we get back, you're getting a drop of Aunt Rachel's lavender oil to calm your furry butt down. You're acting ridiculous." I clench the opening of my knitted cardigan closed. The mustard yellow sweater was last year's handmade Christmas present from Aunt Rachel. It's about a size too large, and drapes over my small frame, making it one of my most comfortable—and favorite— pieces of clothing. Wisps of cold breeze wind through the gaps of yarn and rake across my arms. I shudder. "Let's go." I tug gently on Jax's faded blue collar.

He doesn't budge. Instead, his lip ripples, revealing his long, white clenched teeth.

Or not.

"Maybe it's time to get your ears checked." I give a nervous chuckle.

Jax's eyes are fixated on something I can't make out. There are no bears in these woods. But there are hikers. Maybe someone wandered away from a trail. "Hello?" I call out. "Anyone there?"

The silence, growing heavier by the second, is the only thing that answers.

I let out a long breath to relieve the pressure of my tightening chest. A chill ripples across my skin. I grab Jax's collar and tug hard in the opposite direction. "This is dumb," I tell him. "We're not going to stay out here and play *Panic Attack in the Woods.* Nobody wins that game." I tug his collar, forcing him to trudge along with me.

He snorts his frustration, casting several glances over his shoulder as we resume the path home.

As we get closer to the cabin, I touch the prepaid smartphone tucked in my pocket to make sure it's lying flat so my aunt won't spot it. A fight between Jax and a woodland creature would be the end to my solo "nature hikes" aka "internet time." Without some connection to the outside world, I'd likely join a pyramid scheme, just so I could socialize with people my own age. Lipstick and leggings, anyone?

We emerge from the path into a small clearing. Our faded, one-bedroom cabin sits beside what was once a gravel road, but is now mostly dirt with a few scattered rocks. Aunt Rachel gave me the bedroom when we moved in ten years ago. She sleeps on the lumpy futon in the corner. A bedroom would have been wasted on her, anyway, as she barely sleeps. Each morning she's up making her soaps and lotions before the sun rises, and every night she's tucked into a corner of the futon reading by candlelight when I can fight sleep no longer.

Jax's gaze is still locked on some faraway point through the trees when I drag him inside. Once I shut the door, the dog digs his nose into the crack between the door and frame and chuffs.

Our cabin is three rooms: a bedroom, a bathroom, and an open area that is a divided kitchen and living room. Aunt Rachel has tried her best to make it homey with her vases of wildflowers, homemade curtains, and hand-crocheted rugs. But even with these touches, I can't help but feel that I'm entering a different planet when I walk through the door—one the real world can't penetrate. And it's the real world—not this handmade, organic, granola isolation chamber I live in—that I want to be a part of.

"Hey sweetie." Aunt Rachel smiles, relief visible in her eyes, before she turns her attention to the pots on the stove. The beads knotted in her blond dreadlocks click together as she moves. It's the hairstyle she's worn for as long as I can remember, tied back with the same faded blue handkerchief, while she listens to the same Phish album on the same CD player.

The sameness wraps around me like a hot wool

blanket—itchy and suffocating. I dig my nails into my palms in an attempt to keep from screaming. This *cannot* be my life.

The smell of Aunt Rachel's latest batch of soap wafts over to me. *Ugh. Eau de outdoor music festival.* I wrinkle my nose. "God, I hate patchouli."

She shrugs. *"I* love it. And since mosquitos hate it, it's a win-win in my book."

I flop onto the kitchen chair. Its crooked legs wobble beneath me. I give an inward sigh. The wobbly chair legs, sun-faded curtains, the smells of vanilla and patchouli permeating the air, and the Texas-shaped hole in the linoleum floor—these things are all part of the unchanging, untouchable loop that is my life. And while these things are all I know, the internet has proven there is so much more—shopping malls, amusement parks, museums, and zoos. Those are only a couple of things I want to see.

I touch the phone tucked inside my pocket. Just knowing it's there—my key to the outside—loosens the ever-tightening knots inside my chest.

Stirring the soap, Aunt Rachel asks, "How was your walk?"

"It was okay, I guess." I pick up one of the soap molds strewn across the table—a star—and trace my fingers along the edges. Even the shapes she makes her soap never change.

Aunt Rachel stops stirring long enough to frown at me. She turns the stove burner on low and sets the spoon across the lip of the pot. After wiping her fingers on her apron, she walks over to me, long skirt tangling between her legs as she moves. Her eyes narrow. "Okay, what's eating you?

If it's that time of the month, I have an oil that can help with the PMS."

"Oh God." I make a face. "I'm not on my *period,* okay? I'm just—bored. I walk the same path *every day.* I know all the trees by heart." I pause. "Maybe I could take the truck to one of the public hiking trails? Just for a change of scenery."

"No." There's no hesitation in her answer. "Public or not, hiking alone is incredibly dangerous. That's why I only want you using the trails surrounding the cabin. If you're so bored, I've invited you to my knitting circle a hundred times. Marnie's daughter is there and she's your age."

"The girl who pretends her knitting needles are making out? Uh, no thanks. Jax is better company."

At the sound of his name, Jax looks away from the door, only to ram his nose back in the crack a second later.

Aunt Rachel rolls her eyes. "She's a very sweet girl." When I don't respond, she slices a hand through the air. "You're still not allowed to walk the public trails. If something were to happen—"

"Nothing *ever* happens," I cut in. "And if you're so worried about it, I could get a cell phone."

She jerks back as if I had suggested using a puppy as a soccer ball. "Absolutely not. Cell phones are trackable. I've explained this to you a thousand times."

"You've explained it, but it doesn't make sense." Frustration builds inside me, forcing me to my feet. I stand so suddenly, the stupid wobbly chair falls over. It doesn't break, and for some reason, this makes me sad. I need one dumb thing to change, even if it's a chair. "It's not like we're criminals, or that we're hiding from anyone. I say, let them track me."

Aunt Rachel presses her lips together. She grabs one of the many beaded bracelets on her wrists and twists it around and around. "You have no idea what you're talking about."

I inhale sharply and let it out in a long, slow whoosh. From the moment I began researching colleges on the computer at the library, I knew this was a conversation I needed to have. But the words jumble into knots. "I'll be eighteen in a couple months."

My aunt opens her mouth, as if she might argue about my age, too. Finally, her shoulders sag and she looks up at the ceiling. "Shit," she mumbles. I wonder if she's been expecting this moment as well. "I know you're not a child anymore, Charlie, but there are things you don't understand. It's just—"

"I can't stay here forever," I cut her off. "I want to go to college."

She's quiet for several heartbeats before sucking in a deep breath. "Okay. We can talk about this rationally." She picks up the fallen chair and slowly lowers herself onto it. Swallowing hard, she smooths her skirt across her legs. "There's a great community college thirty miles away. You can commute."

What she really means is, *You can stay here with me, in these woods, making smelly soaps and lotions until we both die, alone, in this stupid cabin with the ugly curtains.*

As much as I love her, I can't do it. This forest and this cabin are a puzzle of which I'm a piece that doesn't fit. There's something unseen, something *more* pulling me, like rope tied around my heart. I need to see where it will lead.

Clearing my throat, I lick my lips. If I don't do this now, I know I'll lose my nerve. "I've applied to several universities."

Her face pales. "But there are no universities nearby."

"I know." I pick at my thumbnail. "That's—that's kind of the point."

"Oh." Her face crumples, and for one terrifying moment I'm sure she's going to cry. Her fingers twist into the folds of her skirt, knuckles white, like she's desperate for something to hold on to.

I hold my breath, watching as the tears well in her eyes. I don't know what I expected. Maybe anger, maybe a fight, but not this. This is infinitely worse. "I'm sorry," I say automatically. But I'm not sure what I'm sorry for. Wanting more? Is that such a bad thing?

Aunt Rachel slumps against the chair like a deflating balloon. "Sweet girl." She holds out a hand.

I take it without hesitation. For the first time since my walk, when the cold seeped into my veins, I feel a flicker of warmth.

She squeezes my fingers with one hand. With the other, she dabs at her eyes with the corner of her apron. "You have nothing to be sorry for. *I'm* the one who should be sorry."

I can only blink. Of all the possible outcomes to happen, this is the strangest.

Aunt Rachel traces a finger along the woven bracelet on my wrist. It's identical to the bracelet on her own arm. We made them together when I was fourteen. "I know you feel trapped, Charlie. I never wanted that for you. I never wanted this." She lets go of my arm and motions around the cabin. She swallows several times before she releases me.

"What are you talking about?" I ask.

"Did you know I used to travel?"

I shake my head.

She smiles, and her eyes get the faraway look of someone falling into their memories. "I've been to Germany, Italy, France, Spain, and Ireland. I'd planned to visit every country on the globe. But then—"

I don't need her to finish. Guilt winds an angry fist into my gut. *I'm the reason she stopped traveling. I'm the reason for this.* "My parents died in the car accident," I finish for her.

She jerks her head back, eyes wide. "Don't say it like that, Charlie. I wanted to protect you." She tugs on the edge of my cardigan, pulling me toward her. "I love you. You're the most important thing in my life, do you understand?"

There's a desperation in her eyes that tightens my throat. Swallowing hard, I nod.

She lets go of me with a sigh. "Maybe I took it too far." She sweeps her dreadlocks over her shoulder and twists them tightly. "All I've ever wanted was to keep you safe."

Safe. The word spirals, cold and slippery, down my spine. "What are you so afraid of?"

She opens her mouth only to shut it again.

Jax growls.

We turn as he claws at the door.

"The only thing there *is* to be afraid of," she whispers. "The *monsters.*"

Chapter
Two

"Monsters?" A laugh bubbles up my throat.

Aunt Rachel opens her mouth when Jax lets out a growl that reverberates throughout the cabin. With his nose still in the crack of the front door, the German Shepherd's lips curl back, revealing his tightly clenched teeth.

Aunt Rachel pales. "Jax?"

He keeps his nose pressed to the door.

"Don't worry about him." I wave dismissively. "He picked up the scent of an animal in the woods, and he's been acting weird ever since."

Aunt Rachel whips her head around, beads clacking like rainfall. "What kind of animal?"

"I don't know." I shrug. "I didn't see anything."

She reaches for me, gripping my shoulders so tightly it borders on pain. A small cry escapes my throat.

"The birds." She gives me a small shake. "What were the birds doing?"

"The birds?" Fear twists through my

ribs before pulling tight with a sharp snap. "What are you talking about?"

"Please, Charlie, think." She gives my shoulders another jerk. "Were the birds chirping at all? What were they doing?"

I try to pull free from her grip, but her fingers hold me like a vice. "Nothing. They were quiet. The entire forest was quiet."

Aunt Rachel's lips part and she releases me. "Shit."

"Aunt Rachel?" I rub my sore shoulders. This is another time I wish we had the internet so I could look up the symptoms of a stroke.

"After all these years—they found me."

"Who found you?"

"The monsters." She spins a small circle, her eyes taking in every inch of the cabin, like she's expecting a creature to jump out at any moment. "We don't have much time."

What the hell is going on? Could she have accidentally poisoned herself with one of her soap ingredients? Maybe she drank some bad wine? My knees wobble as I stand. "Are you feeling okay? You're kind of scaring me."

Jax's growls deepen.

Aunt Rachel licks her lips, her chest heaving from her shallow breaths. "You're my niece. You need to remember that."

My heart pounds against my chest, rattling my ribs. "Of course, I'm your niece."

"As long as they think that, they'll leave you alone. It's me they want." Her eyes are wild, the pupils nothing more than black pinpricks.

"What does that mean, *as long as they think that*?"

She ignores the question and instead whirls around, pulls open a kitchen drawer, and rummages through it with shaking fingers. "Shit. Shit. Shit," she utters over and over. "I was so stupid to think we could stay hidden. We stayed in one spot for too long. This is all my fault."

I take a step toward her only to stop. I'm afraid to touch her. The wildness rolls off of her in waves so thick they prickle against my skin. Is she losing her mind? Am I?

"Here we go." She withdraws a small blue glass bottle like the ones that hold our essential oils. Unlike the oils, this one is not labeled.

I inch away. "What is that?"

"My own special blend." She unscrews the lid and dips a dropper into the bottle. "Dogwood, the cursed tree, and Palo Santo, the blessed tree. Here, put it on your pulse points." She snatches my wrist and squeezes three drops onto my skin. "Rub it in good. It doesn't take much."

The mixture burns, but I do as I'm told. "What's this for?"

Ignoring me, she drops oil onto her own wrists, rubbing them together, along with the back of her neck.

"What's going on?" I ask again.

She shoves the bottle into my hand, curling my fingers around it. "Keep this on you at all times. They don't like the taste."

"The *taste*?" The last word comes out a squeak. I shove the bottle into my pocket where it rests beside the phone. Is this my fault? Did I do this to her when I said I wanted to leave? I nearly have my phone pulled out of my pocket to call 9-1-1 when I hear tires crunching over gravel.

Aunt Rachel's face pales to the color of a full moon. "We're too late. They're here."

Something sour burns up my throat. "*Who* is here?"

"The monsters." She snatches the worn baseball bat she keeps beside the stove. She told me it was for wild animals. Now I'm not so sure. "Stay behind me, Charlie. If you run, that will only make it worse. They get off on the chase." A strange sound, something between a whimper and sob, escapes her throat. "I didn't want this. I never wanted this."

I can't stand it. I pull the phone out of my pocket.

Aunt Rachel recoils like it's a viper poised to strike. "Where did you get that?"

"At the gas station. I'm calling the police."

"How could you—never mind." She shakes her head. "The police can't help. No one can."

The car's engine turns off. The silence that follows is so heavy, for a moment I wonder if I've fallen deaf. Then Jax lets out a series of sharp barks. I flinch at each one.

The knock at the door is much softer than what I'd expect from a monster. Jax lowers his head, teeth bared in a snarl. His normally dark eyes are wide and bloodshot. A line of drool hangs from his lips.

Aunt Rachel raises the bat. "Remember, *don't run*."

I dial 9-1-1. A message appears on the screen to let me know the call failed. "Shit," I mutter.

Aunt Rachel glances at me and then the phone. "It would have been pointless, anyway."

"Rachel Keegan?" A man calls from outside the door. "We know you're in there." There's a lilt to his voice, betraying a smile.

Aunt Rachel snatches me by the arm and shoves me behind her with enough force to nearly knock me over. "Do *not* touch that door," she hisses.

The man clucks. "Don't be like that, Rachel. We have, after all, missed you so much all these years. Who do you have in there with you? I should say we'd like to meet them as well."

Before I can wonder how it was he was able to hear us, the door handle jiggles.

Aunt Rachel inhales sharply and raises the bat higher. A line of hair has risen from the top of Jax's skull all the way to the base of his tail. His growls sharpen.

"Please contain your animal, Rachel," another man calls out, "or there will be consequences."

"What is going on?" Fear rockets along every nerve in my body, frying them to a crisp.

"Hush," she spits at me.

"Pity," the first man says. "This could have gone so easily. But as you wish."

Aunt Rachel grabs my arm and squeezes until pain shoots up my shoulder. "Remember, do *not* run. They love the chase."

Before I can ask her what she's talking about, an ear-shattering crash sends me staggering backward. Aunt Rachel releases me and I scream—or at least I think I do. Splintering wood and shattering glass blow inward, as if a truck had rammed through the front door. But when the rubble settles, instead of a car, two men stand in the hole that was once our door. The night sky illuminates their tall frames.

"Jax?" I twist around, searching for my dog. I spot his legs from beneath a large chunk of what's left of our door. My gut wrenches. "Jax!" I jerk forward only to be stopped by my aunt.

"No sudden movements," she whispers in my ear.

Dusting themselves off, both men tilt their heads, studying me in a way that makes my insides crawl. Even afraid, I can't help but notice the blistering beauty of their chiseled jaws and angled noses. They're both so beautiful, in fact, the word *unnatural* comes to mind, raising the hairs along my neck.

"Rachel, I can't tell you how good it is to see you." The first man steps carefully over the splintered wood. There's a hint of a smile on his lips. He adjusts the leather gloves on his hands, even though it's not nearly cool enough out to need them. He wears a dark, tailored suit, with a crisp navy tie, and spotless shoes. The black lenses of his sunglasses are every bit as dark as his hair.

"What do you want?" my aunt snarls, pushing me farther behind her, forcing me to peer over her shoulder.

The man grins. "Don't be coy. Where is the boy?"

"Dead," she practically spits. "You know this. You monsters killed him."

Killed? My fear is a solid ball of ice wedged inside my ribs. I bring a hand to my chest as if I might dig it out. Aunt Rachel told me her son died when he was a baby from sudden infant death syndrome. What else did she lie about?

The second man steps forward and sweeps his gaze around the cabin. His dark skin contrasts against the light gray of his suit. The overhead light reflects off his shaved head and black sunglasses. He sniffs loudly and wrinkles his nose. "Despite the disgusting odor permeating place, I don't smell anyone else."

"Well, that's a pity," the first man says, clasping his hands in front of him. "Still, the Queen expects us to be thorough.

Rachel, you're coming with us."

"What?" I snake my arm through my aunt's. "No. You're not taking her anywhere."

Removing my hand, Aunt Rachel clutches my wrist so tightly I wince. There's no mistaking the warning in her grip.

"Who is the girl?" The dark-skinned man asks.

"My niece." Aunt Rachel edges in front of me, almost as if she's trying to shield me from view. "She has nothing to do with this."

The first man continues to study me. Even though I can't see his eyes behind the dark lenses of his glasses, I can feel them slide along my body, taking in every inch. It's all I can do not to shudder. Finally, he shakes his head. "The girl is not important." He walks forward and takes Aunt Rachel's chin in his hand. "This is our prize."

She squeezes her eyes shut.

"The queen is really looking forward to seeing you again, Rachel. It was impolite to leave without saying goodbye." He raises his sunglasses, revealing blue-gray eyes the color of ice. "Look at me, Rachel."

"No." She struggles in his grip, his fingers digging into her skin.

"Maybe you would prefer if I spoke privately with your niece?" The man smiles at me, revealing long pointed fangs like those belonging to a snake.

Yelping, I scuttle backward. My heart ricochets against my sternum. "What—What are you?"

Aunt Rachel's eyes fly open. "Leave her alone."

"Then look at me."

"Please." Aunt Rachel whimpers. The sound of it digs claws into my chest. "Don't do this in front of her."

"Do what?" I press myself against the wall, fingernails digging into the wood. "What's going on?"

The man ignores me. "Sorry, Rachel, you don't get to make the rules." He squeezes her face until the skin beneath his fingers turns white. She gasps. "Look at me."

I should run to her. I should stop this. But fear snakes around my legs and keeps me rooted to the floor.

Aunt Rachel meets my gaze. The desperation in her eyes carries a message I can't make out. Slowly she turns away and looks up at the man. He stares at her for several heartbeats. Her face slackens, her shoulders slump, and her eyelids droop.

"There we go," he coos. "Now, you're going to drop that silly weapon of yours and come along without a fight. Is that understood?"

The bat falls to the floor with a thump.

My pulse echoes like thunder inside my head. "Aunt Rachel." I reach out and tug on her arm. "Aunt Rachel, look at me."

She doesn't move.

"Time to go." The man snaps his fingers.

Wordlessly, my aunt heads for the door. Her head sways on her neck as if she drank one too many glasses of strawberry wine.

"No!" I dig my heels against the floor and try to anchor her in place. "What's wrong with you?" My voice cracks as the sob building in my chest threatens to break free.

She doesn't look at me and yanks her arm from my grasp.

"Don't leave me." I reach for her, only to be stopped when the man grabs my neck. His fingers dig into my skin, squeezing hard enough that fire burns in my throat and black spots pepper my vision. I cough.

"Now, now." He pulls me toward him, his eyes of ice penetrating my own. "I want you to stand still and be a good girl."

He flings me backward. My shoulder hits the wall first, followed by my head. The sound of a crack fills my skull as I slide to the floor. Lightning bolts of pain jolt through my body. I cough several times as air returns to my lungs. "You're not taking my aunt." Fighting the dark curtains of unconsciousness that threaten to close, I crawl forward and grab the discarded bat.

"Interesting," the second man says, tilting his head. "The girl doesn't obey. Why wasn't she compelled?"

The first man shrugs. "Rachel loves her concoctions. Maybe she crafted something to ward compulsion." With arms folded, he watches me as I struggle to stand.

I have no idea what they're talking about and I don't care. I raise the bat and, with a scream, I bring the weapon down on the man's shoulder.

He doesn't flinch, even though shockwaves from the impact roll down my arm. "You're beginning to annoy me, girl." He rips the bat out of my hands. The wood snaps and splinters in his clutched fists.

With a yelp, I stumble backward. *It's not real. It can't be.* "You drugged us." It's the only thing that explains Aunt Rachel's behavior and my hallucinations.

He laughs, his fangs gleaming. "Oh, poor, sweet child. Has she not told you anything?"

Monsters. Aunt Rachel's earlier warning blasts through my head. I scramble backward until my spine meets the wall.

The man waves a hand over his shoulder. "Sebastian, come."

A third figure appears in the doorway. He looks like one of the cologne models in the gas station fashion magazines I leaf through. His nose is sloped and slightly pinched at the tip. The angle of his jawline is sharp enough to cut bread. He's younger than the other two, maybe in his early twenties to their forties. "Yes, Frederick?" His wavy chocolate-brown hair is swept away from his forehead, curling at the edges of his shirt collar.

"We're taking Rachel to the Queen. I want you to stay behind and search the cabin. Rachel claims the boy is dead. See if you can find evidence to prove or disprove the claim."

Sebastian pulls his sunglasses off and tucks them into the pocket of his jacket. He turns his icy-blue gaze on me. Arching an eyebrow, he asks, "What about the girl?"

Frederick shrugs. "She has no value. Eat her. Kill her. I don't care. Just make sure she's disposed of."

chapter Three

My breath catches in my throat. *I'm seventeen, I've barely left these stupid woods, and now I'm going to die in them.*

Sebastian's eyes narrow. "I didn't agree to a disposal."

"You don't have to. Consider it an order." Frederick slides his glasses back into place. "Meet us in St. Louis when you are through."

Studying me, Sebastian frowns. "I'll take care of it."

My heart leaps inside my throat, threatening to choke me. This has to be a nightmare. *Wake up, Charlie. Wake up. Wake up. Wake up.*

With my shoulders pressed flat against the door, I don't move as the first two men leave, taking my aunt with them. Minutes later, car doors slam and an engine roars to life.

Studying me, Sebastian removes his suit jacket and drapes it across the couch. "What's your name?"

I clamp my mouth shut. Fear laces through my ribs. With as much as they've taken—my dog's life and my aunt—I'm not about to give them one more damn thing.

"All right." Sighing, he perches on the arm of the couch. "Maybe I can guess. Sarah? Michelle? Olivia? Am I getting warmer?"

"Screw you."

"Interesting name," he says, revealing his own set of sharp fangs. My stomach lurches. "Is that German?" There's a bit of humor in his eyes, a flash of humanity that the other men didn't have. I wonder if I can convince him not to kill me. Better yet, maybe I can convince Jax to eat him.

I turn toward the door, only Jax's feet no longer protrude from the pile of rubble. "My dog." Whipping around, my fingers clench into fists. "What the hell did you do with my dog?"

He looks to the rubble and shrugs. "What would I want with a disgusting animal? Your dog ran off."

"No. Jax would never go anywhere without me." I start for the door, only to have him snatch me by the arm and whirl me around. My heart leaps into my throat.

"It doesn't matter what you believe." There's a gleam in his eye that sends my pulse into a frenzy. "You're not leaving this cabin unless I say so."

"I'd like to see you stop me." I slam a fist against his chest with enough force to make me wince.

Sebastian doesn't budge. He sighs. "It's almost cute how you think you stand a chance, but you're only wasting my time." With his hand still clamped on my arm, he drags me across the room and thrusts me on the sofa. "Sit."

I stand. "No."

His eyes narrow. "You're starting to annoy me."

"I don't see how that's my problem."

"I'm happy to show you." Looking around, he snags one of Aunt Rachel's handkerchiefs off the top of a nearby laundry basket. "Hands behind your back."

I fight to keep my fear from showing on my face. "Screw you."

He snags my wrist and wrenches it behind my back. Even as I struggle, he easily grabs my other arm and ties them together so tight, I can feel the blood pooling in my fingertips. After pushing me onto the couch, he takes a scarf from the same basket and winds it around my feet.

"Now," he says, standing, "let's try this again. *Sit*."

I struggle to pull my tingling hands apart, but the handkerchief doesn't budge. "So how are you going to do it?" Tears well in my eyes. "Stab me? Shoot me?" Other worse ways that I'm too scared to speak out loud cross my mind, and I shudder.

He stares at me for several heartbeats before shaking his head. "You humans are all so afraid to die. You spend your entire lives dreading it—fighting it. If only you would learn to embrace death for the gift it is, you would have nothing to fear."

"Easy to say when you're not the one tied up."

"Maybe." He inclines his head. "Can I be honest with you?"

I glare at him.

"Thank you." He chuckles. "I don't really enjoy killing like the rest of them. It's messy and I just don't understand the thrill the others get."

The world shifts beneath me, leaving me dizzy. "Is that what those men are going to do to my aunt?" My voice trembles.

"Truthfully?" He rakes his fingers through his hair. It's such a human action that I almost forget he's a monster. "I don't know. I try to avoid court politics."

"Court?"

He shakes his head. "Nothing you need to worry about." He turns a small circle, taking in the room. He frowns. "What I do need from you is the proof the Queen is looking for—proof that your aunt's son is dead."

I snort. "If she had a son, don't you think I would know about it? There is no *proof* of anything here."

"Maybe." He tilts his head. "Maybe not." He pulls open a nearby closet, pulls the coats off hangers, and throws them onto the floor. Next, he runs his hands across the top shelf. "If you did know something, I'd be willing to make a deal with you in exchange."

I shift on the sofa, no longer able to feel my fingers. "What kind of deal?"

He stops rummaging. "Your life in exchange for information about your cousin's whereabouts."

"I already told you, there is no information. My cousin died when he was a baby. End of story."

"We'll see." He lifts a cardboard box off the shelf and dumps wool hats and gloves onto the floor. He kicks them aside and grunts. "This is going to take a while."

"Great," I mutter. Leaning against the couch, I squeeze my eyes closed. This can't be happening. It's too crazy. A bad dream is the only thing that makes sense. All I have to do is open my eyes, and Aunt Rachel will be at the stove pouring a new batch of soap into molds. Jax will be curled up on the rug by her feet, snoring softly.

When I open my eyes, nothing's changed. Aunt Rachel

is gone. Jax is gone. And I'm here, in my broken cabin, with a monster.

Sebastian opens the bi-fold pantry doors. He picks up a bag of chips, sniffs, winces, and quickly sets them aside.

I lean back against the cushions as best I'm able with my hands tied behind my back. My shoulders throb from the strain. I wonder if Aunt Rachel is just as scared as I am. She used to hum a song when I was little and heard something bump outside my window. It's the same song I hum now, just so I can feel like a part of her is still with me.

Sebastian jerks upright. "What is that?" He whirls around, his eyes narrowed.

I stop humming.

"No." He shakes his head. Returning a jar of tomato sauce to the pantry, he moves toward me. "That song—it's familiar. What is it?"

"I don't know." I shake my head. "My aunt used to hum it when I was little."

"Interesting. I don't remember anything of *before*. But this song—I know it." His brow creases. "I'm just not sure how. Do you know the name?"

"No. Aunt Rachel never said. It was just something she did when I was upset."

Exhaling loudly, he sits in the chair across from me, resting his elbows on his knees. "Scaring you was never my intention."

"Yeah, well," I shift in my restraints, "you're not really great at making friends."

He cracks a smile. "I have no desire to make friends."

"That's good, because you suck at it. I've only known you for a short while, and I hate you."

He laughs. "Fair enough. But I'm afraid you're stuck with me until I find something. The Queen won't like it if I return empty-handed."

"Sucks for you, because there's nothing here."

"No." His eyes flash. "That would suck for *both* of us."

His words settle like a ball of ice inside my stomach. I shift uncomfortably.

"Where would someone hide something of value in this hovel?" Sebastian stands, his gaze sweeping over the room, before settling on the bookcase. "Is that your violin?"

I follow his stare to the case on the bottom shelf. "Yes."

He retrieves the case and flicks open the latches. He withdraws the instrument by the neck, turning it over in his hands. "You know how to play?"

"No. It's for decoration."

He scowls at me.

I roll my eyes. "I've taken lessons through the home-school co-op since I was four. I can play."

He gets that faraway look of someone who's fallen into a memory. "The violin— That song you were humming— could you play it? Maybe then I could remember where I've heard it."

As much as I despise him, there's not a damn thing I want to do for him. But on the other hand, agreeing would be my ticket out of my binds. I shrug. "Sure. You have to untie me."

He hesitates. "I will, but you have to promise not to run. I *will* catch you, and it won't be pretty."

"Fine."

He sets my violin aside and kneels in front of me. He unwinds the scarf from my ankles first. Next, he motions me to the side with a jut of his chin, and unties my wrists.

With my hands free, I roll my shoulders several times to loosen the knots.

Sebastian picks up my violin and holds it out to me. "Remember, do not run."

Scowling, I snatch the instrument from him. "This is a waste of time."

"Maybe."

With a huff, I withdraw my bow from the case and wind the horse hair tight. Placing the violin beneath my chin, I run the bow across the strings and make minor adjustments to the pegs. Nearly every night for the last thirteen years, I would practice the violin while Aunt Rachel watched, perched on the couch with a glass of wine pinched between her knees.

That empty spot on the couch brings a lump to my throat.

Closing my eyes, I rest the violin beneath my chin, poise my fingers above the neck, and draw the bow across the strings. I don't need the notes. Aunt Rachel's song has long woven itself into my heart. Bringing forth the melody feels as natural as exhaling a breath—releasing something that was long inside of me.

Maybe it's because I've been so afraid up until this point, but I surrender to the music. I become the notes drifting from my fingers, filling the cabin and spilling out into the night. It's only in this moment, alone in the darkness inside my head, that I finally feel safe.

The song ends and I keep my eyes closed as the pieces of myself fall back into place. When I do open them, Sebastian sits on the arm of the love seat, an unreadable expression on his face.

I set the violin aside and loosen the bow.

"You play beautifully," he says, his voice lower than before.

While zipping my violin back into the case, I shrug. I'm not so pathetic I'll thank my aunt's kidnapper for a compliment.

"That was *exactly* how I remember the song—played on a violin."

I straighten. "So?"

"*So,*" he stands, "it's the only memory I have from before."

I shake my head. "I don't understand."

"When I was human," he explains. "And you don't know the name of the song?"

"I already told you I don't. It's just something my aunt used to hum." I catch myself. "*Hums.* It's something she will continue humming." I lock eyes with him, daring him to argue. "Because I will save her."

The look he gives me is full of pity. "You know that's not going to happen, right? The most you can hope for is your own survival—and that's providing you help me."

My fingers tighten into fists. "You're wrong."

He laughs. "If that's true, what is your plan?"

I open my mouth to answer, but the words don't come. I have nothing.

He shakes his head. "You can't fight them. No one can."

Outside the cabin, off in the distance, a dog barks. My heart stills. *Jax!*

Sebastian turns toward the sound.

New plan! a voice inside my head screams.

Even as my veins flood with relief for my poor dog, I realize this is the only shot I have. I push off the wall and launch myself toward the open door with every ounce of strength I can muster. Despite Aunt Rachel's repeated warnings, I do the one thing she told me not to do.

I run.

Chapter
Four

My eyes don't immediately adjust to the darkness of night, and I sprint straight into a sticker bush. Shielding my eyes, I push through, even as the thorns rake across my arms and legs and rip the hair from my top knot.

The forest, usually alive with nocturnal activity, is hushed. The only sounds are my pounding footsteps and gasping breaths. It's too dark, and I'm running too recklessly to stay on the path, so I create my own, tearing through brush and branches. I fight for my footing when my feet sink into the damp mud hidden beneath leaves.

My heart is a loose thing that slams against my ribs, no longer anchored inside me as I run for minutes, or maybe hours. Fear devours all sense of time. I'm not sure how much distance I've gained when a cramp rockets up my torso. The pain pierces like needles beneath my ribs, forcing me to slow my gait to a near-hobble as I clutch my side. I don't dare stop.

Moving slower gives my eyes time to adjust to the night, but it does little good.

Nothing looks familiar. An endless line of trees and brush stretches before me, fading into the dark.

I stop to listen. The small hairs on my neck and arms stand. The normal sounds of the forests are muted. I clutch my sweater tightly to ward off the chill that has nothing to do with the temperature. *I'm safe,* I try to convince myself. But safe no longer feels like a word that exists on the same planet as me.

A force slams into me from behind. I cry out as I'm thrown to the ground, face pressed against soft mud and slimy leaves. Before I can scream, a hand clamps over my mouth, fingers digging into my flesh.

"Don't yell." It's Sebastian's voice, or at least I think it is. The words are more growl than human. He flings me onto my back, kneeling over me on bended knee.

Despite his warning, the moment I see his face, a scream bubbles up, only to be smothered by his fingers.

Sebastian's pupils have dilated, giving his eyes the hollow appearance of empty sockets. His lips are curled in a snarl. It could be my imagination, but his fangs appear larger and sharper, the points gleaming under the moon.

He swallows hard. "I'm trying really hard not to kill you right now. But when you run and, even worse, scream, I lose a bit of control. Can't be helped." His voice is a strange mix of gravel and nails.

I whimper.

His hand moves from my mouth to the back of my head. He hoists me up by my hair and jerks my head to the side, exposing my neck. He brings his nose to my throat and inhales deeply. His breath is hot on my neck. "She made you wear that disgusting oil," he growls. "Even it can't help you if you don't stop making those noises. It's taking every ounce of strength I have not to eat you."

"No," I whisper. I don't want to die among the rotting leaves and decaying logs. I don't want to be another dead thing disappearing into the forest floor. "No." I place my palm against his cheek to push him away. The second my skin connects with his, a series of sparks leap from my fingertips.

I cry out at the same time Sebastian grunts. He releases me, both of us falling apart onto the soft earth.

"What did you do?" he asks, blinking. The black bleeds from his eyes, returning them to their previous silver.

"What did *you* do?" I say, panting.

"That wasn't me." He stands and takes several steps away, as if I'm the one to be feared. His watches me with wide eyes, chest heaving. "So I'm going to ask again, what did you do?"

I stand as well. "Nothing."

"Not nothing." His voice carries the edge of panic. "First the song, and now this. I saw things—flashes—memories?" He runs his fingers through his hair. "I don't know."

I take a step backward.

"Don't do that." His head snaps up. "If you run, it triggers the bloodlust. Besides, you're not going anywhere until you tell me what the hell is going on."

"I don't know."

He's quiet for a moment before saying, "You have to do it again." He doesn't wait for me to answer before striding toward me.

"What?" Trembling, I clamber away until my spine bumps into a tree. I dig my fingers into the bark, hoping to somehow anchor myself back into the real world instead of this nightmare I've fallen into.

"Who *are* you?" He rakes his fingers through his tangled hair. "How do you know these things?"

"I've already told you, I don't know *anything*."

"Do it again." He grabs my hand and places it against his face. His skin is soft and warm beneath my fingers. "I'm sorry for scaring you earlier." There is a hint of desperation in his voice. "I mean, it's actually your fault because you ran. But none of that matters, because you did something just now, and I need you to do it again."

"I'm sorry," I say, my hand resting on his face. "I don't know what I did or how I did it."

He grabs my wrist with his other hand. "Maybe if you just concentrate." He hesitates, face softening. "Please."

There's that humanity again, that subtle glimmer in his eyes that the others didn't have. I have to wonder, is he really different? Or is he just playing me to get what he wants? "Let go of me." I jerk my hand out of his grip. "I can't do — whatever it is you want me to do."

He stares at me for several long heartbeats. "What *are* you?"

"Not a monster like you," I snap.

He's quiet. The silence itches along my skin like a wool blanket. "I'm not a monster — I'm a vampire. And I wasn't always," he says finally. "I think — I almost remembered — " His gaze drifts and he bites off the rest of his words.

Vampire. The word floats through my brain, unable to take root. How could it, when the very idea of a vampire is insane. And yet, the proof stands in front of me. "Are you — are you going to eat me?"

"Honestly?" Folding his arms, he leans against a tree beside me. "I have no idea what to do with you. I don't even know what *you* are."

"Stop saying that. I'm human."

He laughs. It's a wonderful sound, like warm honey on my skin. "If you're human, then I'm Santa Claus."

"Screw you." I raise my middle finger.

His smile disappears. "Why make this more difficult? Why not just tell me what you are?"

"I already told you, I'm *human*. Even if I wasn't, why the hell would I tell you anything? You think I owe you answers?" I snort. "I'm the one who doesn't know what's going on. You're one of the monsters, remember? You helped them kidnap my aunt, you made my dog run away, and you tied me up. I hate you, and I don't owe you a damn thing."

He exhales loudly. "You can hate me all you want, but I'd strongly advise against running. You have a choice here. You can run, trigger my bloodlust, and I'll probably end up killing you and ruining a perfectly good suit. Just so you know, I'll only be upset about the suit. Option number two, you can come with me to your cabin, and maybe we can find a clue about what you are and how you were able to do that—thing."

"Have you not been listening?" I make a face. "Spoiler alert. I'm human. And I can't do any *things.*"

His eyes darken, making me shiver. "Then we go back to the cabin and prove it."

"What about my aunt?"

"There's nothing we can do now." His jaw flexes. "She's well on her way to the farm."

I *do not* like the sound of that. "What the hell is the farm?"

"Every question you ask brings us closer to daylight," he replies with an edge to his voice. "And time is something we can't waste. If you want me to help you, you need to help me."

I lick my lips. "Why the hell would you help me? You're one of the monsters."

He's quiet for so long I'm sure he's not going to answer me, but then he says, "I have no memories of my human life. I'm the only vampire I know who can't remember my past." He looks away. "But then you hummed that song and it stirred something inside of me—a sense of familiarity I've never experienced. When you touched me I saw something—just for a second. A woman with golden hair. And all I could feel was her love. I wonder—I wonder if she is my mother. I always assumed my mother was dead—but now I'm not so sure." His eyes search my face, as if he might find the answers to his questions there.

As a girl whose mother died when I was a baby, I can almost relate. A part of me has always wanted to know what my real mother was like, and longs for a memory. But a larger part of me—the *smarter* part—knows I can't help him and he's still a monster. "I'm sorry. Whatever it is you think I can do, I can't."

"Would you be willing to try?" he asks. "My Queen plans to use your aunt as a pawn in a centuries-old war. I cannot help you myself, but I could take you to someone who might be able to."

My chest tightens. "You would do that?"

"Yes."

I'm not a complete idiot. I know he can't be trusted and he'll probably kill me no matter what I do. But I also know my aunt is getting farther away by the second, and I'm fresh out of other options. "Fine." Despite my quivering muscles, I raise my chin. "I'm going back to the cabin to look for nothing—because that's what we'll find." I take several steps before he clears his throat. "What?"

Sebastian points in the opposite direction. "Your cabin is that way."

A flush burns up my neck, igniting my cheeks. I turn in the direction he pointed and trudge through the woods. Sebastian catches up to me in several long strides. He reaches in front of me, lifting branches and vines out of my way as I walk.

"I'm not helpless," I snap.

"Maybe not, but you're not exactly graceful. The way you're scratching yourself up—I might have some restraint, but I'm still a vampire. You keep slicing open your skin and I might as well be walking beside an all-you-can-eat buffet."

Duly noted. Slowing my pace, I maneuver a little more carefully around branches and sticker bushes.

We walk the rest of the way in silence. Occasionally he grabs my arm when I drift in the wrong direction, or jerks me to the side before I tumble into a hole. When the lights of the cabin flicker through the trees, guilt coils inside my gut, and I have to fight to keep from sprinting toward the door. I enter the gaping doorway only to have my chest deflate when I find the house empty. "Jax? Here, boy."

He doesn't answer.

I whirl around, facing Sebastian. "Did the other vampires do something to my dog?"

His face reveals nothing. "If your dog isn't here, then he ran off. Animals have a natural aversion to vampires. They're smart, unlike humans."

I glare at him. "You don't understand. Jax won't let me take a shower alone. There's no way he wouldn't be here if he was okay."

"My kind do not eat dogs." He makes a face. "We're not disgusting Anima."

"A what?"

"You really don't know anything, do you?"

Grunting, I snatch a piece of splintered wood from the floor. "Then tell me something. I read books, are the stories true? Can I kill you with this?" I raise the stake in the air.

"You?" Sebastian smirks. "Never. A more skilled hunter, maybe. And only if they caught me off guard. Care to guess how many times that's happened? Now put that down before you hurt yourself."

I throw it at him. He easily bats it away. "The sooner you quit wasting time, the sooner we can find what I'm looking for."

With a sigh, I flop onto the couch. "There's nothing to find here. I know, because I've already searched."

Sebastian arches an eyebrow.

I shrug. "I was curious about my parents. Aunt Rachel doesn't talk about them unless she's had more than three glasses of wine." Even then, she doesn't say much. What I do know from her is this: my father was Hispanic with dark hair and smile lines etched around his eyes. My mother shared Aunt Rachel's blond hair and freckles. She studied dance and wanted to go to Julliard—until she got pregnant with me at eighteen.

Because of the pregnancy, Aunt Rachel's parents disowned my mother. Aunt Rachel lost contact with her until the day she was notified of the car accident. Sideswiped by a semi in St. Louis. I was the only survivor.

"I thought maybe I could find a photo or something," I continue. "There's nothing."

"We'll see." He strides to the bookshelf in the corner and pulls out a book. He flips through every page before replacing it and grabbing another.

"This is dumb," I mutter. Standing, I walk into the kitchen, pull open a drawer, and sort through the silverware and cooking utensils. "We should be going after my aunt. What are we even looking for?"

"Evidence." He pulls out another book and shakes it open. "I was ordered to find proof your aunt's son is really dead. But I'm more interested in anything that explains what *you* are." He meets my eyes with his own. They take on a weird silver glow in the cabin's dim light. My pulse races.

"Of course he's dead. He'd be here if he wasn't, right?" Turning back to the drawer, I slam it shut. "And why do you keep calling me a *what*? I'm human. What else could I be?"

He shrugs. "Vampires aren't the only creatures to look human."

The thought makes my heart flutter inside my chest like a frightened bird. "I don't believe you," I say, nearly choking on my words. Because the truth is, I do believe him. I just don't want to.

He replaces the book and leans against the shelf. "What is your name?"

I lick my lips. "Charlize. But nobody calls me that."

"Then what do they call you?"

I hesitate. "Charlie."

"Charlie." For some reason, my name sounds different when he says it—richer. "I don't remember my human life, but I do remember where I was when the Mentis clan found me. I was being held captive, and it wasn't by humans."

Don't ask. Don't ask. Don't ask. But the voice in my head is no match for my mouth. "Who was holding you captive?"

"Not a *who.* A *what.*" He holds my gaze a few heartbeats longer. Abruptly, he walks a circle around the room, taking in every corner. "The faster we find something, the faster I can get you to the person who can help you."

I'm almost relieved he didn't answer my question. The veil that's hidden a strange, darker world from what I know has only been pulled back a fraction.

I'm not sure I'm ready for more.

Chapter
Five

"Charlie."

The strangeness of a male voice cutting through the darkness makes me bolt upright. The purple light spilling through the windows is the color of a bruise. The couch cushion lumps jab my muscles in all the wrong places and my neck is so stiff I can barely turn it. How the hell does Aunt Rachel sleep on this torture device? "Aunt Rachel? What time is it? The sun's not even up yet."

Monsters. Fangs. A dark forest. These are all fragments of a nightmare falling to pieces as I rub the sleep from my eyes.

"Actually, the sun is just setting."

Gasping, I whip my head around so fast pain jolts down my neck. Sebastian stands in the doorway to my bedroom, like a Michelangelo sculpture brought to life. He's careful to stand in the shadows that grow longer by the minutes. The top three buttons of his shirt are undone with his tie hanging loose beneath the gap. His dark hair hangs in disheveled strands across his forehead. I have the insane urge to brush them back with my fingers.

Stop it, Charlie! Just because the homicidal monster is nice to look at is no excuse for losing your shit. You're smarter than that.

"Dangit." I pull the hairband out of the bun that hangs limp at my neck. "I didn't mean to fall asleep." After combing my fingers through my knotted hair, I rewind my hair in a knot at the top of my head and tie it in place.

Sebastian watches me with interest. "I decided to let you be. It is my understanding that humans need rest. My kind do not sleep. While the sun kept me confined to the bedroom, I was able to search every inch."

Sunlight hurts them. Making a mental note, I store that little tidbit away. "That's my room." I stand and stretch my arms above my head. "There's nothing to find in there."

"Actually—that's not true." He inclines his head. "Come see."

I snort. "Impossible. You think I don't know what's in my own room?"

He steps farther into the dark room, his eyes glowing silver. "Then there's nothing to be afraid of."

Understatement of the year. I push my shoulders back and follow him into the room. "Fine. Show me this *thing* you think you found."

Sebastian stops beside my nightstand and picks up the framed photo next to my alarm clock. I was seven years old the day it was taken. Aunt Rachel and I were standing on the riverbank about to push our kayaks into the stream when she wrapped her arm around my neck and crushed me against her. "We need to remember this," she said, pulling out one of those old, disposable cameras that you took to the pharmacy to get developed.

Her cheeks were flush with the hint of a sunburn. I didn't want to smile and reveal the gap from my missing front tooth. But Aunt Rachel wormed her fingers against my ribs, tickling me. She'd snapped the photo right when I opened my mouth to squeal.

Sebastian lowers the frame. "Rachel is very cunning."

I make a face. "This is your big clue?"

He taps the photo. "Sometimes the best way to hide something is in plain sight."

Inside my gut, a flicker of anger fans into a flame. "Are you kidding me? That photo doesn't prove anything. And now we've wasted an entire day looking for nothing, while Aunt Rachel is God-knows-where with monsters."

"Vampires," he corrects. "And you're right, *this* photo doesn't prove anything. But the one behind it does." He turns the frame over and unclips the back, tossing it aside. From there, he tilts the frame toward me and reveals another photograph behind the first.

Impossible. Bile burns up my throat. "What is that?"

Sebastian removes the photo from the frame and hands it to me. "I was hoping you could tell me."

I take the photo with trembling fingers. The edges are slightly bent, but the color is still glossy and sharp. The photo was taken at night, dimming the colors. Even so, there's no mistaking my aunt, though she appears much younger, with her dreadlocked hair, beaded necklaces, and long skirt. She's sitting on a park bench beside a man. He's wearing flip-flops, and his jeans have holes in the knees. His long dark hair is braided and falls over his shoulder.

His rich skin tone, sloped nose, and dark eyes hint at a Hispanic heritage—just like my own father.

The man has an arm wrapped around Aunt Rachel's shoulder. Her head rests in the crook of his neck. The man's other arm holds a baby dressed in blue onesie. Aunt Rachel holds an identical baby dressed in pink. On the ground, resting between their feet, is a large German Shepherd that looks *exactly* like Jax.

"I don't understand." The photo feels dangerous in my hands. My fingers shake and the frame slips from my grasp onto the floor. My legs feel weak, but at the same time, my feet remain rooted to the floor. "I've never seen this man before in my life."

Sebastian's face softens. His fingers twitch as though he might reach out to me before he balls them into a fist. "I'm afraid this photo is the proof the Queen was looking for."

"What proof?" I spit. "It's just a photo of my aunt and some guy I don't know."

Holding my gaze, he plucks the photo off the floor. He studies it and, if I didn't know better, I'd swear his eyes flash with sympathy. "Charlie, you know exactly what it means."

A whirlwind of thoughts spins through my mind, making it impossible to cling to a single one—until I do. Hugging my arms around my chest, I drop onto my bed. "You think Aunt Rachel is really my mother?"

His silence is my answer.

All the questions and feelings swirling through my brain become too heavy to bear. I let my head fall into my hands. "I don't believe it. She would have told me."

Sebastian tucks the photo inside his shirt pocket. "Not if she thought she was protecting you—because of who your father is."

I look up. "My father is dead."

"Your father is *undead*. His name is Matteo, and he is king of the Anima Clan."

I burst out laughing, which only makes Sebastian frown. "Of all the things I have heard and seen these last twenty-four hours, that is the most insane."

"Sometimes the truth isn't what you expect."

I stand. "My father can't be a vampire. That's crazy. What would that even mean for me? I'm human, aren't I?" I hold my arms in front of me, as if I could somehow peer through my skin into the blood beneath.

"It would make you a dhampir," he replies. "It's nothing to worry about. Dhampirs are rarely gifted with anything more than heightened sight and smell." He cocks his head. "Though I've never heard of a dhampir doing what you did to me last night."

"I didn't do anything." Venom laces my voice.

"Denying it won't make it untrue."

Swallowing hard, I stare at my hands, as if I can somehow shrug out of my own skin. For the first time in my life, I feel like I don't belong inside of it. "Even if what you say is true—and it isn't—why does your queen care about me or Aunt Rachel?"

"Because of who your father is. War is brewing, Charlie, and you both are leverage in a very deadly game."

"What does that mean?"

He sighs. "It *means,* she is going to use your aunt as bait to lure Matteo into an unfair fight. She will do the same to you if she knows your connection."

My throat turns to ash and it takes me several tries

before I'm able to swallow. "What do I do?"

"You?" He gives a small laugh. "Nothing. When I return to the Queen I will tell her I found nothing and killed you to save her the trouble."

"Then what? I just sit here in the cabin and pray your freaky buddies don't kill Aunt Rachel?"

He makes a face. "No. You can't stay here, it's not safe. If *my freaky buddies* found you, others can, too."

I fold my arms. "Maybe I should take my chances with the others."

His face darkens. "You called my kind monsters. There are others that make us look like kittens."

I fight to ignore the chill racing down my vertebrae. "You got a better idea? It's not exactly as if I'm flooded with options."

"I told you I would take you to someone." He's quiet for several heartbeats. "Matteo. He can protect you. And he's the only one who might be able to rescue Rachel." He walks to the open doorway and peers out into the darkness. "The Anima Clan would kill me on sight, but I can get you as close as I can. Grab your things. We have to leave before others arrive."

"Are you kidding? Your entire plan is to drop me off with another vampire? As in, another one of the monsters that *eats* people? What could possible go wrong?"

He looks at me, silver eyes unblinking. "Like you said, you don't have a lot of choices. You want to call the police and explain all of this to them? You go right ahead and see how fast they place you in a mental institution. I offered you a solution that will save your life—and possibly your aunt's. It's the best I can do, so if you're going with me, you need to hurry."

Something about the urgency in his voice jolts me to action. I snatch my backpack off my desk and shove an extra pair of jeans, a sweater, and my phone charger into the bag. In the kitchen, I open the cookie jar and remove Aunt Rachel's stash of emergency cash—a whopping fifty-three dollars. Next, I snatch her special oil—the one the monsters aren't supposed to like—and tuck it in my pocket.

Sebastian raises an eyebrow. "I already told you that stuff won't actually keep me from biting you."

Shrugging, I zip everything in place and hoist the bag over my shoulder. "It doesn't matter. I would smother myself in garlic if I thought it would piss you off."

He shakes his head. "While that would be amusing, we're running out of night. Are you ready to go?"

I lick my lips. There's a question keeping my feet rooted to the ground. "Why are you helping me?"

He appears startled for a moment, as if he's been wondering the same thing. I hate that he's not the ugliest monster in the world—that my eyes are drawn to the crease above his nose when his brow furrows. "I don't want you to think what I'm doing is some sort of noble undertaking. I need you alive, Charlie, for selfish reasons only. That thing you did in the woods—I need you to do it again. This gap in my memory, it's haunted me my entire existence. Not knowing is its own type of prison. And I think you might be the one to set me free."

Chapter
Six

Before leaving the cabin, Sebastian grabs my violin case. Of all the things to take, it's got to be the weirdest, but I don't pretend to understand vampire logic. I follow him outside. The sun has fallen below the trees, leaving the sky an inky blue.

It's so strange, following him down the gravel drive. I've never been anywhere with a regular boy, yet here I am following a vampire to God-knows-where. Despite everything Sebastian's said, the logical part of my brain pulls every muscle in my body tight, urging me to run.

As if he can read my thoughts, Sebastian sighs. "Please don't. I'm not human, Charlie, I'm a hunter. Remember what happened last time you ran?" He fishes keys out of his jacket pocket.

I raise my middle finger. I've flipped him off more than any other creature on the planet.

His lip twitches in an almost-smile. "For being so weak, you're quite brave. I can't decide if this makes you intriguing or stupid."

"You're a dick."

He shrugs. "Stupid it is." He points to a bend in the gravel road. "The car is parked beyond there."

"Whatever." I adjust the backpack on my shoulder and follow him. The crunch of our shoes against the gravel is the only sound to echo through the trees. Even so, I keep my eyes trained on the woods, hoping to catch sight of any movement.

"Your dog isn't here," Sebastian says, as if reading my mind.

"How could you possibly know that?"

He points to his left. "A raccoon is hunkered down in a hollowed log over the ridge, there." He shifts his hand right. "Three squirrels in that tree. And a quarter mile away, a doe and two fawns are doing their best to avoid my detection. They are failing miserably. Can't you smell or hear any of this?"

I wait for a sign that his question is a joke. When his face doesn't change, I shake my head. "Of course not."

He looks almost disappointed. "Then you haven't inherited anything from your father. Too bad."

I snort. "Because he *isn't* my father. You might consider that a bad thing, but it's not. I don't want to be anything like you."

He laughs. "Matteo is Anima. He is nothing like me or any other member of the Mentis clan."

"You keep talking about these *clans*—how are they different?"

He gives me a long look before answering. "Believe me when I say you don't want the answer."

Despite the warm night, a chill settles into my bones, and I hug my cardigan tighter. I follow him around the bend of trees to find a silver car parked on the side of the road. I don't know enough about cars to guess what kind it is, only that it looks sleek and dangerous—just like Sebastian.

I glance over my shoulder at the cabin I'm leaving behind. The broken door lays in pieces, revealing the hollow insides. Once, I thought our cabin was cozy. Lately, it's felt suffocating—crammed full of my aunt, her oils, and ideals. I couldn't wait for the chance to break free. But now that I'm leaving the empty shell that was my home, my heart feels just as hollow.

The vampire withdraws a key from his pocket. The car's headlights flash on, and the engine ignites. He walks to the passenger door and holds it open for me. On another planet, in another life, it's something I've imagined a guy would do for me on a date.

"Why bother being nice to me when you're only using me?"

"I'm a vampire, Charlie, not an animal."

"No, you're not an animal. You're a monster." I look around one last time, hoping catch sight of Jax. But there's only dark, endless woods. "I'm so sorry, boy. I'll find you. I promise," I murmur as I climb inside the vehicle.

Sebastian watches me with a curious expression before closing the door. "With everything going on, you are worried about the animal?"

"Yes."

"Worrying about your dog is energy wasted. You should be more concerned about yourself."

"Caring about someone is not wasted energy," I snap. "If anything, it makes me more determined to survive this."

He stares at me for several long heartbeats before putting the car in drive. He murmurs something too low for me to make out—not that I care.

Shifting my body, I face the window. My thoughts turn from my missing German Shepherd to the dog in the picture. It's eerie that my aunt had a dog that looked exactly like him. Maybe that was why she didn't object when I plucked puppy Jax out of the cardboard box outside the Gas Mart—Jax reminded her of her former dog. I wish she would have told me about him. I wish she would have told me about any of this. Then again, maybe there's nothing to tell and this is some horrible mix-up.

A green sign appears in my mind.

Delusionville: Population 1.

I try and shake it away. "The photo could be misleading," I say, as Sebastian pulls the car onto the road. With tinted windows, leather seats, and a working air conditioner, his car is drastically different from Aunt Rachel's diesel-burning truck I nicknamed the rust-bucket. "Maybe she was holding someone else's babies in that photo. Maybe my mother is the one taking the picture. Besides, even if the babies in the picture *are* Aunt Rachel's, there's no proof I'm one of them."

Sebastian makes a face. "If the photo is harmless, why hide it? And why not tell you the truth?"

I have no answer, so I turn back to the window, hugging my arms across my body, and stare out into the night. For over an hour, I watch as dense trees turn into cow pastures and fields, and then change into glowing suburbs. "I did this," I murmur, my breath creating a cloud on the glass. "This is my fault." The thought is so absurd, and yet so accurate, it pulls a giggle to the surface like a string.

Frowning, Sebastian turns to me. "Are you feeling okay?"

"Oh yeah," I reply with another laugh. "This is a dream come true. You see, more than anything I wanted to get away from the cabin. I thought my only escape was college—who knew it only took a vampire kidnapping to do the trick. Could have saved me some agonizing over application essays."

Maybe it's exhaustion, maybe it's terror, but I feel as if I'm falling inside myself, further from reality, and deeper into the darkness. My giggles take on a hysterical edge. "It's crazy, right? It can't be real, can it? Are you real?" I grab his arm, all solid muscle beneath his jacket. *Okay, definitely a little too real.* I let him go. "Am I losing my mind?" I press my hands to my face.

Sebastian's eyes widen, and he hits the blinker. Engine revving, I'm jerked against my seat as the car swerves over two lanes onto an exit ramp.

The jolt releases me from the clutches of hysteria, back into the moment. "Where are we going?"

"It's been hours—I didn't think." He shakes his head. "I'm rarely around humans—we have servants that do the farming for us."

"*Farming?*" I wrinkle my nose. Whatever he's talking about, it doesn't sound good.

"I forgot how weak your species is," he continues. "You're emotional and hungry. I'm going to feed you and that will make you better." His jaw is set at a sharp angle as if he's worried—but about me?

I bark out a laugh. "Yeah. That will fix everything." Even so, my stomach rumbles to life at the mention of food.

"My apologies." He shifts uncomfortably. It's such a regular, human movement that for a moment I almost forget he's one of *them.*

Sebastian pulls into the drive-thru lane of the first fast-food restaurant we come to. Even though it's close to midnight, three cars are in line ahead of us. Humans living human lives, with no idea there's a monster lurking behind them. What would happen if I bolted from the car? Would Sebastian let me go? Would the other vampires kill my aunt? I slump against the seat. As much as I hate to admit it, I *need* Sebastian if I have any hope of finding my aunt.

Sebastian puts on his sunglasses and rolls down the window as we pull up to the speaker. He turns to me with a worried expression. "I've never done this before."

Before I can respond, an eardrum bursting voice asks if they can help us. *God, if only they served something enough to make me forget everything that's happened.*

Sebastian flinches. "I want one serving of food."

I stare at him with my mouth open. "You can't be serious."

The speaker is quiet for several moments before we hear a sigh. "Look, buddy. I'm making minimum wage, here. I'd really love one night where I didn't have to deal with jokers like you."

Turning to me, Sebastian's brow furrows. "What did I do wrong?"

"Just when I thought things couldn't get any weirder," I murmur, crawling over him to the window. My shoulder grazes Sebastian's chest and he stiffens. From this close, I can smell him. I don't know what I was expecting—maybe the scent of blood or decay—but he actually smells pretty damn good. Years of crafting lotions and balms with Aunt Rachel has given me a nose for scents, and I'm able to pick out notes of cedar and orange. Still, his cologne is no match for the smell of French fries and beef wafting through the window.

"I want a double meal," I yell into the speaker. I'm no stranger to a drive-thru. While we don't go often, Aunt Rachel would usually swing through one on our way home from selling soap at the farmers' market. "Extra pickle, no onions. Make it a large with a chocolate shake." I settle deep into my seat. If I'm going to die, I'm not going to die hungry.

Sebastian blinks at me.

"Your total is seven fifty-two," the speaker barks back. "Please pull around."

"Ordering food is surprisingly complicated." Sebastian pulls a wad of bills from his inside pocket and flips through them. Each one is a hundred-dollar bill.

"I guess human blood only comes in one flavor?"

He shrugs. "Different blood types have different flavor notes, but basically you're right. I'm partial to A positive."

"Gross." Re-fastening my seatbelt, I pause to wonder what type of blood I have. And is it strange I don't know? I shake my head, pushing the thought from my mind. "How is it you've never ordered food before?"

Frowning, he keeps his eyes on the car in front of us. "Like I said, I don't remember my time as a human."

"Do you know how long you've been a vampire?"

He shakes his head.

Damn. "That sucks."

"I don't like not knowing my past." He shrugs. "But I *think* I prefer being a vampire. Who wants to be prey when you can be the predator?"

"You drink blood instead of milkshakes. There's no way that's better."

He almost smiles. I wish he would. I bet it's a good look on him.

When we get to the window, a skinny guy not much older than me hands Sebastian my shake as he grumbles about making change from a hundred.

"I don't like him," Sebastian mutters after the worker closes the window. "If we had more time, I'd eat him just to shut him up."

I nearly choke on a laugh, which makes Sebastian raise an eyebrow. It's strange the easiness we've fallen into considering he almost tore into my neck only twenty-four hours ago. It's not that I've forgotten he could kill me in seconds, I only want to believe in his ability to help. At this point, hope is the only thing I have left to hold on to.

The worker reappears and hands Sebastian a bag of food. Sebastian sniffs the bag, makes a face, and hands it to me. "Disgusting."

"Says the freak of nature who eats people." I reach into the bag, stuff a handful of fries in my mouth, and groan in relief.

"I can smell every chemical. That food is loaded with them."

"It's the chemicals that make it so delicious." I take a long drink from my straw. "Mmm. Chemical goodness."

"You're the strangest—whatever you are—I've ever met." He shakes his head, the ghost of a grin on his lips.

Sebastian pulls into a parking spot while I stuff my face. If I wasn't so hungry, maybe I would be self-conscious about shoving fries into my mouth with him watching. Then again, why the hell should I care?

His head tilts. "The weirdest expression just crossed your face."

Shrugging, I take a long sip of chocolate shake. "I was just wondering if vampires dated. Do you go to the movies and split a bag of blood with a single straw?" I snort at my own joke.

He makes a face. "We have physical needs that we satisfy, but we have little use for dating. The Mentis have no use for emotional bonds. They make you weak."

"That's gross, and extremely sad."

He tilts his head. "What's gross about it?"

"I don't know." I take a bite out of my burger. "I guess the way you said it—*physical needs*—it's so cold and sterile."

"You're telling me you don't have physical needs?"

A pickle lodges inside my throat and I nearly choke. "I didn't say that. I mean—I don't know. Not yet—that I know of, anyway."

"How can you not know?"

A blush burns up my cheeks. "I'm not exactly experienced in that department, okay? I've never even been on a date. You saw my cabin, it's not like it's crawling with eligible guys."

He snorts. "Humans and your ridiculous ideals. You don't have to have an emotional bond to share physical gratification."

"That's stupid. Why would I want to be physical with anyone I don't have a connection with?"

"It's wasted energy," he answers. "Human religions spread the lie you need to be bonded with a mate. It's those ties that make you so vulnerable. Love is an illusion, a chemical released in the brain that gives a sense of euphoria. And when the euphoria fades, all that is left of love is obligation, which eventually leads to resentment."

I finish chewing before answering. "You might not remember your past, but I'm willing to bet you were a philosophy major."

His brow furrows. "What does that mean?"

"It means, I'm sure you were super fun to have at parties."

His frown deepens.

"Look." I shift in my seat so I face him. "Everything you just said? Total bullshit. You're a monster, so you probably don't have a soul. That's why you don't get it."

"Is that so?"

"Yup." Smiling, I take another bite of my burger.

"All right then." He leans toward me. "Let's put your theory to the test."

The burger becomes a lump wedged inside my throat. I sputter several times before I'm able to speak. "What are you doing?"

"An experiment." He grins, showing a flash of fangs.

My throat goes dry.

He reaches forward and brushes a strand of hair off my cheek. My skin tingles beneath his touch.

I jerk back. "Stop that."

"Stop what?" There's something smug about the way he

arches his eyebrow. I want to smack it off his stupid face.

He grabs me suddenly, snaking his arm around my back and hitching me against him. The bag of food crinkles between us. My own wide eyes stare back at me, reflected in his glasses. I inhale sharply. For a monster, he's surprisingly warm. His hair falls forward, framing his face. With his lips parted, the moon reflects off the points of his fangs. He lowers them toward my neck.

My hands shake where they rest against his chest.

"You're a smart girl, Charlie." A trail of goosebumps rises beneath his breath, hot on my neck. "You don't like me. You've made that much very clear. And yet, I can hear every beat of your heart racing in your pulse. Right here." His bottom lip grazes my throat. Electricity sparks where we connect.

"It's because I'm terrified of you," I say, voice wavering.

"Really?" His lips brush my ear, leaving me shivering. "Or is it simply your body reacting to mine? Responding in the simplest, most primal nature, nerves firing beneath your skin leading to the chemicals released in your brain? All of this telling you my touch can't be a bad thing, because we know it's not *love*."

Anger boils through my veins and I shove him hard. "Get off of me, you creep."

Smirking, he falls back against his seat. He raises his hands in surrender. "Whatever you want. I think I proved my point, anyway. Love doesn't exist. Hormones do." He shifts the car into drive and pulls out of the parking lot.

"You're an idiot, a soulless idiot who will never understand what it's like to experience love." Glaring at him, I shove fries into my mouth as he turns onto the highway. I'm afraid of what more I might say if I don't keep chewing. What I feel for my aunt, and even my dog, is real, and there's no way he can convince me otherwise.

When I'm finished eating, I wad the empty wrappers and shove them inside the bag. Now that my belly is blissfully full, exhaustion creeps over me. Or maybe it's the anger that has me so worn out. Either way, I rest my head against the window and watch the lines of the road disappear beneath the car.

"I would have fed you sooner if I knew it would shut you up." Grinning, he pulls off his sunglasses and tosses them onto the dash. His eyes glow silver in the dark.

Something pulls tight low inside of me, which only pisses me off more. I want to give a witty response, but tiredness muddies my brain. After several minutes, a single thought pulls to the surface. "Do you think I'm going to make it out of this alive?"

Sebastian's smile dissolves. His hands flex tightly on the steering wheel. "We have a deal. I'm going to take you to Matteo and he'll keep you safe."

"What about my aunt?"

"That's a little more uncertain." Several seconds pass that feel like an eternity before he speaks again. "They'll have her secure at the farm."

A cold, prickly feeling crawls across my skin. "What's at the farm?"

Sebastian doesn't answer.

"Is she—is she going to die?"

He doesn't look at me, but he doesn't need to. Underneath my skin I'm cracking into a million pieces.

Without saying a word, he's given me my answer.

Chapter Seven

A bump in the road jars me awake. While I can't believe I fell asleep, I guess it's not a huge surprise. After all, the leather seats are warm and cushy, a world of difference from my aunt's lumpy sofa. How did she manage to sleep on it all these years? If I ever see her again I'll be sure to give her my bed. I'll sleep on the floor every night and promise never to leave her side if it means she survives. I'll even forgive her for lying to me all these years if it turns out she's my mother. *Anything,* at all, if it means she's okay.

A quick glance at the dash shows it's just after midnight. Sebastian pulls up to a gas pump nestled between two buildings. While I've never been to St. Louis, I have to assume this is it. I've never seen so much concrete in my life. I always imagined a big city would feel like an escape from my cabin. But all around me steel and concrete stretch to the sky. Maybe a city is just a bigger cage.

"We're out of gas," Sebastian says, sliding on his sunglasses. "Do you need anything?"

"How close are we?"

"The Anima live just west of the city. Their camp is forty-five minutes from here."

Forty-five minutes is all that separates me from an entire compound of vampires—one of whom *might* be my father. My throat runs dry. "I need water."

Sebastian pulls out his wad of money and hands me a hundred-dollar bill. "Buy whatever you want."

"I'm keeping the change," I tell him, crumpling the bill in my fist. "Call it hazard pay for nearly ripping my throat out and just being a dick in general."

He sighs and exits the car. "You triggered the bloodlust. You were warned not to run." He presses his lips together, the corners turning down. Is it possible he actually feels bad?

"That's victim blaming, Sebastian, and that is not cool." I open the car door.

"You're not a victim, you're *food*."

"And *you're* an asshole." A cool breeze brings smells of garbage and rancid water. I wrinkle my nose.

Watching me, Sebastian shakes his head as he opens the gas cap. "You're not making this any easier."

"I wasn't trying to." I climb out of the car. The moment my sneakers hit the pavement, my muscles tighten with the need to sprint. It's the farthest we've been apart in hours. My body remembers last night's encounter in the woods, even as my brain tries to rationalize the benefits of sticking with the vampire. So I concentrate on each step toward the gas station, forcing myself to walk even as my muscles scream at me to flee. *Don't run. Don't run. Don't run.*

I'm almost to the door when a figure moves just outside my line of sight.

"Hey, you."

I turn with a gasp.

"Man, you're jumpy." From the corner of the gas station, a girl shuffles out of the shadows. She looks roughly my age, with short, bleached-white hair that falls across her face in jagged strips. She wears a dark, tattered jacket with the hood drawn up, black jeans, and dirty sneakers. Thick black lines of eyeliner circle her lids. A silvery scar stretches from her left eye to her jaw. "That your boyfriend?" She jerks a chin toward Sebastian.

"Uh, that's a hard *no*." Even as I answer, the memory of his lips against my neck floats through my brain, warming my cheeks. *Stupid hormones.* "I'm sorry, is there something you want?" I slowly inch away. I might not be from the city, but surely this isn't a normal greeting.

"Looks rich." The girl chews on her lip. She twitches her head, eyes darting from Sebastian, to me, back to him. "He got money?"

"What does that have to do with anything?" A pressure I can't explain swells inside my chest.

The girl shifts her weight from foot to foot. "If he's not your boyfriend, then maybe he wants to party."

Sebastian glances up from the gas pump. "You, there." His eyes narrow. "Who are you and what do you want?" There's an edge to his voice I recognize from last night. The hairs on the back of my neck rise in response. *Shit.* He's going into vampire mode.

The girl steps in front of me before I can warn her. "I was wondering if you wanted to party. I can show you a good time."

Sebastian makes a disgusted noise. "Leave." It's more

of a growl than a word. I would bet my life that behind his sunglasses his eyes are turning black.

"You should go," I whisper, grabbing her wrist. "He doesn't like partying. Trust me, he's one of the most boring guys I've ever met—philosophy major. Bye now." I give her a small shove.

"Hold up. I have a feeling about this one. He likes to party. *Hard.*" She smirks at me before turning her attention to Sebastian. That little shiver down the spine that warns impending death? Yeah, this girl was born without it. "Come on. I'm tons of fun." She jerks free from my grip and walks toward him, swaying her hips. "Drop the hippie chick and spend a little time with me. I can tell I'm more your speed. What do you say?"

Hippie chick? I recoil, unsure why the insult stings like it does.

Sebastian returns the nozzle to the pump. "I'd say if I had more time, you'd be dinner. But since I don't, you need to leave. I won't ask you again."

"Come on." She steps in front of him. "At least let me show you the goods." She flings her jacket open, revealing two guns holstered against her ribs.

"The hell?" I squeak.

In a blink, she pulls one out and aims it at Sebastian's chest.

He snarls, baring his fangs. "You're a hunter."

She smiles. "And you're a vampire. Want to guess what comes next?" She fires.

A shot rings out and Sebastian crumples to the pavement. His glasses fall to the ground beside him.

I scream, my mind racing to make sense of what just

happened. "Who—what—?"

"Come on." The girl runs toward him, holstering her gun. She kneels in front of Sebastian and glances at me over her shoulder. "Help me get him in the car. Hurry. Before someone calls the cops."

Sebastian hisses in pain, clutching at his chest. A crimson stain spreads beneath his fingers.

Fear roots my feet to the asphalt. "I don't understand. Who are you? What did you do to him?"

She huffs. "Look, I'm going to cut you some slack here because you have wide-eyed traumatized look about you. But here's the deal, you can help me load him in the car, or you can explain this," she waves a hand toward Sebastian, "to the police. And they're not really what we call 'in the know,'" she air quotes with her fingers, "with the whole vampire thing."

"No—wait. You can't do this." I want to run to Sebastian, but just looking at the gun strapped to the girl's side keeps me frozen in place. I swallow hard. "He was helping me."

The girl snorts. "The leeches don't help people, they eat them. I, on the other hand, just saved your life. You're welcome."

I glance over my shoulder to find the gas station attendant watching us from behind the glass doors. Should I signal him?

The girl follows my gaze. "Don't worry about him." She holds her hand up and he waves back. "He's a friend. He's going to erase the security footage while we make our getaway. Grab the corpse's feet."

Sebastian writhes on the ground, clutching his chest. Logically, I know he's a monster, he nearly killed me last night. But this—shooting him and taking him God-knows-where—doesn't feel right, either.

The girl makes a face. "I'm sensing some hesitation. Look, I don't know what the bloodsucker told you, but I can promise you it was a lie. They're murderers. You get that, don't you?"

"I—" A lump wedges inside my throat.

Sebastian's eyes lock onto mine. "Don't do this, Charlie." He takes a shuddering breath. "You won't be safe with the hunters. They're not as they appear."

The girl lets out a sharp laugh. "Not safe? Coming from a demon that eats people? Just when I think I've heard it all." She slides her hand beneath his arms and looks at me. "What were you doing with him, anyway?"

It takes me several swallows before I'm able talk. "They have my aunt."

"Bastards." The girl sneers. "Charlie, is it? Let's get him to the base. Patrick should have some ideas on how to get your aunt back."

When I pause, she sighs. "Look, it's either this or wait for the cops. Think about this logically. Who do you think you can trust? Me, a human, or one of the monsters that took your aunt? I don't know where he told you he was taking you, but his vampire compound is only a couple miles that way." She juts a finger over her shoulder.

My mouth drops. "What?"

"I wasn't taking you there, Charlie," Sebastian says, wincing. "I swear. We were just here to get gas."

"Well isn't that *convenient*," the girl replies.

I don't want to believe her, but everything she says makes sense. He was playing with me, just like he did in the car outside the fast food restaurant.

"Charlie," Sebastian says, "you *have* to listen to me."

The realization that I'm an idiot hits me in the face like a stone hurled from a slingshot. "You lied to me."

"I didn't—"

"You must think I'm so stupid. You were never going to help me, just like I'm not going to help you." I bend down and grab his ankles, keeping my eyes locked on the ground to hide the flush burning across my cheeks. God, I'm a moron. Of course, he intended to eat me all along. The scary vampire told Sebastian to kill me—he didn't say *where*. It turns out I was food to-go. All those years of homeschooling and seclusion—they made me infinitely more naive than I ever realized. How could Aunt Rachel think for a second that she was protecting me?

"On the count of three." The girl counts down, and together we lift Sebastian.

As we shuffle to the car, I can't help but feel as if I'm making a mistake. Still, I write the feeling off as a combination of trauma and exhaustion. Who wouldn't question everything after going through what I've been through?

"Charlie...don't do this." Sebastian closes his eyes, his head falling back. I look away, nearly dropping him. The blonde opens the back door to his car and we shove him across the seat, slamming the door behind him.

She stares at him through the window, hands on her hip. "It's so pathetic when they beg like that. Do they really think we're that stupid?"

"I guess I am that stupid," I mutter. "I believed him." An invisible hand rips into my gut.

"Aw, honey." She wraps an arm around my shoulder and guides me to the passenger door. "They're conniving sons of bitches. There's no shame in being deceived the first time. It's just lucky I was here to save you."

"Yeah," I say as she opens the door and ushers me in. "That's me. Super lucky."

The girl either doesn't hear me, or doesn't care to respond. She skirts around the hood and climbs into the driver's seat. Once the door is closed, she throws back her hood and smiles. "I'm Opal." Before I can respond, she whistles as she runs her hand across the dash. "They may be demon spawn, but they sure have good taste in vehicles. Am I right?"

"I guess?" I catch sight of Sebastian in the rearview mirror. The blood seeping through his fingers has nearly soaked his entire shirt. His face has taken on a grayish hue. I force myself to look away. *He's a monster, Charlie. Don't be stupid because he's pretty.* Still, I ask, "Is he going to die?"

Opal makes a face as she starts the car. "Sweetie, he's already dead. But if you're asking if I terminated him, the answer is no. I'm too good a shot for that. The object is to get the wooden bullet just close enough to the heart to incapacitate. Patrick will want to talk to him before he's exterminated."

For reasons I don't understand, my heart shudders. "Why do you have to exterminate him?"

She makes a face. "Okay, I'm sensing there's some Stockholm syndrome going on here, so I'm going to break it down for you. You know what he is, right—what he was going to do to you? He was going to eat you."

Sebastian didn't bite me the night in the woods. After

that, there were plenty of times he could have killed me—when I was sleeping, for starters. So why didn't he?

The tires squeal and I'm thrown against the seat as the car peals out of the gas station. Opal laughs. "Oh man, I love this car."

I clutch the door handle as Opal navigates the streets of St. Louis at breakneck speed. A man on a crosswalk shouts and jumps for the curb as Opal screeches by.

Opal pats my arm, seemingly oblivious to the late-night bystanders we nearly clipped while cornering a turn. "I was almost finished with my patrol for the night. I'm so glad I found you before he got you to the farm. You would have been so screwed."

There's that word again. "What *is* the farm?"

Sebastian groans from the back seat.

The humor drains from her face. "Exactly what it sounds like. These Mentis fucks are too prissy to get their fangs dirty. They capture humans, and keep them locked up like cattle. They have slaves use IVs to harvest and bottle the blood. I heard they drink it in fancy glasses like wine or some shit. Isn't that the sickest thing you've ever heard of?"

Nausea slams into my gut like a fist. I twist around in the seat to face Sebastian. "And that's where they took my aunt?" My voice takes on a high, hysterical edge. "That's where you were taking me?"

He opens his mouth as if he might answer, but only manages to grimace in pain. "Answer me, you asshole." My hands curl into fists and I lean toward him, ready to propel myself onto him and make him talk.

Opal winds a fist into my sweater and yanks me back

into the seat. "Don't damage the goods." She stops the car in front of a tall chain-link fence. A sign bolted to a gate with faded-red letters spells CONDEMNED. Razor-edged wire spirals around the top. "Patrick will have some ideas on how to get your aunt back — I'm sure of it." She flashes the headlights twice. The dark figure of a man appears from the shadows and pushes the gate open. I'm thrown against the seat as the car bounces over potholes and chunks of broken asphalt. Ahead of us, a dark brick building looms. Several windows are boarded with plywood, and graffiti decorates almost every inch of brick.

I find myself curling my fingers into the edge of my seat. "What is this place?"

Grinning, Opal stops the car behind a crumbling parking block. "Isn't it great? Welcome to hunter HQ. It used to be a high school."

The little alarm inside my head turns into a blaring siren as a sense of wrongness blankets over me. If the past twenty-four hours have taught me anything, it's to trust my instincts. Whatever happens here can't be good.

My apprehension must show on my face because Opal laughs. "I knew you'd love it. Come on."

The men that approach when I exit the car make me want to jump back inside and lock the door. Dressed in black, they each wear an assortment of leather, from boots to vests and jackets. Except for their faces, a mix of tattoos and scars decorate their visible skin, including their necks and knuckles. One man with a jagged scar across his cheek lets out an appreciative whistle. "Where'd you get the sweet ride, Opal?"

She tilts her head to the car. "Bagged and tagged a live

one, boys. The car came with it. Mind carrying the leech inside so I can show the new girl around?"

Another man pushes through the group clustered around us. The other men immediately move aside. His white hair is braided down his back, nearly touching his belt, while his beard grazes his chest. The lines on his face look deep enough to have been etched with a knife. The patch on his leather jacket declares him a member of the Night Stalkers—whatever the hell that is. He looks us over. "You hurt?"

Opal snorts. "What am I, new? See for yourself, Patrick." She holds her arms out. "Not a scratch."

Patrick jabs a finger at her. "You've only been here a couple of months, Opal. You get cocky, you get dead. How many times have I told you that?"

She rolls her eyes. "Don't worry. I played it by the book. I assessed the situation, came between the target and the civilian, and immobilized the leech before he knew what hit him."

"Who's the girl?" Patrick gives me the once over.

I bristle. "My name is Charlie."

Patrick smiles at that. "You got some fire, that's good. You'll need it to survive."

"She was on her way to the farm." Opal presses her lips together. "Bloodsuckers already got her aunt. I told her you might be able to help."

"Dammit, Opal." Patrick's expression turns dark. He rubs a hand across his head. "Don't go making promises you know nothing about."

"But—"

He shakes his head, cutting her off. "We'll talk. *Later.*

Right now, you two go inside. Opal, get Charlie some food and a bed. We'll take the leech from here."

"C'mon." Opal grabs my arm and gives me a gentle tug.

"No." I dig my heels against the ground. "I'm not going to eat and I'm definitely not going to sleep. My aunt is with them. Right now. We have to do something."

He arches an eyebrow. "I understand. But I also know charging into a nest will only get you one thing—dead. Let me and the boys interrogate the bloodsucker and we'll go from there."

I jerk out of Opal's grasp. "And in the meantime you expect me to—what? Pretend everything is okay? How can I do that when they have my aunt and they're—" The possibilities are too horrible to speak out loud. The seed of doubt Sebastian planted sprouts into a bud. What if coming here was a mistake? "I have to help her."

The other men exchange grim glances. Patrick sighs and claps a hand between my shoulders. "We'll talk about it in the morning, kiddo. Promise. For now, get some rest."

"But—"

"Let's go." This time Opal wraps her arm around mine so tightly there's no chance of escape. "Patrick's right. We can't do anything until the boys interrogate the bloodsucker." She pulls me toward the building.

Over my shoulder, I watch Patrick open the back of the car. Sebastian snarls and the men laugh. A prickling sensation starts in my chest and ripples outward across my body. I look away. If I didn't know better, I'd swear I felt bad for him—which is completely stupid. Maybe Opal was right about the Stockholm syndrome. He might have been planning to kill me all along, but apparently my loyalty can be bought with a cheeseburger and a milkshake. How pathetic.

Opal squeezes my arm, her lips pinched in a frown. "You okay?"

"No." I squeeze my palms against my temples. "I feel like I'm going crazy. I keep waiting to wake up."

She laughs. "I was literally in your shoes a couple months ago. Ambushed in an alleyway, Patrick and his crew saved me. Reality is fucked up. You'll feel better after some rest, though." The rusted metal door she pushes open groans angrily. The inside isn't much better than the outside. Graffiti covers the walls, missing tiles dot the floor, and several lockers have been turned over on their side. Above us, a buzzing fluorescent light blinks on and off, casting dark shadows all around us.

Still, as freaky as this place is, there are signs of life. Voices come from inside several open classrooms. The smell of something sweet and meaty—chili?—permeates the hallway.

"Do you live here?" I ask.

"Yep—at least this week, anyway. We move around a lot." Opal releases my arm and skips ahead. "Sure, it's not much to look at, but the people are totally cool. You can bunk with me."

"Or you can give her your room and *you* can bunk with me." A guy with wavy brown hair and a torn AC/DC shirt steps out of a classroom marked Art Studio. He leans against the doorframe, crossing his boots at the ankles.

Opal stops in her tracks, a flush burning up her cheeks.

Tattoos of devils, skulls, and corpses decorate both of his arms. A silver hoop pierces his eyebrow. "Hunting must be bad if you're back so late. I can console you, if you like."

"Shut up, Scott," Opal says, her tone playful. Her lip twitches as if fighting off a grin. "Maybe you haven't heard, but I single-handedly bagged and tagged a bloodsucker, and saved this one"—she nods at me—"from the farm."

Smirking, he folds his arms across his chest. "I'm supposed to be impressed that you bagged a Mentis? Try two Corpus fifteen minutes after the sun set."

"*Please*, all you need to bag a Corpus is a little blood and a net. Mentis require skill—which is why you've never caught more than two, right?" Opal grins. "And did I forget to mention this particular Mentis came with a Mercedes CLS-Coupe?"

"Shut up." Scott's eyes widen, and he gives Opal a lighthearted shove. "I got to see this."

She giggles. "Patrick and some of the others are unloading the leech from the car as we speak. If you ask nice, he'll probably let you take it for a spin. You might have to clean leech blood off the back seat."

"Worth it. This is awesome." He hooks an arm around Opal's neck, plants a kiss on the top of her head, and takes off toward the front of the building.

Opal's cheeks burn crimson as she watches him go.

Only when I shift awkwardly from foot to foot does she seem to remember I exist. "Sorry." She shakes her head and starts down the hallway. "Scott and I, we kind of have this *will they or won't they* thing going on. So far it's *won't*. The hunter life isn't exactly ideal for dating. And it doesn't help he's a man-whore." She sighs. "It's dumb, I know. But it's not like you get to choose who stokes your fire, right?" She stops at the last door on the right. An old plaque labeled

SCIENCE LAB hangs sideways from a single bolt.

Opal enters the room. Inside, stuffed bears are perched on several lab tables along with beakers and test tubes. The teacher's desk has been pushed to the side, and the chalkboard is covered with more graffiti. Rainbow Christmas lights hang from the ceiling. Some loops dangle so low we duck to walk beneath them.

A cot with a sleeping bag knotted up on the end has been shoved in the corner. Posters of spiky-hair, eyeliner-wearing musicians decorate the wall above it. Beside it lays a rainbow rug and a pair of fuzzy pink slippers. The ghost of formaldehyde and dissected frogs tickles my nose.

I quickly cover my face with my hand.

"I know, the smell, right?" Sighing, Opal snatches a bottle of air freshener off the nearest lab table and douses the room. The overwhelming scent of chemical watermelon makes my stomach lurch.

"Better, right?" She grins.

Dropping my hand, I force a smile that feels more like a grimace. "Much better." I cough.

"It was the last available room when I got here." She touches one of the built-in faucets on a lab table. "Even so, I kind of love it. Science has always interested me. It has rules, you know. In a world full of monsters, it's nice to know at least some things make sense."

I nod even though nothing makes sense to me right now. I grab an empty test tube off a rack and give it a sniff. The smell burns my nostrils, and I quickly replace it.

Opal laughs. "You have to be exhausted. Take my bed." She points to the cot. "I'll have the boys bring in an extra one for me later."

The last thing I want to do is sleep, but if Opal thinks I do, I might have the opportunity to explore on my own a little. Maybe I can even find out where they're keeping Sebastian. I might not trust him, but the hunters aren't exactly giving me warm fuzzies, either. "Aren't you tired?"

"Nah." She shakes her head. "I'm always a little juiced after a bag and tag. Think I'll go to the common room and play some Xbox. You can come with, if you like."

I walk over to the bed and force a yawn. "If it's okay with you, I think I'm going to crash."

Her face softens. "Totally okay. You've had a hell of a night." She walks to the cot and smooths the sleeping bag. "But you're safe now. And Patrick and the boys are interrogating the leech as we speak. I bet they'll have a plan to get your aunt back real soon. Go to bed, and things are going to be a lot brighter in the morning. You'll see." She winks and heads for the door.

I count to twenty after she leaves and head for the door and poke my head out. Down the hall, a door opens. I can't be sure, but I think I hear Sebastian shout from inside the room. My heart lurches. Despite everything he's done to me, I can't stand the thought of anyone being tortured. One of Patrick's men walks out into the hallway. He leans against a row of lockers with a gun in his hand. Spotting me, his eyes narrow. "You need something?" he calls out.

My throat tightens. "Um, just wondering where the bathroom is."

"First door to your right." He pushes off the lockers. "I'll escort you."

"No. That's okay." I shuffle away from the door. "I don't have to go, I just—thought it would be good information to have in case."

His frown deepens. "Then I expect you'll be going to bed. It's not safe to *wander.*"

"Right." Turning, I retreat into Opal's room. *What the hell did I get myself into?* While I might not be wearing chains, I'm every bit the prisoner that Sebastian is. The weight of this realization overcomes me, and my knees give out. I fall onto the cot.

I'm so incredibly stupid. I drop my head into my hands. I did this. I wanted away from Marion, our small town. I wanted to be in a real school. And here I am, getting exactly what I wished for, at the expense of my aunt, my sanity, and possibly even my life.

This is my fault, I think, as footsteps pace outside the door. I wanted something out of my reach. And now, I'd do anything—even make a deal with the devil himself—to take it all back.

Chapter
Eight

I can't sleep. Opal's room has no door, so my muscles tense every time the clatter of footsteps come down the hall. Every so often I'll hear the door to Sebastian's room open and close, angry voices emanating from within.

The worst is when the footsteps head in my direction and pause outside the door. I have to keep my eyes shut and breathing even though all I want is to pull the covers over my head and hide. Especially when I feel the heated stare of the guard watching me from the doorway.

"What do you think about the girl's story?"

Somehow, I manage not to flinch when the man's voice cuts through the silence of the room. On the bed, with my back to the door, I hold my breath to keep from moving.

"Not sure," a voice I recognize as Patrick's answers. "We'll keep pressing the bloodsucker in the meantime. If we can't crack him, we'll crack the girl. We'll get the answers we want sooner or later."

I fight to keep my breathing even. Am I the girl? If so, whatever they have in store for me, it doesn't sound good. I count to ten before their footsteps echo down the hall. Even then I hold my breath until my chest burns before finally exhaling.

I crack one eye open, then another. I have no idea what time it is, only that Opal's been gone for several hours. The clock on the wall doesn't move, and probably hasn't for a long time. Peeling the blanket back, I slide my feet over the side of the cot. My first priority is figuring out who these hunters really are. If they're not on the up and up, my second priority is going to be escaping.

Without shoes, I'm able to silently pad to the doorway and look out. No one stands guard outside Sebastian's room. My pulse quickens. I know the hallway won't remain empty for long, so if I'm going to move, it has to be now.

It's not until I'm darting across the hall that I realize I don't have a plan. I've only made it several feet down the hall when the sound of approaching footsteps echoes ahead.

Crap! Sliding to a halt, I grab the first doorknob within reach and duck inside the room.

Plywood boards are nailed across the windows. Several beams of moonlight filter through the knotholes, allowing enough light for me to see what appears to be a large dog cage sitting in the middle of the room. Locked inside, Sebastian sits hunched over, his head ducked so his wavy brown hair hangs across his face like a curtain. His legs are crossed, his arms resting on his knees.

I slap my hands over my mouth to smother a gasp.

Snarling, he looks up. When he sees me, his lips slowly uncurl. "Charlie? What are you doing here?" Before I can answer, he holds up a hand. "Someone is coming. Quick, stand behind the door. They won't like it if they find you here."

Nodding, I duck into the corner. The door swings open, hiding me from view. My heart beats so loudly I'm sure it's going to give away my position.

"Enjoy your last moments on the planet, bloodsucker," a man's voice I don't recognize says. "Tomorrow you die. Course, you could save us all the trouble of torturing you by telling us what you were doing with that girl."

From the crack between the door and the wall, I see a flash of fangs as Sebastian smiles. "Already told you. I was enjoying a midnight snack."

"Seems you traveled an awful long way to pick up a meal."

Sebastian shrugs. "Why wouldn't I make the trip? I have suspicions the local cuisine is inbred."

"Crack your jokes," the man says, a growl in his voice. "Your time is running out." He slams the door hard enough to rattle the walls.

I let my breath out in a whoosh as I peel off the wall.

Despite being threatened, Sebastian watches me with an almost amused expression on his face. "What are you doing here, Charlie?"

I slowly approach the cage. "I don't trust these guys."

He laughs, tipping his head back. "What gave you that impression? The large guns? Their thirst for violence?"

"Yeah, well, I don't trust you, either." I crouch down beside his cage. The door is bolted shut with a large padlock.

"Then what are you doing here?"

"The hell if I know." I rake my fingers through my hair, only to find a mess of tangles. "I thought I could find some more information about these guys, and I wound up here."

"You need to leave," he says, his eyes glittering in the dark. "They won't like it if they find you talking to me. It's not safe."

I make a face. "Please don't pretend you care about my safety."

"I'm not pretending." He lowers his chin, leveling me with his gaze. "You have answers, Charlie, answers I've been seeking for a very long time. I will stop at nothing to protect you."

Something about his words makes my pulse flutter. "Shouldn't you be more concerned about your own safety? I mean, you're the one in a cage."

He sighs. "For *now*."

"Can't you bust out of this thing?" I grab one of the thin bars and tug. "You're super strong, right?"

"Yes. But the bars are made out of silver. I'd tear myself apart if I tried to escape."

I let go of the bar and settle onto the ground. "Why aren't you afraid? You heard the guy—they're going to torture you tomorrow."

He laughs. "You act as if this will be the first time I've been tortured."

I'm quiet for a moment before responding. "Being a vampire sounds super fun."

He smiles, but there's a sadness to it. "You should go. You've already put yourself in great danger by being here."

"Yeah, you're probably right." I move to stand, but something keeps me rooted in place. "I have to know, were you going to take me to your farm and kill me?"

"No," he answers simply. "And you can see I have

nothing to gain by telling you the truth. I needed your help as much as you needed mine."

Maybe it makes me an idiot, but I swear I hear the truth in his words. A tremor of something—fear?—ripples down the length of my spine. While Sebastian isn't exactly my favorite person on the planet, I hate the thought of him being tortured and killed. "What if this is the last time I see you? How will I find my aunt?"

"If something happens to me, get away from here as fast as you can. Find Matteo. He's the only one who will be able to help you."

A lump wedges inside my throat. Nodding, I turn for the door.

"Charlie?"

I pause.

"In case they do kill me tomorrow, will you take my hand again? To see if I'm able to remember any more of my past?" He stretches his arm through the cage, careful to keep from touching the bars.

I swallow several times before answering. "Okay."

His shirtsleeve is rolled up to his elbow, his fingers stretched wide and waiting.

I kneel beside the cage, my hand shaking slightly as I place it inside his. Sebastian looks from my hand to my face, his expression unreadable. His fingers curl around mine, and I flinch, waiting for the shock of light to blast us apart.

But it doesn't come.

Closing his eyes, Sebastian gives another sad smile. "Thank you for trying."

"I'm sorry I couldn't help." I move to stand, but Sebastian's hand tightens on mine, keeping me in place.

"Charlie, you have nothing to be sorry for." His silver eyes catch the moonlight, making them glow. "You trusted me enough to try. That means something."

I try to speak, but the words don't come.

"I need you to do something else for me," he says. "Trust me again." He releases my hand, leaving me alone and suddenly cold.

I hug my arms to my body. "What do you mean?"

"I'll get you out of here. I'll keep you safe. Do you trust me?"

I almost laugh. "What are you going to do? You're locked in a cage."

"Do you *trust* me?" he repeats.

"Yeah, sure." I can't keep the skepticism from my voice. "You're somehow going to get out of that cage and free us from an entire building of scary guys with guns."

Grinning, he settles back to the center of the cage. It's only then I notice the red welts on his arm where his skin touched the bars. "Go now. Before they find you. And whatever you do, don't tell the hunters *anything*."

I open my mouth to argue, only to have him cut me off with a hiss. "*Go.*"

I stand and go to the door, opening it a crack, and I find the hallway miraculously empty. Before I dart into the hallway, something compels me to turn back for one last look.

"*Go,*" Sebastian mouths, his eyes narrowed.

I nod and slip into the hallway, closing the door behind me. I sprint to Opal's room and bury myself beneath the covers, breathing hard. While my entire body is wracked with chills, the hand I touched Sebastian with remains warm, as if I somehow carried a bit of his heat back with me. I hold it against my chest.

Do you trust me? His words echo through my brain. Logically, I know he's a monster who can't be trusted. And yet, there's some part of me, probably the stupid part, that believes him. Or maybe it's only that I want to believe him. Because without a super-powered vampire on my side, what the hell chance do I have of saving my aunt?

Chapter Nine

I keep my eyes shut for several minutes when I wake. As long as I stay submerged in darkness, I can convince myself that the last forty-eight hours were a bad dream. At least, that's what I think until the smell of formaldehyde and watermelon air freshener lets me know how real everything is.

Without lights, long shadows drape across the science lab floor, growing longer by the second. It will be night soon.

I jerk upright. With everything going on, how could I have fallen asleep?

"Hey, roomie. Sleep okay?" Opal walks into the room holding bowl. Grinning, she plops onto a stool next to a lab station.

I stand, tendons popping as I stretch my sore neck from side to side. My first thought is Sebastian, and whether or not he's okay. Still, I push that aside. Sympathizing with a vampire is not going to get me very far in a hunter camp. "Have you heard anything? I really need to find my aunt. I've already lost so much time."

"You can't do anything without a decent breakfast." Opal slurps the milk from the bowl. "It's the most important meal of the day. We have Lucky Charms, Cheerios, and Frosted Flakes. The bad news is we're all out of regular milk. We have almond." She makes a face. "But it's not the same."

"Thanks, but I don't want food. I want to find my aunt."

"Are you sure you're not hungry?" Her eyes dart to the door and back. A man dressed in leather stands just outside the room holding one of the biggest guns I've ever seen. His back is to us, but his tight shoulders let me know he's ready for anything.

A nauseous wave rolls through my gut as my earlier fear is confirmed. "I'm being held prisoner, aren't I?"

"What?" She gives a nervous laugh. "That's ridiculous. Reggie out there is protecting you, not guarding you."

"Really?" I edge toward the door. "So I can leave right now if I want?"

"You can leave anytime you want. Just—not right this second." She sets her spoon aside. "At least not until you talk to Patrick."

There's something about the way she's avoiding eye contact that tickles my stomach with unease. "What does Patrick want with *me*?"

She chews on her lip. "Turns out the bloodsucker that kidnapped you wasn't as easy to crack as Patrick hoped. He wants your help interrogating him."

The knot of worry inside my chest loosens a fraction. At least I know Sebastian is still alive. Still, the fact Patrick wants to see us together can't be good. What if he knows I spoke with him last night? "What does Patrick think I can do that you guys can't?"

"I told Patrick to give you a break, considering everything you went through." Sighing, Opal picks up her spoon and stirs the milk inside the bowl. "He's just all up in arms right now. Says things aren't adding up, Charlie."

Something cold and slippery winds around my stomach. "What kind of things?"

She looks at me, and the intensity of her gaze makes me want to flinch. "When the bloodsuckers go harvesting for their farm, they usually stick with homeless people and runaways—people no one will miss—that's why they went after me." She looks away, but not before I spot the pain that flashes through her eyes. "What doesn't make sense is why they'd go after you and your aunt. We saw the last address entered in the Mercedes's GPS. Why go an entire state away to kidnap some woman and her niece?"

Don't tell the hunters anything. Sebastian's warning from last night replays through my mind.

Reflexively, my fingers curl into my sweater. What if I do have vampire blood in my veins? What would the hunters do to me if they found out? What have they already done to Sebastian? "I have no idea."

Opal says nothing, only continues to search my face until I'm forced to look away. "You have to admit, it's all very weird," Opal says, as I stare at my shoes.

"I wish I had the answers," I say. "Two days ago, I didn't even know vampires existed. As far as their motivation goes, your guess is as good as mine."

She nods, her expression carefully blank. "That's what we'll tell Patrick."

"Okay." I'm careful to keep my voice even as my pulse

skips inside my veins. Despite my best effort, my eyes are repeatedly drawn to the gun holstered to her hip.

"Great. They're in the interrogation room." She starts for the door, pausing long enough to make sure I'm following.

I trail her out of her room and into the hallway on shaky legs. The man guarding the door gives Opal a nod, his lips set in a grim line. We pass several open classrooms as we walk. Inside one, two women sit around a desk cleaning a stack of guns. In another classroom, a man sits against the wall carving a long piece of wood with a gleaming knife.

"He's whittling wooden arrows," Opal says, answering my unasked question. "We also carve bullets out of wood. You get a vampire in the heart with one of those?" She mimes an explosion with her hands.

I can practically feel the blood drain from my face. We walk in silence, my thrumming pulse beating in time to the sound of Opal's boots slapping the linoleum. My heart grows heavier inside my chest, weighing me down, making each step more difficult than the one before.

"I wish I could go back, too," Opal says.

"What?"

"To before," she continues. "When I didn't know *they* existed and the only monsters were the revolving door of foster parents I was placed with." She stops in front of a pair of double doors and places a hand on the peeling paint. *Varsity Gymnasium Home of the Wasps* is stenciled in faded letters across the top. "But there's no going back." She pushes the door open.

A sickly sweet smell of decay barrels into me. I quickly cover my nose with my arm. "What the hell is that?"

"Death." Opal raises an arm, gesturing me forward.

Like an idiot, I walk inside.

The large room reveals hints of its past life as a gymnasium. A single basketball hoop hangs from the ceiling on the far side. A rusted scoreboard is perched beside it. Half of the overhead bulbs are missing, casting various patches of light and dark across the room. The floor bears traces of lines that once marked boundaries for different sports. But those lines are mostly hidden beneath the dried and flaking dark stains soaked into the wood that are too numerous to count.

If there were bleachers, they're now long gone. Instead, rows of chains are bolted to every wall. To my right, a figure huddles against the wall, head buried in its arms, a chain bound to its neck. Patrick, along with a woman and man, stands in the middle of the room. They don't look up as we approach. With guns raised, all three are focused on a figure crouched between them.

Bile burns up my throat. "What are they doing?"

Without looking away, Patrick smiles. "Oh good, you're here. Give us a minute to finish up with this Corpus, and we'll get to the Mentis you bagged last night."

Opal shrugs. "Take your time." She acts as if we walked in on them baking a cake or something equally as boring.

The figure has its head bowed, lines of greasy black hair draped across its face. I don't even realize I'm moving forward until Opal catches my arm and jerks me back. "Not too close," she cautions.

I don't see what the fuss is about. The creature is skinny, its bones practically protruding from beneath its gray skin. But then, as if reading my mind, its head snaps up.

My blood turns to ice and I gasp. "Is that—is that a

zombie?" I can't tell if it's male or female. Yellowed nails curl out from its fingers, hooking into pointed claws. Large black orbs peer out from behind sagging eyelids. Peeling back thin lips, it hisses, revealing fangs longer and more deadly than Sebastian's.

Opal laughs. "Zombies don't exist, silly. This is your garden-variety vampire."

"No." I hug my arms to my body. "I've seen vampires and that *thing* doesn't look anything like one."

"You've seen *Mentis* vampires," Opal says. "This is a Corpus."

"A *what*?" The creature continues to stare at me, unblinking. I hear a rumbling sound and it takes me a second to realize the *thing* is growling at me. I inch away.

Watching me, Patrick cocks his head. "You sure you've never seen one of these before?"

I shake my head. "I think I would remember seeing a moving corpse."

"What do you know about the other clans?" Patrick asks.

"Other—*clans*?"

"There are three clans of vampires." Opal steps toward the creature on the floor and studies it. Its lipless mouth curls back in a snarl. Resting her hand on the gun at her hip, Opal chuckles. "This piece of rotting flesh is a member of the Corpus clan. The vampires who kidnapped you are Mentis clan. The third clan, the Anima clan, is the hardest to identify as they look the most human. All three clans have different abilities and appearances."

The creature on the floor looks as if it might decompose at any moment. How could it be related to Sebastian? "I don't understand. How is that possible?"

"The best we can tell is diet," Patrick answers. "The Anima clan's fangs are small and their eyes are a dark emerald, almost passing for human-green in certain light. We guess this is because they don't need to hunt. They only eat from animals and willing humans."

"They can also transform," Opal says.

"No, they can't," I whisper, because I don't want it to be true. The monsters are scary enough without other freaky attributes.

"They can and they do," the woman across from Patrick says. Streaks of gray line her braided hair. Hoops are pierced through her lip and eyebrow. "But only into certain animals—birds mostly, not just the bats of legend."

Opal continues to walk around the kneeling vampire. While its eyes are devoid of color, I get the eerie feeling it's watching her every move. "The Mentis clan—which you've already met—only consume human blood. Some are willing donors, most are held captive on their farm. Like the leech we found you with, they all look like Instagram models. They use their beauty to lure prey. Their eyes glow blueish-sliver, and their fangs are longer and sharper."

"They have the power of persuasion," Patrick says. "They can compel people to do their bidding."

I nearly choke. "I *knew* my aunt wouldn't willingly leave me. They must have compelled her."

He nods. "Slippery suckers. The trick is not looking them in the eyes."

"And this rancid, foul-smelling, living corpse," Opal gestures to the monster on the floor, "is a Corpus vampire. They eat anything and everything; animals, humans, other vampires, even their own kin." Opal draws her gun, and the three other hunters step aside. She fires, hitting the vampire in the chest. Blackened bits of flesh and dark ooze splatter across the floor. It lets out an ear-splitting shriek before falling over.

My stomach clenches painfully tight as I fight to keep from getting sick.

"Show her," Opal says, cleaning the muzzle of her gun with the edge of her shirt.

Despite the overwhelming urge to run from the room, I manage to stay rooted to the floor with my hands pressed against my mouth. I have no doubt whatever comes next won't be any better.

The man hoists the monster up by its shoulders and drags it to the other creature chained to the wall. Its head snaps up as they approach. It's another Corpus vampire, with equally long fangs, gray skin, and a gaunt face. This one, however, is noticeably female, with a slender frame and small breasts.

They drop the corpse in front of her. With a yowl, she uses her claws to rip into the other vampire's chest. I feel as if my own bones are breaking with each crack of the dead vampire's ribs as they're snapped apart. With its ribs splayed wide, the female corpus buries her face into the gut, slurping noisily.

I press my hand against my nose and mouth. "I'm going to be sick."

Patrick clamps a hand on my shoulder. It should be a reassuring gesture, but instead I flinch. "No shame in it," he says. "Most of us were the first time we witnessed a feeding."

The creature continues to rip and slurp, breaking bones and tearing into organs in its desperation to feed. Finally, it sits up, tilting its head back so lines of black liquid and meat drip down its neck. It meets my gaze with its jet-black eyes and grins.

I recoil. "You said every clan has an ability…what can a Corpus vampire do?"

Patrick releases my shoulder. "They can pass almost undetected in shadows."

As if in response, the creature appears to dissolve into the shadows behind her, reducing her figure to a dark outline. Her giggle echoes around the room. "They're coming for you, to feast on your insides."

Her voice scrapes across my brain like an icepick. I shudder.

Patrick sighs. "Shut it up."

Opal nods. Withdrawing her gun, she aims toward the huddled black mass and fires. The creature materializes as it falls from the shadows only to collapse on the ground in a heap.

"I definitely do not like Corpus vampires," I whisper.

Patrick smiles. "Hey Opal, what's the only good kind of vampire?"

"A dead one," she answers, holstering her gun.

He laughs. "That's right, kiddo." He claps her on the back a couple of times when she returns to his side. "Now let's get that Mentis leech out here and see if we can figure out why he traveled such a great distance for you." He wags a finger at me, and my heart does a summersault. "Unless you know why—sure would save us a lot of trouble."

My throat is too constricted for words, so I shake my head.

Patrick frowns. "Guess we'll have to do this the hard

way." He turns to a set of double doors in the back of the room. "Bring 'em out."

Seconds later, two men push through the doors. They each hold a chain that connects to a metal collar, which is clamped securely around Sebastian's neck.

My blood freezes into ice. Sebastian's face is a blank mask. The only sign of emotion is the silvery fire blazing in his eyes. Despite the collar around his neck, he moves with his shoulders back and head high, like he's out for a walk, instead of the prisoner of some crazy biker gang. His shirt is ripped and stained crimson, but there are no visible wounds on his skin except for the raw-looking red welts on his neck from the collar. Something inside of me twists at the sight.

"Pure silver chains," Opal whispers into my ear. "All vampires are allergic. Silver is the only metal that can weaken a vampire enough to hold them."

The two men stop with Sebastian between them. They tighten their hold on the chains while he tucks his hands in his pants pockets, appearing at ease. His eyes lock onto mine for just a moment before he turns his attention away. "Patrick." He nods to the older man.

Grinning, Patrick cocks his head to the side. "I don't believe I gave you my name during our earlier *interviews*."

Sebastian gives a slight shrug. "No, but your reputation as a nuisance precedes you. I knew exactly who you were when I first laid eyes on you."

Patrick laughs. "I'll take that as a compliment." He paces in front of Sebastian, looking him up and down. The vampire's chocolate hair hangs in disheveled strands across his forehead, and his skin is noticeably paler.

Sebastian catches me looking at him and winks before turning his attention to Patrick.

I clamp my lips together even as my cheeks warm.

"You can take it as you like," Sebastian says, "but if you were smart, you'd take it for what it is—a threat."

Patrick gives a small nod. The man on Sebastian's right withdraws a gun. Sebastian arches an eyebrow right before the gunman fires a bullet into his leg.

I inhale sharply. Patrick frowns at me and I quickly try to muffle my breathing with my hands.

Sebastian's wince lasts for only a second before it's buried under a mask of indifference, even as blood oozes from the hole in his pants. "If you're trying to kill me, you're failing miserably. I know most of you are lacking an education, so I'll make it simple. My heart is here." He taps his chest.

"How dare you," Patrick spits. "How dare you come into *my* house and mock me. We all know you're going to die here tonight. Question is, how long do you want us to drag it out?"

"Please don't do this." Before I realize what I'm doing, I find myself creeping toward the door I came in from. I know I need to do something—but I'm not sure what. There are too many hunters between us, and I know I'd never be able to stop them from killing Sebastian. That doesn't mean I have to stand here and watch it happen.

Opal catches me and quickly loops her arm through mine. "You don't have to be afraid. This is all part of the process."

Patrick gives another nod, and the man shoots Sebastian in his other thigh.

The vampire grunts, but remains standing.

I clench and unclench my fingers, fighting the urge to reach out and snatch the gun aimed at Sebastian. "Opal, this is—this is torture. I can't watch this." I glance at the door. Something moves along the wall, just outside my peripheral vision, but when I turn to look, nothing is there.

"Don't worry." Opal grips me tighter. She licks her lips, leaning almost eagerly toward Sebastian. "It'll all be over soon."

Fear grips my chest like a vice. I'm not sure who the true monsters really are.

Patrick spits at Sebastian's feet. "Your wounds won't heal with a wooden bullet in them. If you talk, we can end your suffering real quick. Stay quiet and we can bleed you out for days. Why did you travel all the way to Marion, Illinois, for the girl?"

Sebastian's eyes blaze. "I was in the neighborhood and thought I could use a little snack."

"Liar." Patrick juts his chin and the gunman fires again, this time hitting Sebastian in the shoulder. Sebastian inhales sharply, his expression carefully blank. Ribbons of blood wind down his chest and legs.

"Opal checked the girl for bite wounds," Patrick says. "She doesn't have any."

"Wait. You *checked* me?" I pull my arm free of Opal's. "When?"

She shrugs. "You're a sound sleeper. I was just making sure you weren't hurt."

I hug my arms across my chest. Inside my head, alarm bells sound off. "You don't think that's invasive?"

"Not as invasive as if you were infected, turned into one

of those things, and ripped my throat out. Relax, Charlie. It was for your own good."

"I warned you," Sebastian says, with a smug tilt of his head. "Hunters are not to be trusted."

Patrick laughs out loud. "Oh, that's rich. The murdering bloodsucker says *we're* not to be trusted."

The alarm bells in my head reach near-deafening volume. I take another step back. This isn't right. *Nothing* about this feels okay.

"Now, hold up there, sweetheart." Patrick turns his narrow-eyed gaze on me. "I'm going to need you to relax and stay put. There's plenty that needs figuring out here."

Coming here with Opal was a mistake. I can feel it now in the electricity humming through my veins. This was a stupid, dangerous mistake. "Or what?" I shake my head and take another step back. "You're going to shoot me, too?"

Patrick shrugs. "If I have to, yes." He slips a hand inside his jacket and withdraws a gun.

Every muscle in my body collectively tightens as my lungs lock up and I fight to draw breath.

"You see, Charlie, my job is to keep people safe." Raising the gun, Patrick takes long, slow strides toward me. "And to do that, I need to eliminate all threats." He cocks the trigger. The click echoes in the hollow space where my heart was before it fell to the floor. "So how about it, Charlie? Are you an asset? Or are you a threat?"

chapter
Ten

"You will not touch her," Sebastian yells, straining against his chains. The two men gripping the chains wince and fumble in a struggle to restrain him.

I can't move. I can't breathe. All I can do is stare at the empty darkness that is the barrel of the gun pointed at my head.

"What the fuck, Patrick?" Opal darts to my side. "What the hell are you doing?"

"Being cautious." He keeps the gun trained on me. "Thought I taught you the same."

"You *taught* me to protect people," she snaps.

"And that's exactly what I'm doing. Something strange is going on here, and this girl knows more than she's saying." He takes another step toward me. "You better start spilling."

"Drop your weapon," Sebastian growls. "If you so much as scratch her, I will introduce you to your still-beating heart."

"See?" Patrick points a finger at Opal. "Vampires do *not* protect humans. Explain that."

Opal frowns. "Charlie, what is going on?"

Again, I think I see something move outside the edge of my vision. I glance over my shoulder. Several dark shadows cast by nothing I can see are clustered together in the corner. At least a dozen more line the far wall, blocking a door marked *Emergency Exit.*

"Opal?"

"Yeah?"

"Don't Corpus vampires have the ability to hide in the shadows?" My voice quivers.

Patrick gives an impatient huff. "Answer the damn question. What the hell is your connection to the vampires?"

"Yes," a deep hissing voice interrupts. "By all means, answer the question."

The shadows appear to peel off the wall, solidifying into more than a dozen Corpus vampires. Dressed in ripped, dirt-streaked, and sweat-stained clothing, they have the same corpse-gray skin and identical snarls—or maybe they're grinning? Without lips, it's hard to tell.

One vampire stands ahead of the rest. His mostly-shaved head sports a foot-long blue Mohawk. He wears leather boots that buckle up to his knees and a large, gold hoop through his nose. "We've been searching for your little hideout for quite a while." His is the voice that spoke from the shadows. "We don't mind waiting another couple of minutes before devouring you all. Please, finish your conversation."

Opal grabs my arm, her nails digging into my skin like claws. This, more than the vampires surrounding us, shoots terror into my veins like a drug. I didn't think fear was an emotion Opal could feel. Even Sebastian's usual cocky expression has been replaced with that of concern. If they're worried, that can only mean one thing—we're all going to die.

Patrick shifts the aim of his gun toward the mass of approaching vampires. The color has bled from his face, leaving his skin the same hue as his glassy eyes. "Opal, you get the chance, you run."

Still holding my arm, she draws her gun with the other hand. The other hunters do the same. "Patrick, I won't leave—"

"Dammit all to hell, girl." The flush returns to his face. "For one goddamn minute can you do what you're told. RUN." He fires his gun, striking a female vampire in the chest. She falls to the floor and doesn't get up. The two vampires standing beside her pounce on her fallen corpse, ripping apart her chest with their teeth.

Mohawk bares his fangs. "That was the last of your many, many mistakes." He raises a hand in the air and snaps his fingers. "Kill them all."

With a collective growl that vibrates from the walls into the soles of my feet, the Corpus vampires charge.

Sebastian yells, straining against the chains. "Charlie, run!"

In response, the gunman holding his chain fires another bullet, this time striking him in the chest. Sebastian falls to the ground.

"No!" I start toward him, only to be jerked by Opal. She fires a bullet into the chest of a Corpus vampire running toward us.

"Leave him," she says, shooting a round into the head of another vampire. "He's dead. And we will be, too, if we don't get out of here."

Next to us, a Corpus vampire sinks her teeth into the woman hunter. She cries out before collapsing to her knees.

"Tammy!" Opal releases me and fires at the vampire, shattering the back of its skull. It slumps forward, falling on top of Tammy, who doesn't get up. "No." Opal's face crumples.

Terror squeezes my throat, threatening to suffocate me.

"Keep shooting," Patrick yells. He's across the room, kicking the head of a vampire on the floor while trying to pull a Corpus off the hunter who shot Sebastian. From the pale color of the hunter's skin, lines of blood running down his neck, I can tell it's too late for him, too.

Screams and gunfire erupt from beyond the gym doors.

"The whole place is under attack," Opal whimpers. A male Corpus grabs her arm with a clawed hand. Opal heaves it over her shoulder onto the ground and shoots it in the chest.

A week ago, I never realized how useless and weak I am. Then again, I didn't really have a reason to be anything but. I whirl around, looking for a weapon—any weapon—when my eyes find Sebastian. He's on his back, chest heaving, struggling with the chain around his neck.

Across the room, a Corpus vampire wearing torn fishnet stockings with a miniskirt and combat boots stalks toward him, licking her lips.

No. I've seen what Corpus do to other vampires. Monster or not, I won't let that happen to Sebastian.

Something rams into my shoulders and I sprawl to the ground. A shot fires and a Corpus collapses beside me. Its gray tongue rolls out of its gaping mouth, only inches from my face. I suck in a quivering breath, push onto my knees, and keep crawling.

Sebastian frowns when I reach him. "What are you doing?"

"Saving you." I fumble with the clasps of chain with shaking fingers. From this close, I can smell the copper tang of the blood that soaks his shirt. I hope I'm not too late.

The female Corpus must smell it, too. Her grin widens with each step.

Sebastian's brow furrows. "Why risk yourself?"

"I don't know." I shake my head. "But if there's some *Too Stupid To Live* award out there, I want to make sure I secure my nomination." The clasp pops open. I unwind the chain from his neck.

The moment I drop the chain to the ground, Sebastian tackles me.

I really do deserve that award, I think as I fall backward. My shoulder hits the floor with enough force to make spots flood my vision.

On my back, Sebastian straddles me with arms on either side of my head. "Stay down," he orders, "and don't leave my sight."

"Wha—" I don't get to finish before the female Corpus lands on his back—the exact spot I was sitting only a second ago. He grunts before whipping her to the ground beside me. Rolling off me, he punches a fist into her chest. The sound of bones cracking raises bile up my throat. He pulls out a shriveled black organ—what I can only guess was her heart. It pulses several times in his hand before he squeezes it, black ooze dripping across his fingers, and flings it across the room.

"The hell?" I squeak, crab-crawling away.

"Stay close to me. I will keep you alive." A second vampire rushes him. Sebastian dodges their outstretched hands, grabs them by the neck, and twists. After the body falls to the floor, he rips out the heart and drops it to the ground. For all the chaos erupting around us, he almost looks *bored.* Sebastian flings the black liquid from his hand and winces. Hissing, he digs his fingers into each of his wounds, pulls out the bloody bullets, and drops them to the ground. With the bullets gone, his skin weaves together before my eyes, without so much as a scar left behind.

A man's scream echoes throughout the gymnasium.

I whirl around to find Mohawk, the last vampire standing, ripping into Patrick's throat with his fangs.

"No!" Opal's shriek is a mixture of anguish and rage. She fires her gun.

Mohawk takes a bullet in the shoulder. With a snarl, he drops Patrick's limp body to the ground and faces Opal. "I can already taste your blood."

"Taste this." Opal fires. The first shot goes wide. The second shot never comes. Instead, the empty chamber clicks over and over as she squeezes the trigger. All color drains from her face, leaving her ghostly pale. "Shit." She squeezes the trigger several more times before throwing the gun at the vampire.

He catches it one-handed, crumpling the metal in his fist before tossing it aside.

Opal whimpers.

I turn to Sebastian and tug on his shirtsleeve. "You have to do something."

He grunts. "No, I don't. She ambushed me, remember?"

"Fine. Then I will." I stalk across the gymnasium only

to be jerked backward by my shirt collar.

"Do you have a death wish?" Sebastian says with a growl. "I promised I would keep you safe, but my patience has a limit."

"I don't care." I shrug out of his grasp. "Opal doesn't deserve to die like this. No one does."

Pinching the bridge of his nose with his fingers, Sebastian sighs. "Fine. I will save the girl, but only if you *stay put.* Agreed?"

I nod. "Hurry."

Mohawk has his yellow claws hooked around Opal's neck. He opens his jaws wide, a line of saliva dripping from his fangs onto Opal's cheek.

"Enough," Sebastian shouts, striding toward Mohawk with his fists clenched. "Corpus, leave this place. Your point has been proven."

Mohawk snaps his jaws together and laughs. Jerking Opal by her neck, the Corpus swings around to face Sebastian. Opal trembles in his grasp. "You think this was about proving a point?" he asks. "Maybe a Mentis would care about something so juvenile. This was about protecting my family and *revenge.* This group has murdered more than twenty of my brothers and sisters. I have orders from my Queen to devour all humans I find. That includes the two remaining girls." The Corpus turns his onyx gaze on me, running a tongue over his fangs.

A shudder ripples across my body.

Sebastian raises his chin. "I'm afraid I can't let you do that."

Mohawk's claws dig into Opal's neck. She whimpers as thin lines of blood trail down her skin from his fingers.

"You think a weak Mentis such as yourself can stop me?"

With eyes glowing, Sebastian unbuttons his sleeves and rolls them up to the elbows. "It's cute how you assume *I'm* the weak one." His eyes bleed black and he snarls, baring his fangs.

Again, Mohawk laughs. "Pathetic fangs for a pathetic excuse of a vampire." He flings Opal aside. She slams against the wall with a grunt.

I run to her side. "You're okay." I slide my hand under her arm and pull her to her feet.

"I'm *not* okay." She wobbles before leaning heavily on me. "Everyone is dead, Charlie. I couldn't save them." Her voice hitches in a sob.

"I'm going to rip your heart out," Mohawk says to Sebastian, "and shove it down your throat while it's still beating, so you might know the sugary-sweet taste of Mentis blood before you perish."

Sebastian smirks. "It's sad, but also pathetic, how you think you have a fighting chance."

Opal pulls away from me, and I latch on to her arm. "Where are you going?"

"Scott…" She blinks with unfocussed eyes. "I have to check on—to make sure that he's—" She withdraws a wooden stake from her waistband. It falls from her trembling fingers onto the floor.

"Opal." I give her a shake. "We need to stick together. It's our only chance for survival." I scoop the stake off the floor.

Mohawk yells and charges Sebastian with outstretched claws. Sebastian ducks beneath the Corpus's grasping fingers and lands a kick to Mohawk's calves, sending him sprawling. The Corpus snarls and jumps to his feet. "You're only delaying your death," Mohawk says, stretching his neck back and forth.

Sebastian rolls his eyes. "Are all Corpus this disillusioned, or is it just you?"

Mohawk growls. "I am more than two-hundred years old. You don't stand a chance, baby vampire. Your newness reeks."

Surprise flashes across Sebastian's face before his brow furrows. "*Baby* vampire—?"

Mohawk tackles him before he can finish. They roll on the ground, fists flying. The crunch of knuckles connecting with bones echoes off the gymnasium walls as blood splatters the floor at their feet. Mohawk thrusts his fist into Sebastian's gut. He crashes against the wall with a grunt before sliding to the floor.

My heart races and I clutch the stake tighter. I know if Sebastian loses, Opal and I are dead.

Mohawk launches with clenched fists. Sebastian ducks, and Mohawk's fist crashes through the wall. When he pulls it out, bits of plaster rain onto the ground. "Enough of this," Mohawk snarls. "Now you die." He grabs Sebastian's shirt collar and rears back his free hand, claws extended toward Sebastian's chest.

Before I realize what I'm doing, I'm running toward them, stake clenched so tightly my fingers throb.

Sebastian spots me over Mohawk's shoulder and his eyes grow wide. "Charlie, no."

With a yell, I plunge the stake between Mohawk's shoulders.

The Corpus vampire sputters. He releases Sebastian's

shirt and stumbles backward. Turning, his onyx eyes find mine. A low gurgle erupts from his throat, and he coughs, spraying thick, black liquid across my face.

I gasp and scramble away.

Sebastian shoves Mohawk aside. The Corpus vampire lands face-first on the ground and doesn't move. A pool of black ooze seeps out from beneath his body. "We have to go. Now." Sebastian grabs me by the arm and pulls me toward the double doors.

"No." I dig my heels into the ground. "Opal will die if we leave her."

He folds his arms over his chest. "And that's my problem, why?"

I square my jaw. "Because I'm not leaving without her."

I'm not an idiot. I know if Sebastian really wanted to, he could throw me over his shoulder and carry me kicking and screaming from the building. He sighs. "Fine." He crosses the gymnasium, stepping over the bodies of fallen vampires and hunters. Opal stands in the middle, eyes unblinking, rocking back and forth on her feet. Sebastian grabs her wrist. "Against my better judgement, you are coming with us."

"Patrick's dead," she mutters. "Scott, too, probably. Everyone." Her lip quivers.

Sebastian gives her a shake. "If you mourn the dead now, you will join them. Focus instead on surviving."

His words appear to get through. She blinks, her eyes slowly falling into focus. "You're a leech. Why should I trust you?"

Smiling, he releases her. "What other option do you have?"

She frowns.

"He saved us. Come on." I loop my arm through hers and pull her toward the gymnasium doors. "We need to get the hell out of here."

Sebastian reaches the double doors first, but pauses before opening it. He lifts his head in the air and sniffs. "There are more coming. Even through the carnage I can smell their stench." He pushes them open, revealing a hallway littered with blood and bodies.

Opal draws out a breath.

"Stick close to me," he hisses.

Dark shapes spill like ink from shadows cast by the lockers. They solidify into more than a dozen snarling Corpus vampires.

"New plan." Sebastian pushes us backward and slams the doors shut. "I will hold them off while you retreat out the back doors." He jerks his chin toward the emergency exit at the far side of the gymnasium.

"Won't there be more of them outside?" I ask.

"I'm not sure," he replies. "There is too much blood for me to scent through. So be careful. Head straight for my car. I'll meet you there as soon as I dispose of them." Grimacing, the door handles jerk beneath his grasp.

My heart hammers against my ribs. "There are too many of them."

He chuckles. "No, there's just enough to make it a fair fight." His hair hangs across his forehead in disheveled strands clumped with blood. My own skin is streaked with blood and darker bits. "Remember, don't die." He thrusts open the doors and pushes into the grasping hands. The doors slam shut behind him.

Please don't die, either, I think in response. Worry

weaves through my ribs as shrieks and growls erupt from the other side. I tell myself it's because Sebastian is the only one capable of keeping us alive—it would be dumb to care for any other reason. I've survived this long, that proves I have a *few* functioning brain cells, right? And smart girls don't crush on dead boys.

"Charlie, snap out of it."

Blinking, I find Opal skirting around the bodies of hunters and vampires, plucking weapons off the floor. She finds a knife and two guns that she tucks into the holster on her waist. A third gun, still dripping with blood, she tosses to me.

"Jesus," I cry, catching it with two hands, then immediately wish I hadn't when the blood squishes between my fingers. "I don't think you should be throwing guns around like that."

"Don't be a baby." She presses her lips into a grim line. "You ever fired one before?"

"No." After wiping my hand off on my shirt, I thrust the gun back at her. "I'll just end up shooting myself."

"No, you won't. It's easy." She pushes it away. "Just point and pull the trigger."

The door at the back of the room slams open. A Corpus with stringy black hair and sagging jeans stands in the doorway. It snarls, lines of black drool dripping from its fangs onto its chin.

With a yelp, I raise the gun and fire. The vampire falls face-first onto the ground.

"See?" Opal claps my back. "Just like that."

"Just like that," I mutter, with my heart rattling against my sternum.

"C'mon." She takes off toward the emergency exit, and I follow. The rusted door whines in protest as we pry it open. Outside, the cool night air is a welcome relief from the stench of blood and rot inside the gymnasium. "Keep out of the shadows," she says, darting under an overhead light.

"How the hell am I supposed to do that? It's nighttime! It's all shadow." Still, I follow her, skipping and hopping from pool of light to pool of light.

Beside the gymnasium door, a shadow rolls forward. Opal fires and a vampire materializes, only to fall onto the ground. She presses her back against mine, gun extended. The next two streetlights are out, leaving an ocean of darkness between us and the parking lot.

A laugh sounds from the distance. It could be from someone walking on the street—or it could be from something terrible.

I hold my gun out as well, though it shakes in my grip. "We're going to die," I say.

"Probably," she answers back.

"Nice pep-talk."

"Go team human," she replies.

I almost smile. This strange, violent girl—I kind of like her. "It's too bad we can't be friends because of our impending gruesome murders."

She chuckles. "I would have like that—being friends."

The side doors of the school open with a bang.

I suck in a breath and tighten my hold on the gun. Opal's instructions float through my brain like a mantra: *point and squeeze. Point and squeeze. Point and squeeze.*

But instead of a Corpus vampire, Sebastian exits the school. He staggers a few steps before finding his footing.

His shirt is nothing more than ribbons hanging from his neck and wrists. Blood and darker stains streak across every inch of his skin. "We need to leave. *Now.*"

Relief floods through me at the sight of him. His eyes meet mine and hold my gaze. My body temperature rises in response.

Opal lowers her gun. "What about the rest of the horde?"

Chest heaving, he flexes his jaw. "I killed them."

"All of them?" Her voice squeaks. "That's impossible."

"Tell that to the dead Corpus."

Opal stares, wide-eyed, at the doorway. Still, nothing else immerges.

"Charlie." Sebastian grabs my arm and I try to ignore the stupid way my heart sputters when he does. "Are you hurt?"

I shake my head.

"Good." His eyes search the parking lot. "We have to hurry. More will be on their way. Where is my car?"

"Just around the side. Follow me." Opal sprints out of the pool of light into the darkness.

Sebastian extends a hand to me. "Stay close to me."

I hesitate before slipping my hand into his. In some bizarre way, his touch is beginning to feel *right*. It's befitting of my completely screwed-up life.

Sebastian squeezes my hand, pulling me from my thoughts. Even though I know he only offered his hand as a means of survival, just like last night, there's something intimate about having his fingers encase my own.

"We're almost there, Charlie."

I look away from our entwined hands, just as the sharp

sting of claws rakes across my shoulder.

Sebastian's eyes widen in horror. "Charlie."

I don't even get out a scream before I'm jerked from his grasp and spun around. I flinch when the Corpus vampire's breath, a mix of blood and rot, fans hot against my cheek.

She opens her jaws wide, fangs gleaming. "You think you can kill my brothers and sisters and expect to live?"

Shouting, Sebastian reaches for me only to be grabbed and have his arms pinned behind his back by another Corpus. This vampire, a male, has the tattoo of a skull inked onto his face.

This time I do scream. I try wrenching from her grasp, but she only tightens her hold. Her claws rip into my shoulder, breaking skin, making me wince.

"Don't be shy, little mouse," the Corpus whispers in my ear. "I like the sound of screams when I feed." With viper-like speed, she sinks her fangs into my neck.

Pain erupts beneath my skin. I try to fight her off, but she only holds tighter. The agony intensifies as what feels like fire burns away my flesh. It starts at my neck then sweeps across my entire body, incinerating muscles and tendons, organs and bone. My blood feels as if it's boiling inside my veins, cooking me alive. Black spots creep around the edge of my vision, and I welcome them. I want to pass out, if that will put an end to the suffering.

Because I know.

There is no coming back from this.

I know with a certainty that only comes at the end.

This is death.

Chapter
Eleven

Shrieking fills my head. Even though I lack the breath to make a sound, I must be the one screaming. Until this moment, I never realized pain could be a tangible thing—something that could wrap around your body and squeeze until you begged for the end.

I'm sorry, Aunt Rachel. I thought I could save you. But I'm just not strong enough. Please God, let it be over soon.

A flash of white light blinds me. *Is this the end?*

Pain rockets along my hip, and the light vanishes. Slowly, my vision falls into focus and I find myself on the still-warm asphalt, loose gravel digging into my palms.

Beside me, the female Corpus writhes on the ground, twisting along with the flames engulfing her body, almost like a dance.

The fire hadn't been inside me, after all.

Slowly, I roll onto my back, blinking to make sure my eyes aren't playing tricks on me. The stars blink back, the same ones that hung over my head all those boring years I spent at the cabin. I wonder, do these stars even recognize me anymore?

Sebastian's hands are on my shoulders, dragging me away. The heels of my tennis shoes grind against gravel. I can't take my eyes off the writhing figure. The flesh drips from her bones like melting wax. "Wha-what the hell happened?" I ask.

Sebastian pulls me to my feet. A flicker of something— fear, maybe—passes through his eyes. "Charlie, she bit you and erupted in flames."

I bring my hand to my neck, expecting blood or puncture holes. Instead, I find nothing. "Why? How?"

"I have no idea." His own gaze stays locked on the burning Corpus. She's stopped moving, barely more than ash as the fire licks across what remains of her bones. "We'll have to figure it out later. Now we leave."

"But—"

He winds a fist into the collar of my shirt and yanks me forward. "No time. More will be on their way."

Tires screech as the silver Mercedes peels around the corner of the building only to stop inches away from my toes. "Get in," Opal yells through the open driver's-side window. Her gaze drifts to the smoldering pile of the former Corpus vampire. "What the hell happened?"

"I think I set that vampire on fire," I say.

Opal's eyes widen. "What? How?"

"Later." Sebastian opens the back door and throws me across the seat.

I land with an *oomph*.

He climbs in and slams the door. "Drive."

The tires squeal and the car surges ahead. Something

smacks the window, and I look up just as gray claws rake across the glass. "Go, go, go," I scream.

"Hang on," Opal calls.

I'm tossed against the door as the car swings wildly to the right. The clawed hand disappears. On either side, the buildings whirl past in a streak of gray and brown. "Where are we going?" I ask.

Opal blinks several times, her knuckles white on the steering wheel. "I—I don't know. The hunters—the school— that was my home. Now—" She bites back the words with a shake of her head. "I can't go back into foster care. I won't."

"We'll go to the Anima," Sebastian says. His eyes meet mine, and the intensity I find there steals my breath. "They will keep you safe."

Opal's laugh is an angry bark. "I've had my fill of bloodsuckers for the night, thank you very much. There's no way in hell I'm going to willingly track down any more."

Sebastian scowls. "I can't take you with me. My clan will imprison you in the farm. The Anima are your best shot at staying alive."

"No. I'm done." Her voice quivers. "I'm staying away from all leeches—no matter their clan." She presses her lips together and shakes her head. "As long as you monsters exist, there is no such thing as *safe*." She glares at him in the rearview mirror, daring him to argue.

Sebastian doesn't say a word.

I remember that dreamy look on her face when we first arrived at the compound and she ran into Scott. He meant something to her—they all did. And now they're gone. I, probably better than most, know *exactly* what that feels like.

I scoot to the edge of my seat and wrap my arms around

the headrest in front of me. After surviving a vampire massacre, seatbelts are almost a laughable safety measure. "Did you see Scott?" I ask softly.

Biting her lip, she shakes her head.

"That's good, right? That means there's still a chance."

"Not much of one," she spits through clenched teeth. "God, I hate *fucking* vampires." She screams the last word, slamming her hand against the steering wheel. The silence that follows swells so large it pushes me against my seat, threatening to suffocate me.

"You know where we have to go," Sebastian says, finally.

Opal inhales sharply. "If you even suggest going to the Anima again, so help me, I'll shoot you now."

"You have a better idea?" he asks.

Opal slams on the brakes. The tires screech, and I'm thrown against the seat. The buildings surrounding us are dark except for the random lit office. "I don't get it. Why do you care what happens to us? You're a bloodsucking *Mentis*. You should want to take us to your farm and drain our blood."

His eyes narrow. "I don't care what happens to *you*. I care what happens to Charlie. And the Anima will, too."

"I'm sorry." She twists in her seat, facing me. "Don't take this the wrong way, but what makes you so goddamn special?"

I shrink against the seat. "I-I—"

Sebastian cuts in, "I believe Matteo, King of Anima, is her father."

"Jesus Horatio Christ the Third." Opal turns around and stomps on the gas pedal. The car lurches forward, making me fall back against the seat. She locks eyes with me in the rearview mirror. "What does that even mean—your *father*? Are you one of *them*?"

The accusation makes me flinch. "No. I'm human."

Sebastian makes a face. "You're a dhampir."

"You don't know that for sure," I spit through clenched teeth.

"Patrick was right," Opal says, shaking her head. "Vampires don't protect humans. I shouldn't have trusted you. Look what it got me."

Her words tear at my heart. "Don't say that."

"To be fair," Sebastian says, "the Corpus that attacked you had nothing to do with us."

She gives him a withering look in the rearview mirror. Leaning back, he shrugs.

Several long minutes pass before Opal slams her hand against the steering wheel. "Fuck," she screams. "I have no family, no home, no money—nothing! Except for a bloodsucking corpse and a half-corpse whatever-the-hell-you-are."

I am all-too-aware of the guns still strapped to Opal's chest. I look to Sebastian, who seems more amused by her breakdown than concerned.

"I'm human," I say again. Though I'm not sure if I'm trying to convince anyone but myself at this point. "And it's not like I asked for any of this, either. I lost my home, and my aunt, too. All I have in this world is a hunter and a vampire. You're not exactly resume-reference material."

Opal blinks, then her lip twitches in an almost-smile. "I don't know. That sounds like a pretty kickass resume to me."

"So, we're screwed together?" I ask.

Opal glances at Sebastian. "What about the leech?"

He exhales loudly. "For the last time, I'm trying to protect Charlie."

"*Why?*" She draws the word out with a huff. "Vampires don't do anything that doesn't benefit them. Crossing your own clan could get you in a lot of trouble."

"If they find out, they will kill me—but only after many days of excruciating torture." His tone is matter-of-fact.

"Exactly." Opal waves a hand in the air. "Why would you risk that—for *her*?" She jerks her chin at me.

"*Hey*," I say.

"No offense," Opal adds.

Shifting in his seat, Sebastian looks out the window. His jaw flexes several times before he answers. "It's like you said, I'm self-serving. I believe Charlie can help me uncover my past life as a human. That's all."

His admission pinches in a way I don't quite understand, and I look away.

"Why do you even care about your human life?" Opal asks.

For several seconds, he says nothing. "I need to know who I was and how I came to be—*this*."

"You don't want to be a vampire?" I ask.

He shrugs. "I don't know. How can I know what is better when an entire part of me is missing?"

Opal laughs out loud, startling me. "Oh my God. A leech with an existential crisis. Just when I thought I'd heard it all." She continues chuckling, drawing a frown from Sebastian. "Look, I'll save you the time and trouble. Your human past? Doesn't matter because it's gone. You're dead. You're a walking, bloodthirsty corpse. I don't trust you. I don't like you. And I sure as hell don't believe you won't hand us over to the Mentis the first chance you get."

He leans back, his eyes glittering in the dark. "Just like I don't doubt you'll shoot me in the heart the second you get an opportunity."

"Did we just all become best friends?" I ask.

Opal makes a face, her eyes flicking to me. "You think *I'm* the one you have to worry about. Apparently, this one," she juts her chin at me, "can set vamps on fire. What the hell is up with that, anyway? Is it a dhampir thing?"

"No," Sebastian and I answer together. "I'm not a dhampir," I say with a huff.

"Dhampir or not," Sebastian says, "combusting a vampire is not something I have heard of before." Raising an eyebrow, he gives me a long look. "That was very strange."

I squirm in my seat and rest my hand on the bottle that miraculously managed to stay in my pocket. "My aunt gave me a mixture of essential oils before she was taken. I wonder if that's what did it?"

Sebastian makes a face. "I would know if there was an oil that could burn vampires. Mentis are schooled in every available mortal weapon."

Opal laughs. "Sorry, bloodsucker, looks like your almighty clan doesn't know everything after all. Charlie, you have to give me some of that oil, especially if we're headed into a vampire lair."

Sebastian scoffs. "I wouldn't describe the Anima compound as a *lair,* just as I would hardly describe the Anima as vampires. They're little more than humans with sharp teeth."

"Speaking of," Opal glances at me, "do you have sharp teeth?"

"Of course not." Reflexively I run my tongue across my teeth. As far as I can tell, they're no different from anyone else's.

Still, Opal watches me warily for several more seconds before returning her attention to the road. A frown pulls at her lips. "Where am I going?"

We stop at a light. To our right is an all-night café. A group of women with tiaras and pink feathered boas laugh at a booth next to the window. I'd be willing to bet vampires are the last thing on their minds. My gut twinges with grief over a life I'll never have back. I place my hand on the window, wishing I could join them, just for the night.

"It would be easier if you let me drive," Sebastian says.

"Dude." Opal shakes her head. "I've lost everything. I just need control over…something. You have to give me this."

I think Sebastian might argue. He nods. "Washington, Missouri."

"Washington is where the wineries are, right?" Opal asks. "That's like, the middle of nowhere." The light turns green and Opal stomps on the gas, leaving the girls, tiaras, and cheese fries far behind us.

"Yes," Sebastian answers. "The Anima prefer isolation. Still, they remain close enough to the city to keep their eyes on the other clans."

She arches an eyebrow. "How do you know this?"

"We know *everything* about each other. We're on the verge of all-out war."

"*Why?*" I ask.

"I—we—we've always been at odds." His brow furrows, almost as if this is the first time he's considered the question. "Our differences in feeding and hunting created the rift in the clans. St. Louis is the largest city in the heart of the country. If you possess the heart, you dominate the body."

"So, there are vampires everywhere?" I ask.

"Yes," he answers, "but the kings and queens of the clans reside here, fighting for control of the heart."

Opal snorts. "All the feuding is pretty dumb, if you ask me."

"Because human fighting makes more sense?" Sebastian asks.

With lips pinched, she looks away.

As we drive, the buildings become smaller, fading into rows of tightly-packed houses. Soon the yards grow wider until even the houses fade, leaving us surrounded by endless dark highway. My mind is a soupy mix of fear and questions. Sebastian stares ahead, eyes trained on the road, his expression unreadable.

"Take the next exit," he says after a long stretch of silence. "In a quarter of a mile, there will be a gravel road on the right. That leads to their compound."

My pulse quickens. I thought we had more time. "Will they try to hurt us?"

"No." He shakes his head. "The Anima believe in peaceful coexistence with humans."

"Will they hurt *you*?" I ask.

His eyes glitter in the moonlight. "Maybe. Anima fight as a last resort. But I'm Mentis, and our clans *are* at odds." He shrugs, clearly not concerned.

Opal rolls to a stop at the top of the exit ramp. She twists in her seat to look at him. "Normally I couldn't care less about the demise of a bloodsucker, but you did sort of save us back there. Maybe it wouldn't be the worst thing in the world if you didn't stick around. I hear Florida is nice this time of year."

He smirks. "Opal, I'm flattered you care."

She wrinkles her nose. "Just enough to not waste a bullet."

"I'm touched. Still, Charlie is my best shot at getting answers about my past. I'm not leaving until I have them."

My stomach clenches with unease. "I already told you I can't help you."

He tilts his head. "That's only because you haven't tried."

I sigh and sink deeper against the seat.

Opal huffs. "Okay, it's your funeral. And maybe ours, too. Who the hell knows." The car moves forward. "Let's get this over with." Following Sebastian's directions, she makes a right onto a gravel road lined with trees. The farther we travel, the more the branches reach over the car until I feel as if we're going to be swallowed whole.

Opal stops the car in front of a rusted red gate blocking the road. Only darkness lies beyond it. A sign hangs from the top rung reading, *No Trespassing. Violators will be prosecuted.*

With a groan, Opal turns off the car. "What now?"

"We wait," Sebastian answers.

"For what?" No sooner is the question out of her mouth than a crow caws loudly, making me gasp. A second later, it perches on top of the gate, tilting its head to watch us with gleaming eyes.

"For a *bird*?" Opal asks dryly.

"No." Sebastian sits up, shoulders tense. "For the Anima."

Another crow lands beside the first, then another, and another, until there are nearly a dozen black birds lined up on the top rail, their beady eyes directed toward us.

Sebastian stares back. "And it looks like they're here."

Chapter Twelve

One of the crows swoops off the gate and lands on the hood of the car. Beside me, Sebastian tenses.

"What's happening?" I ask.

"They're trying to figure out who we are and what we're doing here."

"I highly doubt that," Opal says, making a face. "In case you haven't noticed, those are birds—pretty tame ones at that. Someone must be feeding them."

Sebastian gives a short laugh. "Someone has *definitely* been feeding them." He opens the door and steps outside.

Gripping the wheel, Opal whirls around. "Where the hell are you going?" Panic laces her words.

Sebastian faces the bird on the car with his hands raised. "I have no quarrel with you or your clan this night."

The crow facing him caws loudly, dipping its head beneath its wing. For a second I wonder if it's falling asleep. But then it shivers, and the feathers along its body ripple as it grows larger. The crow throws its wing back suddenly, and feathers fall to the ground like a discarded cloak, leaving a crouched woman where seconds ago a bird had stood. With blazing green eyes, she stares through the windshield at us.

Opal and I gasp in unison.

"Did you know they could do that?" I ask Opal.

She nods her head, skin pale. "I mean, I knew, I've just never actually seen it happen."

The woman rises to her feet, the hood of the car groaning beneath her knee-length boots. Draped over her shoulders is an ankle-length green cloak. She tosses back a long mane of curly, red hair, her green eyes narrowing at us in the dark. The remaining crows hop and caw along the gate, flapping their wings. She clutches a wooden spear, the tip plated in silver. "Why come here then, Mentis?" She spits the last word as if it leaves a sour taste on her tongue. "If not to wage battle?" Her voice bears the faintest hint of an Irish accent.

Sebastian tucks his hands in his pockets. "I come seeking refuge for the two humans in the car. One might have special interest to Matteo, as she is related to Rachel."

The crows on the gate fall still and silent.

The red-headed vampire scowls. "Impossible. Rachel is dead."

"She is very much alive," Sebastian says, shaking his head. "Though for how long, I can't guarantee. That's why you must let us talk to Matteo immediately."

The woman hops off the car, her boots crunching against the gravel. She raises the spear, the tip inches from Sebastian's heart. "*King* Matteo," she says with a growl. "When speaking of him, you will address him as such."

Sebastian's raises his chin. "He is not *my* king."

If he wasn't so far away, I'd plant my elbow in his gut. There's a difference between being brave and stupid, and pissing off the vampires who outnumber us can't be smart.

"Not *yet*," she answers with a smirk. Just like the hunters told me, her pointed fangs are barely longer than my own canine teeth. She rests the spear against his shirt.

In response, Sebastian's hands curl into fists.

The crows on the gate hop and squawk along with the rising tension.

Shit. I climb out of the car. Looks like it's time for me to be stupid, too.

"Charlie," Sebastian warns. "Get in the car."

"No." I shake my head. "Can we please not do this right now?"

The redhead whips her head around, narrowing her eyes. "Excuse me?"

"We really don't have time for another stupid vampire pissing contest. My Aunt Rachel is in trouble and the longer it takes for you to mark your territory, the more danger it puts my aunt in. Sebastian said you would help her. If that's not true, just tell me now so we don't waste any more time."

The Anima vampire frowns. "I wouldn't think it possible—but you certainly *act* like Rachel." Lowering her spear, she turns to the crows. "Go. Tell the King we have *guests.*" She eyes Sebastian warily. "If we allow a Mentis into our compound, you understand security measures will have to be taken."

"You can't be serious," he says.

She raises an eyebrow. "Do I look like I'm joking?" She unties a leather pouch from her belt and tosses it to Sebastian. "Put them on."

He catches the bag with one had. "This isn't necessary. I'm not here to fight."

She folds her arms. "Are you telling me your clan wouldn't do the same?"

He growls, opens the bag, and withdraws what looks like a set of handcuffs without a chain to connect the two. The silver rings sizzle and smoke against his skin.

"What is that?" I ask.

Wincing, he fastens the rings around each wrist. His skin blisters where the silver touches. "Silver cuffs," he answers. "They won't kill me, but they will slow me down."

"We'll be able to subdue him easily if he tries anything," the redhead says.

My stomach lurches as his skin peels away from the silver, revealing the muscle beneath. "That looks awful."

"I'll heal." His face is a blank mask. "Besides, I've had worse." He's quiet a moment before adding, "Much worse."

Somehow, I don't think he's referring to what the hunters did to him.

The redhead walks a slow circle around Sebastian, eying him at every angle. "If you came here with ill-intent you will die."

His eyes narrow. "If I came here with ill-intent, you'd already be dead."

Grunting, she turns to me. "What is your name?"

I swallow past the lump in my throat before I'm able to speak. "Charlie."

"Opal." The hunter steps out of the car and stands beside me. Her fingers twitch over the gun hidden by her jacket.

The Anima catches the movement and smiles. "There

is no need to be afraid. The Anima respect humans and believe in peaceful coexistence between our species."

"But you still drink our blood," Opal says, with a roll of her eyes.

"Only from the willing," the vampire replies. "My name is Delaney." She looks us over, eyes hesitating on the rips and bloody stains in our clothing. "You must be exhausted. Come." She motions us forward with a jerk of her head.

"What about the car?" Opal asks.

"I'll send someone for it later. The rest of the way to the compound is too treacherous for a vehicle that doesn't have four-wheel drive."

"That's not ominous at all," Opal mutters.

Smirking, Delaney opens the gate and pushes it wide. "I thought hunters were fearless."

Opal hesitates. "How did you know?"

She points to her nose. "You reek of Corpus blood."

I hug my arms across my body. Opal raises each of her arms and sniffs underneath.

"I'm not a hunter," I say quietly.

"Then what are you, Charlie?" Delaney's eyes blaze green in the darkness.

Sebastian inches closer to me—a warning not to reveal too much. Reflexively, I lean against his arm. I might not understand his intentions, but after what he did for me at the hunters' camp, I know he'll protect me. Maybe that's enough. "I'm confused," I reply. "I'm scared. And I just want my aunt back."

Delaney eyes me curiously a moment longer before gesturing us forward. "This way."

"Stay by me," Sebastian says, voice low, as he slips

between Opal and me. I cringe at the small wisps of smoke trailing from each of his wrists.

"I thought you said we'd be safe here," I say.

"There is no such thing as safe," Opal mutters, lips set in a grim line. She forges ahead, keeping stride with Delaney.

"She's wrong, Charlie," Sebastian says, once Opal is out of earshot. "I would not lead you into danger, I promise."

I study the features of his face in the dark to see if I can read any hint of truth there. Without meaning to, I find myself closing the distance between us, so that our arms almost brush as we walk. It's as if some part of me has already decided he's my best chance at survival, even if my brain won't admit it.

Delaney wasn't kidding when she said our car wouldn't make it. The gravel path is pocked with holes and craters several feet wide. The shadows cast by the trees keep me from seeing how deep.

Opal glances at me over her shoulder as if to say, *Are you sure this is a good idea?*

I can only shrug and pray we're not being led toward a worse demise than what the Corpus had in store for us.

Sebastian says nothing, his face contorting with pain. When he catches me looking, he smooths his face into a blank mask. "You're nervous. Don't be."

I laugh. "Sure thing. Why would I be worried about that when I'm headed into the heart of a vampire compound?"

"Not that." He shakes his head. "Don't be nervous about meeting your father."

This catches Delaney's attention, and she glances at me over her shoulder.

"He's not my father," I hiss.

Sebastian makes a face. "Charlie, be rational."

"I *am*," I say, tightening my fingers into fists. "I get why you would think Matteo's my father—there's the photograph and the fact that my aunt had a relationship with him. It makes sense, and I understand. But I don't think logic works here." I stop walking. "I just—I don't feel it, okay? I don't know how else to explain, but when I try to dig deep inside me, there's this ache—because my parents are truly dead. I might not know or understand anything else about this messed up world, but I do know that."

Sebastian looks away, shaking his head. His dismissal ignites a flame of irritation inside the pit of my stomach. I drift away from him, concentrating on watching my steps, careful to not slip on the loose gravel as we begin to climb a hill.

Opal reaches the top before I do, halting long enough to let out a low whistle. I hurry to her side and gasp. Below us is what looks like tiny village. Electric lights blaze in the windows of campers and trailers, while several bonfires burn outside of tents. At a glance, it looks like nearly a hundred different tents and RVs have made home in a field surrounding a giant red barn and the accompanying farm house. Groups of humans and vampires—with their glowing eyes—mill about between the tents and trailers. Their laughter wafts to the hill where we stand.

Delaney places a hand on Opal's shoulder and smiles at the field below. "Welcome to the home of the Anima, sanctuary for Anima vampires and their human allies."

"*This* is your compound?" Looking around, Sebastian makes a face. "It's a glorified trailer park."

Delaney scowls at him just as two crows fly overhead,

their caws shattering the silent night.

Delaney nods up at them before turning back to us. "King Matteo has been told of your arrival. He looks forward to receiving you in his home." She motions to the farmhouse with her hand.

Opal sighs. "This might as well happen. Come on, Charlie."

What feels like a ball of lead inside my stomach keeps me rooted in place. It takes me several tries before I'm able to force one foot in front of the other. Dozens of pairs of glowing green eyes turn on me from the valley below. My pulse stalls. "Do you think this is a good idea?"

"Nope," Opal answers. "I'm just fresh out of better options."

Sebastian moves to my side. From this close, I can hear the slight sizzle of the metal burning into his flesh. "Whatever you do, don't leave my sight," he whispers.

The closer we move to the compound, the more eyes turn in our direction—both human and vampire. Their expressions are mostly curious, though some offer smiles. It's hard to picture Aunt Rachel here, surrounded by so many people, when I've spent my entire life in isolation. I thought she enjoyed the solitude, but now I'm not sure. What else could I be wrong about?

"Was Aunt Rachel—was she happy here?" The words escape my lips before I realize they've formed.

Delaney pauses. "I believe so. She and Matteo were very much in love. They lived in the farmhouse together until the babies were born. If it weren't for the attacks—" her jaw tightens as her steps quicken. One of the crows screams angrily overhead. Delaney waves a hand as if to silence it.

"What happened?" I asked.

Delaney shakes her mane of red of red hair. "We thought the Mentis killed her twin infants. We discovered the boy's body, torn to shreds. We never did find the remains of the baby girl or Rachel. We always assumed they'd been killed as well." She opens her mouth as if she might say more, then quickly snaps it shut. "I'll leave the explanations to the King."

Twins. Each beat of my heart brings a throbbing ache that vibrates through my body. Aunt Rachel said she had an infant son who died from SIDS. No wonder she wanted us to stay hidden. I just wish she would have told me. If I'd known, or been more prepared—but of course that's ridiculous. Knowing about vampires would have never prepared me for the nightmare I find myself in now.

As we continue down the dirt path, the crowd of onlookers presses forward. Most of the women dress similarly to my aunt, with long skirts that graze the ground above their bare feet. The men wear loose-fitting pants, and most of them are shirtless. A few children poke their heads through the legs of the adults, only to zip away again when I meet their eyes.

I'm getting a glimpse of so much more than a hidden community; it's a life that could have been. Despite the warm evening, I shiver and pull my sleeves over my hands.

We walk the rest of the way in silence. Several fires over, someone is playing the guitar. The tune sounds familiar, but I'm unable to place it. This entire place is like that—a memory just beyond my reach.

When we reach the door, Delaney grabs Sebastian's arm. "If you so much as look at the King funny, I'll gut you."

He shrugs out of her grasp. "I already told you, I'm not here to fight."

A crow lands on the porch railing beside me, followed by another, and another, until nearly a dozen crows watch us with unblinking eyes. A pressure builds in my chest as Delaney opens the door and nods for me to enter.

A couple of the birds hop anxiously back and forth. While Sebastian made his intentions clear, the Anima haven't been so transparent. Sebastian may not be here to fight, but that doesn't mean they aren't looking for one.

Chapter Thirteen

Grimacing, Opal covers her nose with her hand. "What is the God-awful smell?" she asks.

"Patchouli," I answer. The very fragrance my aunt scented her last batch of soaps before she was kidnapped. She told me she liked it because it kept the mosquitos away—but what if she really favored it because it reminded her of here?

Delaney looks impressed. "We craft soaps and other goods to sell at the farmers' market. Along with the income from our organic produce, we are an entirely self-sufficient community."

I wonder if soapmaking was a skill my aunt learned from the Anima or vice versa. Either way, it's becoming easier to picture her here. Not so easy is wondering where she is now. Just imagining the things she might be enduring weakens my knees.

"Please, come in," a male voice booms from deeper in the house. The voice is warm and inviting, not the sinister tone I imagined for a vampire king. "Would you be so kind as to step into the light so I might see you better?"

Opal hesitates, and I push past her, following the glow of candlelight down a narrow hallway. The hall leads to an open room filled with light from a burning fire. Shelves stuffed with leather-bound books line both sides of the stone fireplace mantle. A faded woven rug stretches across a chipped hardwood floor. The shades are drawn, casting shadows around the figure at the end of the room.

Even in the darkness, I know he's there. I can feel his presence like my own heartbeat. "This is quite the group," the man says. I can't tell if he's talking to us, Delaney, or even himself. "A Mentis, a hunter, and girl who claims to be Rachel's niece."

Walking in front of us, Delaney addresses the shadow. "I've disabled the Mentis, just in case."

Green eyes flicker and glow from the darkness, long enough to find the shackles around Sebastian's wrists, before going dim again. The man laughs. "Something tells me that if this Mentis is with a human and a hunter, he wouldn't dare go looking for more trouble than he's already in."

Sebastian lifts his chin. "You know what a risk I'm taking being here?"

"I do. What I do *not* understand, however, is why."

"That explanation would take some time." Sebastian tilts his head. "Would it be possible for you to come into the light?"

The man is quiet so long, I think he might not answer. Finally, he says, "It is not possible."

"So, the rumors are true," Sebastian murmurs.

"What rumors?" I ask.

"Show them," the man says.

Delaney hesitates long enough for me to see her lips curl into an apprehensive frown. She grabs a lantern from a nearby table and lights it. She feeds the wick high into the canister, creating enough light to uncover the room's shadowed corners.

What she reveals makes me gasp.

Opal yelps. "Jesus." She backs into Sebastian who, in turn, positions himself in front of us.

I fight to keep from gagging. First from the smell of Sebastian's burning skin, and second from the sight in front of me.

He is the man from the hidden photograph. Gone is the smile he wore that day with my aunt. He grimaces at us from a carved wooden throne with red velvet cushions. While he looks as though he hasn't aged since the photo was taken, there are some differences. His eyes flicker in the dim lighting, where Sebastian's and Delaney's glow. He wears jeans and worn leather boots. Dark circles create caverns beneath each eye and his previously bronze skin has paled to an ashy gray.

All of this, I know immediately, must be from the foot-long wooden stake protruding from his bare chest.

Reflexively, I bring my fingers to my own chest, as if I can remove the ghost of a stake that isn't there. "That looks really, *really*, bad," I breathe.

"I bet it doesn't tickle," Opal adds.

King Matteo gives a ghost of a smile. "You're correct in that assumption."

"For Christ's sake," Opal says, "just take it out."

Delaney shakes her head. "We cannot risk it. A splinter has grazed his heart. If we try to remove the stake, we might drive the splinter in farther, risking the King's final death."

"And I'm not ready to go just yet." King Matteo's fingernails curl into the wooden armrests. "There is still much to do."

"Can you transform?" Sebastian asks.

The King shakes his head. "Again, too risky. Any movement whatsoever could drive the splinter deeper into my heart."

My own heart shudders. "You mean to tell me," I say, "you've been stuck to that chair for—"

"Nearly seventeen years," he finishes for me. "I was staked trying to protect my children during a Mentis attack. They killed my son in front of me. Rachel and my daughter disappeared during the battle. For all these years, I thought they were dead, too."

Opal whistles lowly. "That sucks."

He raises his chin. "I've managed. And I'll continue to manage until my work is complete. And that brings me to you three." Tapping a finger, he looks us over. "Before I answer any more of your questions, I do have a few of my own. Let's start with Rachel." His eyes flick to me. "You called her your aunt, correct?"

I nod.

He frowns. "Rachel and I were deeply in love and knew everything about each other. As far as I'm aware, Rachel had no siblings. How long have you lived with her?"

"As long as I can remember." A nervous flutter shoots through my stomach. He opens his mouth to reply, but I cut him off. "I know where you're going with this. I get it. The logical thing to assume is I'm her daughter—*your* daughter." I swallow hard before continuing. "But I'm not. I'm sorry."

He arches an eyebrow. "How can you be so sure?"

I shake my head. "A feeling I have. It's dumb, and I can't explain it. But I just know I'm not, because it doesn't feel *right.*"

He stares at me a long time before nodding. "Feelings are very important, and all too often we don't listen to our gut until it's too late. Sometimes, though, what we want, and the truth, can be opposing sides of the war within us. And if we want something bad enough, we can make it the truth."

"That's super deep," Opal mutters.

I elbow her in the ribs.

"You have to decide, Charlie, if you believe you're not Rachel's daughter because you feel it, or if you simply want it not to be true, because of who—and what—I am. I wouldn't blame you for it."

I open my mouth, though I'm not sure how to answer. King Matteo stops me with a shake of his head. "You do not have to answer that question now. Just think on it. In the meantime, where is Rachel now?" He leans forward, maybe without realizing, because he winces and hisses in pain.

Delaney is at his side in an instant, pushing him back into place. "Careful."

He lifts his hand, waving her away.

"The um"—I look to Sebastian, who gives me an affirming nod—"Mentis have her."

Matteo's lips curl, revealing his short, but still sharp, fangs. He growls, the sound of it echoing around the room.

His eyes glow green, just for a couple of heartbeats, before fading again.

"It's obvious what they intend to do," Delaney says to the King. "They're going to use Rachel as bait—to finish what they started." She motions to the stake.

King Matteo nods.

"What I'm wondering is," Delaney continues, "how do we know it's not a trick? The girls are, after all, accompanied by a Mentis. He could be orchestrating the entire thing, just as a chance to get close to you." She whirls on Sebastian, drawing the spear at her back and thrusting the point against his chest. "I say we kill him."

While my heart wedges firmly inside my throat, Sebastian only looks annoyed. "I've told you, I did not come here to fight."

"Then what did you come here for, *Mentis*?" King Matteo spits the last word through his teeth.

"To ask for protection for the girls. The Mentis have no idea who Charlie is—or what she is."

"*What* she is?" Matteo raises an eyebrow.

"Dhampir, of course," he continues. "And if the Mentis found out, you know as well as I do how much more appealing that makes her."

Despite my attempts not to, I find myself squirming where I stand. "You don't know I'm a dhampir."

"And you don't know you're not." He turns to me, leveling me with his gaze. "You're certainly not human. Humans can't torch vampires with just a touch." He stares at me, as if daring me to disagree.

Instead, I look away.

"Wait—" Matteo raises a hand, his eyes widening. "Are

you telling me she torched a vampire?"

"A Corpus," Sebastian answers.

"It's a long story," I say. "It's not worth getting into when we should be focusing on Aunt Rachel."

The King frowns. "We will return to that interesting piece of information. But I agree, time is of the essence. Before we can do anything, I do need to know, Mentis," his gaze falls on Sebastian, "what is your investment in this? What do you gain by delivering the girls to me, other than your death at the hands of your own clan?"

This time it's Sebastian's turn to look uncomfortable. "When the Mentis found me, I had no memories of my previous life, or anything before they found me. Once, when Charlie touched me, I saw flashes of— I'm not sure. But I believe she can help me figure it out. I need to know who I was before, and what happened to me."

"*You*." The King raises his chin, his eyes wide. "You're the one from the mound—the last mound. I heard stories, but didn't believe them. Mentis have a knack for exaggerating."

Sebastian's lips press into a grim line. "It's no exaggeration."

"Mound?" I ask. "What mound?"

"Faerie," Sebastian answers simply.

Opal begins laughing only to stop abruptly. "Oh, wait. You're serious? There are *freaking* fairies?"

"Not anymore," Sebastian replies.

"Vampires were created over a thousand years ago by the Queen of Air and Darkness to serve as her personal army against the Court of Light," King Matteo says. "Several centuries later, tired of doing her dirty work, the vampires revolted, starting a war that would end in the complete extermination of the Fae."

"That's so sad," I say.

"If you had met the Queen and her thirst for blood," Matteo says, "you would not think so. Thankfully, she was killed in battle nearly four hundred years ago."

"How do you know this?" I ask.

"My sisters and I were there. We were the ones to kill her." He sighs. "Next, we killed the Queen of the Seelie Court. Maybe she didn't deserve to die as the Queen of Air and Darkness did, but we couldn't risk our newfound freedom. The Fae could never regroup without their queens. They fought each other for the thrones while we slowly whittled down their armies. We hunted them until their numbers depleted. The mound Sebastian came from was the last to fall." He eyes Sebastian. "What do you remember of your time there?"

Closing his eyes, Sebastian shakes his head. His hair falls in waves against his cheeks. Something—sorrow maybe?— pinches his face. "Darkness. The taste of blood—still warm, on my tongue. There was a flash, and then Mentis soldiers stood before me. Blood and fallen Faerie surrounded me." Opening his eyes, he swallows. "That is all. My Queen told me I was a prisoner of the Faerie. If so, for how long? How was I captured? And why?"

King Matteo shakes his head. "I don't have the answers."

"I think Charlie might," Sebastian says.

They look at me, and the intensity of their dual gazes makes me flinch.

"Come here, child." King Matteo beckons me forward with a wave of his hand.

I glance over my shoulder at Opal, who shrugs. Holding my breath, I walk forward, concentrating on placing one foot in front of the other. I stop only when my toes are inches away from the base of his throne. "I'm not really sure what protocol is here. I've never met a king. Do I bow or something?"

He laughs, and there's something so rich in the sound, so genuine, my nervousness all but vanishes. His eyes blaze just for a second. "That won't be necessary. But I would like you to lean forward."

My heart skips a beat, but I do as I'm told. From this close, I can smell the tang of blood. I glance down to see small ribbons of blood trickling from around the stake in his chest. He reaches for me, and my muscles tense, only to unwind when he cups my chin.

His skin is warmer than I expected, his fingertips worn with callouses. I've not had many men touch me, but, I find, I don't mind. *This is what fathers do with their daughters,* I think. *It's kind of nice.* The thought opens a scar I didn't know I had, that covers up a want I didn't know existed. It's strange to realize you need things you swore you didn't, and that some part of you is a liar. It makes me wonder what else I've lied about to myself.

"Rachel was the love of my life," Matteo says to me. His voice catches, almost like the words cut his throat as he speaks. "My entire existence before her was fighting and death. When I met her, she brought a clearer understanding to my life—a new *purpose.* She is the reason I became who I am, and the reason I fight this forsaken stake in my chest every single day. I swore to her that vampires and humans could exist in harmony. It wasn't just my dream—but ours together. If the Mentis have her, I will stop at nothing to get her back."

"Thank you," I whisper.

His smile turns sad, and he drops his hand. "I know you say you are not my daughter. But I tell you this, whether you are my daughter or not does not matter to me. You are important to Rachel, and that makes you important to me."

A lump wedges in my throat. I swallow several times before I am able to speak. "I guess we won't know for sure what I am until we get Aunt Rachel back."

Matteo settles his head against the throne. "I have something that can prove it now."

I gasp. "What?"

Closing his eyes, he shakes his head. "I've hidden it far from here. I will send some men to retrieve it right away. With Rachel captured, we can't waste any time."

"Exactly," I say. "Can we really afford to wait?"

"We can't afford not to," he answers. Before I can argue, he continues, "You must be exhausted. I will have Delaney arrange rooms for you."

"And hungry," Opal adds.

Matteo laughs. "I will have food prepared and sent to your rooms. In the meantime, I must make plans for Rachel's retrieval."

"Oh." I take a small step back. "Okay." While I want to protest, sunrise must be just around the corner. The King has grown paler than he was when we first arrived.

Delaney steps forward. "I'll have the guards prepare a holding cell with silver chains for the Mentis."

"No!" I whirl around. "Please don't." I can't stand the thought of Sebastian being put through any more torture.

"He's been through so much and risked his life to get us here. He's already wearing those God-awful cuffs. Please, don't make him suffer any more."

Something flashes through Sebastian's eyes. Surprise? I can't be sure because it's gone as quickly as it came.

Delaney sneers. "Don't be foolish, child. He doesn't care about you. He cares about himself. He is a Mentis."

"But are you?" Matteo asks, head cocked to the side. "The Mentis found you, of course. But were you a Mentis before?"

Sebastian shakes his head. "I don't know. My fangs were smaller when they found me, but who knows what the Faerie were feeding me in captivity."

"If you agree to the peaceful coexistence of vampire and human, you could be one of us if you choose," Matteo says.

Sebastian's jaw tightens. "There is no choice. The Mentis would kill me for even considering leaving the clan."

"We could protect you," the King says.

"And they would slaughter you for it."

Delaney scoffs. "They could try."

"And they would try," Sebastian says. "Are you really willing to risk any of your people for me?"

Delaney presses her lips into a thin line.

"Don't worry," Sebastian continues, holding his hands up. "I don't expect you to. And I don't expect you to trust me, either. I'm willing to wear your chains and sit in your cage for the night. Soon, though, I must return to the Mentis before their suspicions become too great. I'm sure they're already looking for me."

"And what will you tell them when you return?" Matteo asks.

"That I was apprehended by a hunter and escaped when the Corpus attacked. There were no human survivors."

Matteo nods. "You will be punished for allowing a hunter to capture you."

"I know."

"I will make sure you've been fed before your journey back." Matteo says. "Human blood from willing givers. Enough so you can hopefully endure what will come."

An invisible band ensnares my ribs and pulls tight. I can't even imagine how bad the torture will be if the vampires won't even speak of it out loud. "How do you know what will happen to him?"

Matteo's eyes flick to me. "His queen is my sister. She did this," he nods to the stake in his chest, "to me."

Ice fills my veins, and I shudder. "At least you survived."

He laughs, but there's nothing friendly about the sound. "You think she missed her target? No, Seraphina knew exactly what she was doing when she struck. She didn't want me dead—not yet. She wants me to suffer—which is exactly why she took Rachel."

"To make her suffer?" My knees weaken as a thousand terrible possibilities flood through my mind. I stumble backward, only to have Sebastian place a steadying hand on my lower back. A whimper escapes my throat, a disgusting weak sound that proves all too much how helpless I am. "Are they going to kill her?"

"Doubtful." Matteo's eyes get the faraway look of someone falling into themselves and the memories inside. "My sisters and I were the original vampires created by the Faerie. The things we were made to do—the torture we endured—" He swallows. "It left us broken and full of rage. My Rachel saved me. She showed me that I could love and be loved. Seraphina and Cordelia were not so lucky. They are still full of hate. Because of this, they don't want to kill me—they want to *destroy* me. And to do this, they will destroy everyone I care about."

"How would they do that?" I ask.

His eyes blaze green without flickering out. "Seraphina doesn't need to kill Rachel to destroy her—Seraphina only needs to make Rachel a Mentis, just like her."

Chapter Fourteen

Aunt Rachel, a Mentis.

I feel as if I'm falling, though a quick glance shows my feet on the carpet. The flickering lantern flames, the bookcases, even the walls appear to be inching toward me, threatening to tumble down at any instant.

There's not enough air. I pull at my shirt collar to keep it from choking me.

"Charlie?" Opal's voice. And even though she's right next to me, it sounds far away. "Are you okay?"

"I can't breathe." I gasp. My clothes feel too tight—the air too thick. I turn for the door.

"Charlie," Matteo says.

I stumble toward the exit. Have to get out. Have to get air. I hear more voices. Delaney. Sebastian. And Opal again. I can't understand what they're saying, and it doesn't matter. If I don't get outside soon, I'm going to suffocate to death. I fumble down the dark hallway, trying to retrace my steps, until I come to a heavy wooden door with a large, brass knob. I push the door open and plunge into the night.

A crow perched on an overhead branch caws loudly.

I nearly tumble down the porch, grasping the wooden handrail at the last moment. I take two more steps and fall. Cool, damp earth soaks through the fabric at my knees.

"Charlie."

I blink. Between the night and dark spots edging across my vision, I can't make out who's there. I gasp, sucking in breath after breath, but it's not enough. I rake my fingernails across my chest, as if I could somehow pry my ribs open and flood air into my lungs that way.

"Charlie."

I blink again. Sebastian, his silver eyes glowing, crouches beside me. One hand poised above my back, as if he might touch me, but isn't sure.

"Something's wrong," I tell him. I hate the tremor in my voice. "I can't breathe. I need a doctor."

"You don't need a doctor," he says. His voice is low, his eyes unblinking. "You're having a panic attack. You will be fine. I just need you to calm down."

I laugh. "How the hell do you suggest I do that?" I dig my fingers into the dirt, needing to be rooted to something, or else I'll blow away with the wind. "You heard what he said, what they have planned for my aunt."

"I won't let that happen."

I release the earth, leaving little pockets in the dirt where my fingers had been. "How will you stop them?"

"I just will." He sets his jaw, daring me to argue.

"Why would you do that?"

He sighs. "Charlie, would you take a walk with me?"

I glance over my shoulder at the open door to the

farmhouse. "I thought Delaney was going to chain you up."

He stands and holds out his hand. The cuff is missing from his wrist. Already the skin has healed, leaving no trace. "I asked King Matteo to let me talk to you. He agreed."

I take his hand, the touch making my pulse quicken. The earth falls back into place one jagged piece at a time. "I bet Delaney's thrilled about that."

He grins. "It's not like she's leaving me unsupervised." He motions to the six crows gathered in the branches above us. "Come on." He pulls me to my feet and I'm surprised to find that the ground is steady beneath me.

He lets go of me and immediately shoves his hands in his pants pockets. "Shall we?"

I nod, and together we follow a worn dirt path. Trees line one side of the path, while the valley and the camp below are on the other. Most of the campers have gone inside their tents and trailers, leaving behind only tendrils of smoke from their extinguished fires. The crows follow us, hopping and flying from branch to branch, always keeping us in sight. A blanket of clouds masks the dark sky, and the smell of rain weighs heavy in the air.

"Are you feeling better?" Sebastian asks after several minutes pass.

I nod. "I think so." As much as I hate to admit it, just having him near eases the tension in my chest. I pull the sleeves of my cardigan over my hands and twist them into my fists. "How would they do it?"

He frowns. "Do what?"

"Make Aunt Rachel a vampire. How does it work?"

He sighs. "Charlie —"

I stop walking. "No, Sebastian. I have to know. How does it work?"

He stops beside me. "Fine. The transition would have to occur on a full moon. They would drain her of all of her blood. And before she took her dying breath, they would give her vampire blood to drink."

Jesus. "When is the next full moon?"

"Just over a week."

My stomach clenches. That's not much time. "Does it…hurt?"

He shakes his head. "I don't remember my own turning, but from what I've seen, there is a lot of screaming and writhing. So, yes, I would assume it hurts very much."

My throat goes dry. "Death would be better than being a Mentis."

He tilts his head. "I *am* a Mentis."

"No." I shake my head. "I met the other two Mentis who came and stole my aunt. You're nothing like them."

He laughs. "You're forgetting I was ready to bite you in the woods."

I place a hand on my hip. "Bullshit. You were only trying to scare me."

He grunts. "Charlie, it's dangerous to make assumptions. You'll wind up dead."

I whirl on him. "You know what? I hate how everyone criticizes me for following my gut. So maybe I don't analyze everything, but I think there's something to be said for listening to your feelings. It's kept me alive this long, hasn't it?"

He smirks. "Barely. I think I helped a little."

"Right. Because I trusted you. That was a feeling, remember? I could have left you chained up on the floor of the gymnasium, but I knew I had to free you. That was my gut, Sebastian." Turning away from him, I throw my arms in the air. "And please don't say anything misogynistic about how I'm young, a girl, and overly emotional. I swear to God, I'll stake you right now."

Overhead, several of the crows cackle, almost as if they're laughing. "You, too!" I point my finger up at them. They immediately fall silent. With a sigh, I hug my arms across my chest. "Logically, I know it makes the most sense for me to be Matteo's daughter. It would be amazing if my parents were still alive. But I know I'm not, just like I know you're not really a Mentis."

"Charlie—"

"Tell me I'm wrong, Sebastian."

He presses his lips together, jaw tight. He's quiet for so long I don't think he'll speak at all. Then he does. "You're not wrong."

I blink. This wasn't the answer I'd expected.

"But you're not exactly right, either." Sweeping a hand through his hair, he makes a frustrated noise. "By every definition of Mentis, I am one. But ever since you touched me, I've had my own feeling that maybe—" He stares up at the sky. "I haven't always been. Part of me was hoping that when we arrived at the Anima clan, someone here would recognize me, that maybe I once was Anima. But that wasn't the case."

His admission tugs at my heart. Without meaning to, I take a step closer. "I had no idea."

He shakes his head. "It was stupid to hope for that." His shoulders hunch, and for the first time, I spot a crack in his vampire exterior to the guy—the human that could have been—beneath.

"Not stupid." I place my hand on his arm. "Maybe you were in a clan not from around here?"

"Maybe—" But the way his voice trails at the end lets me know he doesn't really believe it. He looks at my fingers resting on his arm and frowns.

I immediately recoil, withdrawing my hand. "Sorry."

"No." His expression softens. "I was just trying to remember a time when a human willingly touched me, and I can't. Mentis don't touch that often."

"I know." I roll my eyes. "Physical need and chemical reactions. Believe me, I remember the conversation."

"Right." He's silent for several heartbeats. "But maybe I was wrong about some of it."

"What part?"

He holds out his hand. "Maybe there *is* more."

I swallow hard, trying to process his words. My heart thrums nervously before I place my own hand in his, fingers entwining.

We both stare at our hands for several heartbeats. My heart is a hummingbird, flitting against the cage of my ribs.

"But of course the physical need and chemicals are still there as well," Sebastian says.

I can't help but laugh.

"Shall we?" Making no move to release my hand, he motions toward the path with the jut of his chin. "I don't think we have long before it rains."

I nod. As much as I don't look forward to going back, the weight of exhaustion presses against me like a cement wall. Morning must be coming soon.

A couple of drops hit my head and shoulders, and Sebastian gives me a tug. "We better hurry."

I pick up my pace, working twice as hard to get my short strides in time with his longer legs.

The boom of thunder shakes the ground, the vibrations rolling all the way up my spine. The sky opens up. Squawking in frustration, the crows abandon their posts as they fly together toward the barn.

Sebastian stops, yanking me gently back by the arm. The rain is so heavy it's like a curtain between us, distorting my view of him and everything around us. The water is cold, soaking my clothes and seeping into my bones. I shiver.

"Wait," he yells over the roar of the rain. "The crows are gone."

I shield my eyes to better see him. "Yeah? So?"

He grins. "We're unsupervised. We can do whatever we want."

I tilt my head, unsure what he's getting at. "You want to leave?"

"No." He laughs.

"What do you want, then?"

His dark curls are matted to the side of his face in wet tendrils. Rain droplets slide down his jaw in silver lines and fall from his chin. He's almost too beautiful to be real. I try and take a mental picture of him, in this moment, to sear on my brain for all time.

"Charlie." His expression turns dark, and it has nothing, or maybe everything, to do with hunger. My breath catches in my throat. "I want this," he says. Before I can move, he slides his hands on either side of my face. My heart trembles, aware of what's going to happen before I am.

My body hums in anticipation as he draws me forward, pulling me to my toes. Right before our lips touch, I stop breathing. The earth, the galaxy, the solar system—it all stops breathing.

His lips touch mine and a wave of heat crashes over my body. I close my eyes. Not just to feel him better, but to quiet the voice in my head asking me what Opal would think. Telling me I'm an idiot for making out with a leech. That he's a killer, a vampire—part of the clan that kidnapped my aunt.

But he also saved me—more than once. And I saved him. Why? Because deep down I know he's not like the other Mentis—I feel it. And as I drown in the warmth and sweetness of him, I also feel the rightness of us being together. And despite what everyone else thinks, our hearts should have as much say as our heads.

Maybe I am stupid. Maybe I just don't care.

The fire inside me grows, consuming all I am. I pull away with a gasp. I might not be an expert, but kissing isn't supposed to hurt. Even in the rain, the water does nothing to stop the burn. "Sebastian?"

His eyes are wide, twin silver sparks in the dark. "Charlie, look."

He motions to our hands, still clasped together, and the orb of light filtering through our fingertips.

"What the—?" I try to pull away, but Sebastian only tightens his hold.

"Don't let go, Charlie. Promise me, you won't let go."

The pain is too much. A million hot pokers jab at my skin, threatening to sear through. The light from our joined hands grows brighter, swallowing our hands in a glowing orb so white it's almost blue. It burns my eyes, forcing me to turn away. My heart is like a pebble, slingshot against my ribs.

I can't take much more. And still I hold on to him until I'm sure my insides are being ripped in two. "Sebastian!"

My scream is cut short by a crack of thunder. A blinding flash follows, and we're ripped from each other's grasp. I fall onto my back against the soft, wet earth. Electricity jolts through my veins, making my muscles spasm. I try to move, try to speak, but I can't do either. I can only lie there, blinking against the rain, as it fills my nose and mouth.

Soon I can't breathe. Water floods my lungs. I gasp, or at least I think I do, as enough sensation returns to my body that I'm able to move my fingers. I claw them into the mud, feeling the cold earth push beneath my nails, and slowly I push myself up. I sit, hacking the water out of my lungs until I'm sore from it. My hair hangs across my eyes like a wet curtain, and I push it back with muddy fingers. "Sebastian?"

He doesn't answer. *Did I hurt him? Oh God.* "Sebastian!" I scream louder, until my voice cracks. Terror swells inside my chest like a balloon. But then I see them, two silver eyes opening nearly twenty yards away.

He climbs onto his feet with more ease than I did. Still, he presses his palm against his temple and shakes his head.

My knees wobble. It takes all my strength to keep from toppling over into the mud. Electricity still tingles along my veins. "Were we just struck by lightning?"

"No. Charlie, that was all you." He drops his hand and walks toward me. When he reaches me, he holds out a hand as if he might touch me and quickly drops it again. It hurts more than I expect it to. "Are you all right?"

Trembling, I hug my arms across my chest. "That wasn't me."

"Charlie, I felt it. I know it." He rakes his fingers through his hair, only to have the wet strands fall back across his eyes.

"I don't understand. What did you feel?"

"I remember." He places his hands on my shoulders. "I know who my mother is."

Chapter Fifteen

Sebastian takes my arm, and I can't help but notice how careful he is in making sure our skin doesn't make contact. We don't speak as we walk back to the farmhouse. Even though I want to know what he's learned, I'm glad for the silence. It gives me time to process everything that's happened, from meeting King Matteo, to the kiss, and the flash of light that happened shortly after.

Everyone wants me to think logically about things instead of going with my gut. But no matter which way I turn things in my head, I can't make sense of anything that's happened. And this terrifies me. Because if I'm not Rachel and Matteo's daughter, then what the hell am I?

Delaney is waiting for us when we return. Leaning against the foyer wall with her ankles crossed, she's more like a worried mother than a vampire guard. She frowns at the both of us, soaked to the bone and dripping on the welcome mat.

Spinning on her heels, she snaps her fingers, which I assume is the signal to follow her, so I do. With Delaney in the lead, we climb a set of mahogany stairs that groan loudly under our feet. "The King has asked that you *both*," she flashes a frown at Sebastian, "stay as our guests. However, as the captain of his guard, I have insisted precautions be made."

At the top of the stairs, a long hallway stretches before us with four doors on either side. Delaney unclips a pair of gloves from her belt and puts them on. "Sebastian, you'll be staying in the first room on the left. The doorknob is pure silver. We ask that you remain in your room until nightfall. You'll find blood and clean clothing waiting for you." With gloved hands, she opens the door and motions him inside.

He enters the room without a backward glance.

My lungs tighten, making it hard to breathe. God, why do I even care if he looks back at me or not? I hate myself a little for being so pathetic.

Delaney shuts the door behind him and removes her gloves, fastening them to her belt. "Your room is across the hall. You'll find an adjacent bathroom, food, and clean clothing all waiting for you inside."

"Thank you." I start for the door when she snatches me by the shoulder. Her usual harsh expression has gone soft. "King Matteo will stop at nothing until he has Rachel by his side. You have nothing to fear."

I smile, because I know she means well. But in truth, her words ring hollow. I've met the Mentis, and they're ruthless killers with the ability to brainwash humans. As badass as Delaney is, this hippie tribe of soap-making, bird-changing vampires really doesn't match up. Especially when their king is staked to his throne.

I dart inside the room before she can read the doubt on my face.

A lantern glows on a wooden desk in the corner, illuminating the bedroom just enough for me to get my bearings. Two twin beds stand against opposite walls. Opal is collapsed on the bed farthest from the door. Still in her clothes, she snores loudly. Even in the dark I can see how puffy her face is. She must have cried herself to sleep.

Guilt wrenches my stomach, and I close the door as quietly as I can, so as not to wake her. This whole time I've been consumed with thoughts about myself, my aunt, and Sebastian, Opal's been suffering, too.

"I'm an awesome person," I mutter. I grab a folded quilt from the desk and carefully cover Opal. She moans softly, but doesn't wake. Next, I flop onto my own bed. Along with my violin and my bag from the car, someone set out a pile of folded clean clothes on the foot. Like Opal must have been, I'm too tired to change, so I set everything on floor.

Against the wall between our beds is a nightstand with two plates. One has a sandwich, bag of chips, and water bottle, while the other is nothing but crumbs. I rip into the sandwich — peanut butter — and devour it in five large bites. Next, I tilt my head back and devour the chips by the handful. When the bag is empty, I open the water bottle and drain it. Finally, with a full belly in what feels like an eternity of being hungry, I collapse onto the bed.

Still, sleep doesn't come. I can't help but count the passing seconds as if they're grains of sand in an hourglass. Each minute that passes is a minute I've lost without my aunt. And each minute lost brings her closer to an eternal life as a bloodsucking monster.

· · ·

I wake to purple and pink ribbons of sky. Staring at the ceiling, I let my eyes adjust to the growing darkness. I'm not sure how long I lay there, trying and failing to convince myself to get out of bed. Another day waits outside the door, and I'm not sure I'm ready to face it.

It's a weird sort of feeling—not knowing what I'll find if I look at myself in the mirror. While I'm sure I appear the same on the outside, the things that have happened to me—kiss included—since leaving the cabin have distorted me in such a way it's almost like I no longer fit inside my own skin. I'm now a stranger posing as Charlie, and I don't think she's ever coming back.

Can you hold a funeral for yourself? Or at least the person you used to be? If not, it should seriously be a thing, because I feel like I need to mourn everything I've lost—especially innocence.

People laugh outside. It's obvious the camp is waking up. All I want to do is close my eyes and pretend this is all a dream—except for maybe the kiss. I'll keep that.

There's a knock at the door.

"Charlie?" The word is muffled by the wood, but there's no mistaking Delaney's gritty voice. "At the camp humans and Anima eat communally in the barn. Will you be joining us?"

Holy hell. A vampire-human communal barn breakfast. When did this become my life? And why did I think it was ever a good idea to leave my safe, little cabin?

"Yeah." I mean, there's no point starving myself. I sit up

and try to access my hair, only to find it matted with clumps of mud. The memory of the flash that tore Sebastian and me apart, flinging me into the mud, flashes through my mind, reminding me that the mystery of what I am still needs to be solved.

And the fact that I'm even considering myself a *what,* even internally, already bumps this day off the list of *Charlie's Top Five Favorite Days.* "I'll be down as soon as I shower."

"Very good," Delaney says. "We'll keep something warm for you."

"Thanks." Last night proved they have real food. Still, an image of Delaney microwaving a bowl of blood comes to mind. I smile, which is good, because I was worried I forgot how.

Opal's bed is empty. I grab the clean set of clothes off the floor and head to the adjacent bathroom. Twenty minutes later, I'm mud-free and feeling slightly more human—which is hilarious. The jeans and black T-shirt I've been given—soft from previous wear—are a perfect fit. Rather than deal with my mess of wet hair, I tie it in a loose braid as I leave the room for the barn.

At least, that's what I intended. But the moment I'm in the hallway I can't help but glance at Sebastian's room, only to discover his door open a crack. The temptation is too great. Or maybe it's that I didn't have much willpower to begin with. As I quietly inch toward the door, I notice something—a strange heavy breathing coming from the other side. And another thing. A noise I can't quite piece together until I have a palm on the door and push it open.

Sucking. The sound is sucking. And the view isn't much

better. Sebastian stands, back to me, arms wrapped around a girl with dark skin, her own encircling his neck. Her eyes are closed, a faint smile on her lips. Sebastian's face is buried in the crook of her shoulder.

Terror barrels into me, and a scream spills from my lips.

Sebastian jerks upright, as does the girl, her arms falling from his neck. Eyes open, she smiles at me. "You must be Charlie. So nice to meet you."

"The hell?" Tremors shake my body. I take a wobbling step.

Ribbons of blood spiral from the puncture on her shoulder. She quickly pulls a handkerchief from her pocket and presses it to the wound. A tiny crease forms above her eyes. "Wait. Haven't you seen a vampire feed before?"

I take another step back. "Well I have, and they were pretty much murdering everyone as they did it."

Her face softens. "Don't worry. Nothing like that would ever happen here. The Anima have a deep respect for humans. We give them life."

"And they give us death."

She shakes her head. "Not here. It's safe. And, if done correctly, a feeding can be quite *enjoyable*." She smiles up at Sebastian in a way that makes me want to punch her in the throat. "And your boy here," she pats him on the shoulder, "sure knows how to do it right." Still holding the handkerchief to her neck, she chuckles softly. "Don't look so upset. It's only natural, honey. They have to eat, same as us. I'm going to go bandage this up." She starts for the door, only to hesitate. "It was great to meet you, Charlie. And I'm so glad my clothes fit you so well. You can borrow anything you want." With that she leaves.

Which is good, because I hate her. She was nice to me. She gave me her clothes. And I hate her. Just add it to the list of reasons I'm winning at life right now.

I direct my attention to Sebastian, who still hasn't turned around, and it's starting to weird me out. "So, that was kind of awkward, right?"

The Anima must have loaned him clean clothes as well. Gone is his shredded suit, replaced with faded jeans and a gray T-shirt that allows me to see every ripple of muscle along his back—and there are plenty. It's pathetic, he doesn't even have to be facing me to make me weak in the knees. "Look at that. You're wearing jeans and you haven't even burst into flames yet. Who'd have thought." I give a weak laugh.

He shakes his head. "I'm still in bloodlust, Charlie." His voice is a growl. "You shouldn't see me like this."

It's the growl that makes my pulse skip and hop. "I've already seen you like this, remember?"

"And it terrified you."

"Because I thought you were trying to kill me. I know better now. I'm not afraid."

"That is a mistake." He whirls around, eyes black and feral, and grabs my arms. "These humans here are foolish, Charlie. Don't think for a second you are safe with a vampire, *any* vampire. Even me."

I try to move away, but his hands hold me like a vice. "We are not humans. We are predators. All we care about is hunting and blood. In fact, part of me wants to rip your throat out right this second."

I jerk out of his grasp. "You're a liar."

His eyes narrow. "Care to test that theory?"

"I don't have to." Anger ignites my blood to near boiling. I shove him, hard, and he doesn't budge. "You're just trying to scare me."

"The truth can be scary."

Squaring my shoulders, I tilt my head and level his black-eyed stare with my own. "You would never hurt me."

He laughs. "You really are a fool. What makes you think so? Another teenage girl *feeling*? Your ridiculous hormones are going to get you killed."

His words sting like a slap. "Why are you being such a dick? If you regret kissing me last night, just say so. This"—I jab a finger against his chest—"is really dramatic."

He snaps his jaw shut, his black eyes fading to gray.

"This teenage girl, hormones and all, isn't an idiot," I continue. "I can tell when someone is trying to push me away. You claim vampires are so tough and scary. So why wuss out when it comes to telling the truth?"

He jerks back as if I struck him. "I've given you the truth. It is not my fault you can't accept it."

"Yeah?" I fold my arms. "Then prove it. Rip my throat out."

He scoffs. "Like I would risk setting myself on fire with your poison blood."

"I'm confused. Either I have to worry about you biting me, or I don't. Which is it?"

His eyes blaze silver fire. "You are an impossible, stubborn girl."

"*You're* the stubborn one. Because you know I'm right."

He's on me in a second, so fast I don't see him move. His hands clamp on to my arms, and he shakes me lightly. "Fine," he spits through clenched teeth. "Maybe you're right. I haven't been able to stop thinking about kissing you, and wanting to do it again. And that is so much more dangerous than any bite."

When I speak, my voice comes out a whisper. "Why?"

"Because vampires and humans don't work. If you need more proof, look at Rachel and Matteo. Their relationship will be her demise."

My hands shake. "I'm not human. You keep reminding me of that."

"True." His smile is sad. "But that still doesn't make you strong enough to survive in my world. Whatever these feelings are—this thing between us—we need to end it before it ends you." He gives me another gentle shake. "And it will end in your death. Do you understand, Charlie?" There's a chord of desperation in his voice.

"Okay," I say, even though it hurts to do it. "But I have to know. Does this have anything to do with what I made you remember last night?"

He drops his hands and backs away. "I'd be lying if I said it didn't."

"Sebastian, what was it?"

His eyes fixate on the ceiling. "When you did—whatever it is that you do—it was more than just images this time, but flashes of feeling. I saw the same woman as before, with honey-gold hair. She shone so bright it stung my eyes to stare too long. I am sure she was Faerie."

"So you remembered your captivity?"

He shakes his head. "No. Despite what my Queen has told me, I don't think I was a captive. I think the Faerie woman was my mother."

I inhale sharply. "How is that possible? You're a vampire."

With a sigh, he pinches the bridge of his nose. "I have no idea. It's just the feeling that came along with the pieces of memory. She loved me, Charlie. And I loved her." Dropping his hand, he looks up at me. "She's dead now. I know that, too. I wasn't strong enough to protect her." He looks at me, silver eyes blazing straight through me, piercing my heart. "Just like I know I'm not strong enough to protect you."

"What if I don't need protecting?" I say, voice soft.

His laugh is sad. "You are a girl in a world of monsters, who just found herself in the middle of a centuries-old vampire war. And I won't be the one to let you down and watch you die."

Before I can respond, he pushes past me, leaving me alone in his room with the weight of his words.

Chapter
Sixteen

I'm not sure I how long I sit on Sebastian's bed before Opal ducks her head in the room, sighing with obvious relief. "There you are." She pushes the door open and steps inside. "I've been looking all over for you. The spread in the barn the Anima put out for the humans? Ah-mazing." When I don't respond, she tilts her head and frowns. "What's wrong with you?"

Shaking my head, I pick at a loose stitch on the quilt. "I think Sebastian just broke up with me. I mean, that's not the right phrase. I don't know what I mean."

Her eyes grow impossibly large. "First off, that's disgusting."

I roll my eyes. "How did I know you were going to say that?"

"Second." She scurries over to the bed and drops beside me. "I have *sooo* many questions. When were you guys even a thing?"

I shrug. "That's just it. We weren't." I chew on my lip for a moment, deciding how many details I should share before resolving to screw it. "We kissed last night. Something happened and he got a few more memories back, and then he made it *abundantly* clear there can never be anything between us."

"Thank God! Because, gross, Charlie." She makes a gagging noise. "If you really want to make out with a leech, I can go pull one out of the pond, their lips are probably cleaner." She tilts their head. "Except I don't think they have lips. Still, you're probably going to want to sanitize because that's nasty."

I scowl. "Do you really think you're helping right now?"

She sighs. "I get that he's hot. But all the Mentis are hot. Their looks are meant to draw us in, get us nice and close before they pounce." She jabs two fingers into my neck, making me flinch.

"And sure," she continues, "Sebastian did save us. He's not high on my list to stake, but a relationship between a human and a vampire could never end well."

I yank on the thread, pulling it from the quilt and leaving a hole behind. "That's what Sebastian said."

"Because he's right." Her voice softens. "Even if there wasn't a deadly war raging, vampires are immortal and humans?" She shrugs. "Not so much. Somebody's going to die eventually."

I make a face. "You're just a ray of sunshine."

"The truth hurts. But you know what might cheer you up? The bacon they have in the barn." She groans. "Two words: Smoked apple. It brings purpose back to this dismal abyss of a monster-filled life."

I can't help but smile, even as my stomach grumbles. "I guess I can go for some purpose."

"Great." She jumps to her feet and grabs me by the arm. "I'll lead the way." She guides me from Sebastian's room, down the stairs, and out the front door. Outside, the hum of voices and laughter can be heard before the barn even comes into view.

Two large doors stand open to the night, revealing rows of tables filled with people and vampires, talking and laughing in the flickering lamplight. At the far end of the room, two women with violins, a man with a guitar, and male vampire with a banjo play an upbeat folk rhythm.

The people sitting closest to the door smile as we approach. Several even call out greetings. The smell of bacon and warm bread wafts from several grills set up at the far side of the building.

The girl who'd been feeding Sebastian stands from the far end of a table. A splotch of blood blooms beneath the bandage on her neck. "Charlie. Over here. I saved you a seat."

Inwardly I groan, even as I force a smile. "Um, be right there." *God, I'm petty.*

"Go sit," Opal says, dropping my arm. "I'll get you a plate."

"You're only doing that so you can get another helping of bacon," I say.

She grins. "If you can't prove it, it didn't happen." She skips off before I can argue. After the condition she was in last night, it's good to see her smile, even if it's only outwardly.

"I didn't get to tell you earlier, but my name is Natalie," the girl says as I sit down.

Probably because you were getting your neck sucked on by the same vampire I'd kissed the night before.

"It's nice to meet you." And then, because I feel guilty for my bad thoughts I add, "Thanks for the clothes."

She waves her hand. "My pleasure. We don't get a lot of visitors, so I'm happy to help. Most people don't know vampires exist, and the ones who do want nothing to do with them. Am I right?" She laughs.

Yeah. Because the other ones will rip your throat out— that's kind of a downer.

I smile back. I do a quick glance around. The vampires are easy to spot with their glowing eyes. Most of the humans have plates of food in front of them while the vampires drink blood from glass mugs. Only a handful of humans, both men and women, sport the same bloody bandage on their neck as Natalie. And there are at least a hundred vampires in here.

"Where do you get all the blood?" I ask.

Natalie picks up a biscuit and begins to butter it. "Cows, mostly. But we also harvest pigs and chickens. The guys have a lot of fun making variations. They'll infuse the cattle blood with alcohol or weed to give it a little kick. Speaking of, I have some smoke if you're interested. Good stuff. We grow it ourselves so you know it's pure."

"Um, no thanks."

She shrugs. "Totally cool." She crams half the biscuit into her mouth. "That's what this place is all about, honoring your truth," she says, words muffled.

And I thought some of the festivals we sold soap at were out there. But at the same time, I can totally picture my aunt loving this place. "So, if you have so much animal blood, why were you giving Sebastian your blood?"

"Oh, that." She dusts the crumbs from her hands. "The

Anima believe human blood is sacred and they reserve it only for special occasions. Obviously, the King receives daily offering because of his condition. The guards on duty will also receive human offering before taking their posts. And blood here is always freely given."

"Why give Sebastian your blood, then?"

She reaches for another biscuit. "Because of the special mission he's going on with Delaney. They're going to need their strength."

"Mission?" I whip around. "What mission?"

Shrugging, she tears the biscuit in half. "Dunno. Something for the King."

Before I can respond, the music stops mid-song and the entire room falls silent. Natalie stands, along with everyone else in the barn, and motions, hurriedly, for me to do the same.

Why not? I think, climbing to my feet.

When in Rome, and all that.

Around me, humans and Anima alike press their right fist across their chest and bow their heads. From the open doors, the sound of synchronized marching fills the barn as four Anima enter, each holding a wooden pole over their shoulder, balancing King Matteo, staked to his throne, on a platform above them. They set him down in the middle of the room.

A crow flies down from the rafters, transforming into a shirtless vampire with feathers woven into his waist-length black hair. The long knife tethered to his waist makes me inhale sharply. "Who among the humans would honor and be honored by the King, by offering upon him their lifeblood?"

Across the barn, dozens of chairs scrape across the wooden floor as women—and a few men—leap to their feet with their arms raised, Natalie included.

"Sit down, girl," a nearby woman hisses. "You know you can only give offering once a week."

Huffing, she folds her arms and sits down.

The knife-wielding vampire points to a woman with shoulder-length blue hair and tattoos decorating both arms. She squeals excitedly before dashing to the throne. Matteo holds out his hand and she places her own within it.

He smiles at her briefly before drawing her to him and spinning her around to face us. "Today we give thanks to Amelia for her gracious offering of lifeblood.

The entire room chants, "With blood, comes life, and life brings hope."

Looking around, I'm starting to get the eerie feeling I've accidentally joined a cult.

"With this offering," the King continues, "I take the life and hope it brings for a peaceful coexistence for humans and vampires alike." He pulls the woman to his face and sinks his teeth into her neck. The barn erupts into cheers. The woman in his arms closes her eyes and smiles.

Holy crap. I did join a cult.

The band begins to play, and the people around me sit, resuming their own meals as Matteo continues to drink.

Opal appears at my side. She drops a plate piled high with bacon in front of me. "How fucked up was that?" she asks.

Natalie frowns. "It was a beautiful gift of life and hope."

Opal drops into the seat beside me. "Simmer down, crazy pants. I'll drink the Kool-Aid as long as it comes with a side of bacon." She elbows me in the side.

A line of blood trickles down Amelia's neck, soaking into the front of her shirt. I shift uneasily in my seat. "I think I lost my appetite." For as long as I can remember, Aunt Rachel taught me how important it was to be tolerant of all people, no matter their race, religion, or sexuality. But blood-drinking ceremonies might be too much for even me.

Still, what they want—a coexistence between vampires and humans—is so much better than the hunting and slaughtering of humans the other clans prefer. Maybe I should be open-minded?

I glance at Matteo, his teeth sunk into the woman's neck. She moans.

Nope. I quickly turn around. *I can't do it.* "I think I'm going to get some air."

Opal makes a face. "The barn doors are wide open. There is plenty of air."

"Not the right kind." Shaking my head, I stand.

"*Okay.*"

I've already started for the door when King Matteo's voice rings out. "Charlie, a word?"

Damn. I force a smile to my lips and slowly turn. "Sure." Even though the ceremony I just witnessed soured my stomach, I can force myself to stay if he has an update on rescuing my aunt.

Humans and vampires alike watch with interest as I approach the throne. Another woman stands with Amelia, taping a bandage to her neck before ushering her away.

I stop several feet away, shifting from foot to foot. "Everyone is looking at us."

Matteo smiles warmly, blood a crimson stain around

his mouth. It takes all of my willpower not to stare. "It's not often we have guests. My people are curious. Already the whispers have begun."

Before I can ask what he's talking about, he shifts, wincing slightly as his eyes dart to the stake and back. "You ran off last night quite upset, and rightly so, but I never got a chance to put your mind at ease. I want you to know that I'm going to do everything in my power to retrieve Rachel *before* any harm comes to her."

"Thank you." I try to smile, but it feels strained.

He frowns. "I'm getting the sense you don't believe me."

I shrug and inch a little closer. "I'm sorry. I want to believe you, more than anything. But I've met the other clans and you—" Without meaning to, my eyes travel to the stake in his chest.

He nods. "I understand. While might and power may be impressive, they lie. True strength comes in compassion and understanding, wouldn't you agree?"

"Well, yeah, that all sounds very well and good on paper, but when a Corpus is trying to rip out your throat, there's no compassion or understanding that's going to make them stop."

He frowns. "That's where you're wrong. While my sisters have been so focused on this damn war between us, they've completely missed the bigger picture. Lurking in the shadows? Harvesting humans like cattle?" He makes a disgusted noise. "Once I bring all vampires into the light, their way of life, their very existence, will be in jeopardy."

I inhale sharply. "Wait. You want to go *public* with your existence?"

"Absolutely. My people have spent too many years

hiding." Murmurs of agreement rise from the tables around. "We want to coexist peacefully with humans. And going public is the only way to do that."

"The humans are going to freak," I say.

"Initially." He nods. "But we are committed to peaceful coexistence. And the humans will come around once they recognize we can heal their diseases with our blood. When they understand we mean them no harm, they will join us to exterminate the ones that do."

His words fall on me like a mountain of bricks. "You want the humans to help you win the vampire war."

Green fire flashes through his eyes. "I want the humans to aid us in peaceful coexistence."

A chill spirals down the length of my body. What an idiot I was to assume Matteo was weak. He may be staked to a throne, but his mind is as dangerous a weapon as any Corpus's fangs.

A single question pushes to the front of my mind. "Where did Sebastian and Delaney go?"

"To retrieve the object I spoke about last night. He volunteered at first dark, and, like you, I have a good feeling about him, despite his Mentis shortcomings."

The item that will either prove or disprove that I am his daughter.

"I don't believe he really is a Mentis," I say.

The King shakes his head. "Nor do I."

"So," I twist my hands together, "what exactly are they retrieving?"

Matteo sweeps his gaze across the barn. Slowly, the room falls silent as the air becomes thick with anticipation. "The cruel Faerie Queen of Air and Darkness created me and my two sisters to be her personal army." His voice rings out, echoing against the rafters.

Chair legs squeak as people lean in.

"Having carried out her atrocities against Fae and humankind for centuries, we could take her slavery no longer, so we rebelled. Together, my sisters and I killed her along with her entire court. The Faerie Queen had three magical items she used to rule and dominate, and my sisters and I split the articles amongst ourselves.

"Cordelia, Queen of the Corpus, took the Faerie Queen's blade. The sword is embedded with stealth magic. Whoever wields it can blend into the shadows.

"It should be no surprise that my sister Seraphina, Queen of the Mentis, chose the crown. The crown was forged with compulsion magic. With it, my sister and her clan can persuade humans to do their bidding.

"I chose the necklace of transformation, which enables my clan to transform into birds." His head falls against the throne, and he turns his gaze to the ceiling. There's something sad about his expression. But if I used to be able to fly, and no longer could, I'd probably be sad, too.

"It soon became clear that my sisters and I could not agree on how to feed and exist among humans. That's when the fighting began. It is the magical objects my sisters war over. They believe that by holding all three, they will be able to rule, and ultimately destroy, the other clans. Because of this, I hid the necklace."

An uneasy feeling coils in my gut. "That sounds like a dangerous mission."

He smiles. "There is no greater warrior in all of the clans than Delaney. She was deadly before I changed her.

Now she's unstoppable."

"Sure, but why take this risk? If there's any chance the other clans might attack you for the necklace, why bring it here?"

"Only myself or someone of my lineage can wield the necklace. If you wear the necklace, and the stones glow green, then we will know for sure if you are my daughter or not."

It's impossible to wrap my mind around—that magic Faeries and glowing stones actually exist. But standing in a room full of vampires does make me more inclined to believe than I would have been a week ago. "And if it doesn't glow?"

He's quiet for several moments before answering. "It is time the necklace returned to me. I am stronger when I wear it. Rescuing Rachel will not be easy, and I need all the strength I can muster."

I have so many more questions, but Matteo waves a hand in the air, silencing me before I have the chance to ask. "Go," he says. "Enjoy the night with my children. Be at ease knowing I will rescue Rachel and all will be well. I must converse with my warriors and prepare them for the battle ahead."

He snaps his fingers and the four large vampires that carried him into the barn return to his throne and lift it from the ground. Marching in unison, they carry him from the barn, their footsteps echoing into the night.

The music begins immediately, as does the talking and laughing. Despite the mood of people and vampires around me, I can't get the itchy bands of anxiety to release their hold of my body.

Be at ease, the King said. *All will be well.*

But as I step out of the barn into the warm summer night, a series of tremors overcome me. I hug my arms tight across my body because I *know,* despite what the King said, the feeling digs inside my brain like a thorn.

Nothing will ever be right again.

chapter
Seventeen

I spend the next couple of days with the Anima clan doing my best to keep busy. If I'm helping to cook meals, then I'm not counting down the days until the full moon and Aunt Rachel's transformation. When I'm assisting the soap makers, I'm not thinking about Sebastian's kiss and the weird place we left things off. When I'm sitting in the barn, talking with Opal and Natalie, I'm not wondering if Matteo is my father, and what it means if he is or isn't.

It's the moments of quiet when I first wake up to the sun sinking below the horizon, that's when the thoughts haunt me. So I move. Throwing on my clothes and dashing from my shared room, hoping if I move fast enough I can outrun the fog of worry always at my heels.

But there are times, like now, that my fingers can't go fast enough to keep the fog at bay.

"See?" I tell Henry, an older man who I learned used to have terminal cancer until he came to live with the Anima and received their blood. "If you wrap the mold in plastic wrap as soon as you pour, and then remove it before it reaches the gel stage, your soap won't crack." I tuck the edges of plastic wrap around the mold and place it on a cut log beside the campfire he built outside his trailer.

"I really appreciate the tip." He smiles.

I shrug. "My aunt taught me. It's not like cracked soap is a bad thing, but I know it doesn't always sell as well."

"And we can use all the sales we can get." He reaches for the plastic wrap and tears off a sheet for himself. "It's funny to think I'd be living in a commune making soap for money."

"Why?"

Shaking his head, he laughs. "Once upon a time, I was a lawyer. If the cancer hadn't killed me, that job surely would have. I was so obsessed with getting ahead in life, I forgot to actually live it."

I consider his words. "This," I scan the various tents and trailers in surrounding us, "makes you happy?"

"No." He laughs again. "And that's what being here taught me. "There is no *this* that can make you happy. No one thing, place, job, or person can make you happy. You know what makes you happy?"

I shake my head.

He places his hand over his heart. "You. Only you can make you happy."

I turn his words over in my head. When I was with Aunt Rachel I was convinced the key to my happiness was getting the hell away from the cabin. But now that I'm hundreds of miles away, I'm not happier, and even more lost.

Shaking my head, I push the thoughts away before

they can take root. *No.* I will not think about Aunt Rachel, Sebastian, Matteo, or anything else that will have me erupt into sobs in front of this nice man.

"Charlie!"

I spin around to see Opal stepping over a couple making out in a sleeping bag. Carrying my violin case, she stops in front of me. "You haven't touched this thing since we've been here, and I'm dying to know if you can actually play it."

I think about the last time I played the violin—for Sebastian—and shrink away. "I'm not really sure I'm in the mood."

"Come on. *Please.*" She clasps her hands together. "Other than a few homeless guys, I've never seen anyone play one of these in real life."

Henry sets his soap mold aside. "It's a beautiful night. The only thing that would make it perfect is some music."

"See?" Opal thrusts the case at me. "Everyone agrees. Now you have to play."

Frowning, I wipe my hands off on my pants before taking the case. "Fine. But just one song."

"Yay." Clapping, Opal drops onto the nearest log.

With a lump in my throat, I remove the bow and run a block of rosin down the hair. Henry said only I can make myself happy. Once upon a time, playing the violin did just that. But now, my days of making music in the little cabin in the woods feel like a lifetime ago.

With trembling hands, I remove the violin. After tuning the strings, I place the instrument beneath my chin. This new chapter of my life should bring new music. But as I drag the bow across the strings, I bring to life the song that's haunted me throughout my existence. The song without words that Sebastian remembered from his past.

"Oh," Henry says, clasping a hand to his chest. "This is one of my favorites."

His recognition of the song almost makes me stop. The melody has a tight hold on me, keeping me from breaking. It calls to the camp in the same way it calls to me. People come, by the dozens, encircling the campfire where I play.

Many sway to the notes as they pour from my fingers, drawing us all closer. From somewhere in the crowd, a guitar rings out. A bearded man emerges with a viola tucked beneath his arm. He raises it and plays along.

It's not long before a girl, slightly younger than me, steps up to the fire. She holds out her hands and begins to sing.

My love said to me
My Mother won't mind
And me Father won't slight you
For your lack of kind
Then she stepped away from me
And this she did say
It will not be long, love
'Til our wedding day.

She stepped away from me
And she moved through the Fair
And fondly I watched her
Move here and move there
And she went her way homeward
With one star awake

As the swans in the evening
Move over the lake

The vocalist pauses as the guitarist picks up tempo, forcing me along in a whirlwind of flying fingers and thrusting bow. The girl twirls, her long skirt spinning in a dizzying array of colors. When she begins the third verse, the crowd joins in.

The people were saying
No two e'er were wed
But one has a sorrow
That never was said
And she smiled as she passed me
With her goods and her gear
And that was the last
That I saw of my dear.

I dreamed it last night
That my true love came in
So softly she entered
Her feet made no din
She came close beside me
And this she did say
It will not be long, love
'Til our wedding day.

Someone shouts, and the tempo picks up again. The people gathered move together, dancing and spinning as a tambourine keeps time with a steady pulse.

Opal hooks an arm through mine, yanking the violin

out from beneath my chin. "Come on," she shouts, laughing. Setting my violin inside the case, I can't help but laugh, too, as we spin and twirl arm in arm through the dancing crowd.

Opal releases me, and I spin away, only to land in Henry's arms. Taking me by the elbow he twirls me, and I'm passed to another boy. We're only together for a moment before the crowd shifts again, and I'm passed to the next dancer.

The moment my hands meet his chest the breath leaves my lungs. Sebastian stares down at me, eyes blazing, before spinning me away, only to pull me tightly against him.

"You're back." My throat is so tight, I'm barely able to squeeze out the words. "When?"

"Just now."

Taking me by the hand, he twirls me. The next dancer in line holds his hand out for me, but Sebastian draws me against his chest. Reflexively, I wind my hands behind his neck, fingers locking. He drops his hands to the small of my back, pulling us together, so my chin rests in the hollow of his throat when I look up at him.

There's something about the expression in his eyes that causes a shiver to run down the length of my spine. I know that him being here means he must have found the necklace Matteo sent him after. There is now proof of my parentage in the camp.

And yet, I can't bring myself to care. I want the music to go on forever, so that I might stay with Sebastian, locked in this moment where I've found a seedling of happiness.

Pressed together, we move as one. The other dancers are nothing but streaks of color beneath the star-filled sky.

"Charlie," Sebastian begins, "the way we left things—"

"Please don't," I say, cutting him off. "Words are always getting in the way and messing things up. I just want to exist in the moment—at least for a little while longer."

He nods, drawing me to him. He rests his chin on my head as the music spirals around us. I close my eyes, and for a moment the rest of the world falls away. There is only music, Sebastian, me, and an entire sky full of stars.

Sebastian's breath, warm on my neck, makes me gasp, and my eyes fly open. Turning, I find his lips dangerously close to mine.

"Before you, Charlie, I didn't believe I could have these feelings." His jaw flexes. "I don't want them."

"I don't want them, either," I say.

A grin tugs on the corner of his lips. "Looks like we're screwed."

"So what do we do?"

"There's only one thing to do." He lowers his mouth to mine. The glint of fang flashes from his parted lips. "This." The moment his lips touch mine my muscles tighten with the need to draw him closer. His arms ensnare my waist, pulling me against him so that the warmth from his body spills into me, setting me awash in flames. My heart comes alive, a fluttering thing that beats against its cage of bones. Electricity jolts through my body. I lift onto my toes, my fingers winding into his hair. I don't want him to ever let me go.

But then the music stops, and he does just that.

The air between us is colder than anything I've ever felt.

Opal pushes through the crowd. "The King wants you to come to the barn right away. He wants *everyone* there."

As soon as she says the words the summoning bell clangs in the distance. Each ring pierces my chest, rattling my ribs. Swallowing hard, I turn to Sebastian. "I'm not ready."

A tendon along his jaw flexes as he places a hand on my arm. "When it comes to finding out the truth, no one ever is."

Chapter Eighteen

"Of course you're not ready." Opal snatches my hand. "Finding out if a vampire is your dad is something nobody could ever be ready for."

Sebastian squeezes my shoulder. "I'll meet you there. I have to do something, first." I want to stop him, but he's already gone, disappearing into the crowd making their way to the barn. Several crows cry as they fly overhead.

"Why do vampires always have to be so damn mysterious all the time?" Opal asks.

I shake my head, wondering that, too, among other things. Still dizzy from the kiss, collecting my thoughts is nearly impossible. We're quiet as we follow the crowd traveling the path. Soon the barn is yards away.

I hesitate, gripping Opal's arm. "What if he's my dad?" I whisper.

"You know, these bloodsuckers aren't as bad as the other ones. It wouldn't be the worst thing in the world. It would make you a vampire princess, right? I mean, how cool is that?

Regardless who your dad is, it doesn't change who you are."

"Yeah? Who?"

"Charlie." She shrugs. "And if Matteo isn't your dad, you're still Charlie. Nothing changes unless you want it to."

"I guess. But now there's all this stuff with Sebastian. I don't know what to think anymore." I drop my hand.

Opal peels back her jacket, revealing the wooden stake holstered to her belt. "Want me to stake him? Because I will. That's what friends do."

I smile. "I really don't think that *is* what normal friends do."

"Really?" Wrinkling her nose, she lets her jacket fall into place. "What type of lame friends did you have before me?"

Laughing, I slide my arm through hers and settle my head on her shoulder. "Really shitty ones, I guess."

"Sounds like it." The doors are open. The inside is ablaze with lantern light. The eating tables have been pushed against the wall, leaving only rows of chairs facing King Matteo on his throne. Delaney stands by his side, hands clasped in front of her and spear strapped to her back.

Nowhere in the sea of faces do I spot Sebastian. *Where the hell did he go?*

"I'm pretty sure we have to go in," Opal whispers.

"I know." I inhale sharply. "I just—I don't know how."

"One foot in front of the other," she says, leading me forward. "I'll be with you the entire time."

We step into the barn and every head turns to face us. The hushed murmuring comes to an abrupt stop. I squeeze Opal's arm so tightly my knuckles turn white. My grip has to hurt her, but she says nothing. She gives me a small smile and walks with me to the front of the room.

The silence smothers me like a wool blanket pulled too-soon from the dryer. Overhead, a crow sitting on a wooden beam ruffles his feathers with a shake. The sound echoes through the rafters.

King Matteo smiles warmly from his throne before turning his attention to the room. "My people, tonight the necklace has returned to my possession, strengthening me, and you, as we prepare for the trials ahead."

A murmur ripples through the room.

"The continued violence between the clans must come to an end, as well as the senseless hunting and slaughtering of humans."

More voices rise in agreement.

"As I'm sure you've heard, the Mentis have kidnapped a woman who many of you remember—my beloved Rachel. They think they can bargain her life for the necklace."

Several people shout in protest as the crows begin to scream.

Matteo holds his hand up to silence the room. "Do not fear. Myself and my trusted warriors have worked tirelessly these last few nights coming up with a plan I believe will bring us victory."

The room slowly quiets.

"You see," he continues, "the Mentis underestimate us, and that will be their undoing." His eyes blaze green. "Charlie," he motions me toward him, "please step forward."

Opal gives my arms a squeeze before releasing me.

The room buzzes with muffled whispers as I walk forward, stopping in front of the throne pedestal.

"Sebastian, please," the King calls out.

Sebastian stands from the middle of the chairs. It's then I notice Natalie has positioned herself beside him. I fight to ignore the flicker of jealousy that sparks inside me. He picks up a dirt-streaked box and walks forward. His eyes meet mine, and my chest squeezes painfully tight.

I keep my gaze locked on the King, even when I feel the heat of Sebastian's body beside my own. I know I should still be angry with him for the way he treated me before he left. But I'll be damned if I'm not drawn to him like a magnet.

"Please, present the necklace," the King says.

Sebastian opens the box, and this time my curiosity gets the better of me, so I look. The necklace Delaney withdraws is shaped like a golden serpent, its head protruding through a loop in its tail, completing the circle. A single large emerald is embedded in its head, while two smaller emeralds sparkle as eyes.

The lantern light ripples off the snake's golden scales, and if I didn't know better, I'd say it appeared to be breathing. Sebastian holds it out to the King.

Matteo raises his arm and the snake uncoils its head from its tail. I gasp, as do others in the room. The snake coils around Delaney's wrist, traveling from her fingers to Matteo's outstretched hand, where it winds up his arm onto his shoulder and coils around his neck. Both Matteo's and the snake's eyes blaze green.

Holy hell. I take a step backward.

Matteo catches my movement and smiles. "Do not be afraid. The necklace will only attack hostile forces. Only a member of my lineage can wield it. If you wear the necklace and its eyes blaze green, we'll know who you truly are." His voice lowers. "Are you ready to find out?"

Not even close. But despite my fear of what the necklace will or won't tell me, I find myself holding out my hand without even realizing I'd moved it. The snake lifts its head and watches me, blazing eyes blinking, as if deciding, before it begins to travel down Matteo's arm to my outstretched fingers.

Every muscle in my body coils as it draws closer. It flicks out a golden tongue, almost touching my finger, when a scream pierces the silence of the barn. With a start, the snake turns, retreating up Matteo's arm and settling onto his neck.

I turn in the direction of the noise to find one of Matteo's guards, a dark-skinned woman with a shaved head, stumbling into the barn. A large stake protrudes from the center of her chest.

Clutching the stake, the woman manages to make it to the throne as terror winds through my chest. "My king," she falls to her knees, hand clutching the stake.

Matteo's eyes widen, his lips drawing back in a snarl. "Alyssa, who has done this to you?"

She coughs, splattering drops of blood across the wooden floor. "I-I have failed," she gasps.

"What do you mean?"

She looks up, her glowing eyes beginning to fade. "They are here."

Chapter Nineteen

The erupting screams hurt my ears as people and vampires jump from their chairs.

"Mentis!" someone shrieks.

"Get the women and children out of here," the King shouts. "Anima, protect the humans at all costs."

A hand snatches my arm and yanks me away from the King. I barely have time to scream before I realize it's Sebastian. His eyes have turned black, his muscles tight. "Do *not* leave my side, Charlie. Do you understand?"

Fear has my throat in a stranglehold, so I'm only able to nod my reply.

Opal runs up to us, gun in her outstretched hands. She waves it back and forth, eyes sweeping over the room. "Is it true? Are the Mentis here?"

Sebastian closes his eyes and inhales. "Five of them. Approaching as we speak." Opening his eyes, he emits a low growl and pushes me behind him.

Opal aims her gun at the door. Beside us, several guardsmen have surrounded the

King. In front of them, Delaney stands with her spear raised. Her eyes have turned as black as Sebastian's. "Protect the King at any cost," she snarls.

Behind us, the barn continues to empty of humans until all that remain are black-eyed snarling Anima. To the front, three men and two women step into the open doorway. I recognize two of the Mentis as the same ones who kidnapped my aunt. All five wear gray suits, the men with ties, and dark sunglasses.

The same man who first stepped into my cabin moves forward. With a smirk, he removes his sunglasses and tucks them into his jacket. His gray eyes blaze. "What a quaint reception, King Matteo. Truly, you shouldn't have."

"How dare you enter my compound and start a fight." Matteo's fingers dig into the wooden arms of his throne. "Let it be known that it is your last."

"Easy, your *highness*." The Mentis clasps his hands behind his back as he surveys the room. "We didn't come here to wage war. We've come to collect what is ours. Unfortunately, your little bird there," he motions to the dead vampire on the floor, "wasn't receptive to the idea."

"Should I kill them now?" Delaney asks, spinning her spear in a slow arc.

Matteo holds up his hand to stop her. "There is nothing of yours here."

"Is that so?" The Mentis turns his attention on me. Sebastian pushes me farther behind him. "Sebastian?" A slow grin creeps over the Mentis' face. "How good to see you're faring your *captivity* so well. The Queen will be most relieved to know you're all right."

Sebastian's jaw tightens. "*Frederick.*"

Frederick faces Matteo. "How about an exchange? We'll take the girl and Sebastian. In exchange, we'll give you Rachel back in human form."

An ice pick of fear drives through my heart.

"Failure to accept our offer," Frederick continues, "will result in our keeping Rachel." He grins, exposing his long fangs. "*Forever.*"

"No." I push in front of Sebastian. "I'll go. Just please don't hurt her."

"Charlie, no." Sebastian grabs my arm. "They will torture you."

Frederick cocks his head. "Now that's not very nice. We've always been more than accommodating to you, our little wayward son."

Baring his fangs, Sebastian snarls.

Frederick laughs. "I think you've spent a little too much time with the Anima, boy. You're turning sentimental."

"Maybe I'm just remembering things clearly for once."

The smile melts off the other vampire's face. "Enough. We've wasted enough time already. Let's go." He snaps his fingers.

"If I go peacefully, then you leave Charlie out of it," Sebastian says.

"No deal." Frederick shakes his head. "The Queen was very specific with her terms. If the girl stays, then her aunt joins us forever."

"Screw you, assholes." Opal runs forward, firing a shot that cracks the silence. One of the female Mentis grunts before falling over. "You're not taking anyone anywhere."

Frederick glances at the fallen vampire and shrugs.

"We'll accept her death as payment for the loss of one of your own. Any more violence, and we'll be forced to take action." He looks at me. "Girl, are you coming?"

Opal aims her gun at him and I push it down. "They'll only send more." If I leave with them, I'm not dumb enough to think they won't torture me or kill me. But if I allowed them to change my aunt, knowing I could have stopped it, I'd never be able to live with the guilt. "Yes. I'll go."

"Not without me," Matteo says.

"What an interesting offer." Frederick tilts his head, considering. "We accept."

There's a collective gasp among Anima vampires, followed by cries of protest.

Matteo slices his hand through the air, silencing them. "You would dare argue with the will of a king." He looks at me, and I swear I see him wink. Or maybe I imagined it.

The Anima fall silent, except for Delaney, whose fists shake at her sides. "You know the Mentis Queen will kill you immediately, if the journey there doesn't do it first. How do you expect to travel in your condition?"

"I need you to cut the part of the stake pinning me to the throne."

"That's insane. If the stake moves, you'll die."

He reaches out and clasps her arm. "Perhaps, but as Anima, we vow to protect humanity, especially when the humans are part of our family. Where Charlie goes, I go."

Snarling, Delaney whips out a knife. "This is suicide."

"Perhaps," Matteo answers. "And if it is, I name you successor. Continue with the mission."

She startles, the black draining from her eyes, leaving them blazing green. "Of course. I-I am honored."

Closing his eyes, Matteo bows his head. "Do it. Make it fast."

Delaney raises the dagger. "Do not move. Do not *breathe.*"

Opal runs up beside me and squeezes my arm. "Get the hell out of here while they're distracted," I hiss.

She has her eyes narrowed at the Mentis. "I'm not going anywhere."

Dammit, she's stubborn, but I love her all the more for it.

We inhale together as Delaney brings the knife down at Matteo's back. There's a crack of splintering wood. With a grunt, Matteo grips his chest and falls forward. Blood trickles between his fingers.

I start forward, but Matteo holds up a bloody hand to stop me. "I am fine—I'll be fine."

"You're going to have to help him," Delaney tells the Mentis. "He can't walk. And if any of you decide to hurt him, I will personally feed you your own hearts."

"What a silly threat," Frederick says. "King Matteo is Queen Seraphina's brother. He will be treated accordingly." Raising his arm in the air, he snaps.

Two of the male Mentis step over their fallen companion and grab Matteo by the arms, hoisting him over their shoulders.

Scowling, Delaney grips her spear. Her lips ripple as a low growl emanates from her chest.

"Come, Sebastian," the Mentis snaps again. "Come, girl."

Sebastian grabs my wrists. "Don't do this, Charlie. Say the word and I will kill them all."

I shake my head. "They'll only send more."

"Then I will kill them, too."

Something in my heart softens. "And then they'd hurt my aunt."

He brings his mouth to my ear, breath tickling warm and hot against my neck. "Then I will kill the whole goddamned clan for you. Just please, don't do this."

Maybe he could do it, and he'd die in the process—something else I couldn't live with. "I can't risk it," I say. "My aunt is only human, and I'm—*not*. I stand a better chance at survival."

Muttering a curse—something about stupid, stubborn girl—he releases me. "If they separate us, I will find you. Remember that—especially when things are darkest."

I swallow hard and nod.

Opal holsters her gun. "I'm going, too."

I whirl on her. "No, you're not. I'm not putting any more people I care about at risk."

"That's a shame." Frederick grins. "There's always room on the farm for one more human. Especially a spunky one." He licks his lips.

Opal jerks forward like she might attack him, and I grab her by the shoulders. "You're smart," I tell her. "You have intel on the other clans, and you know how to hunt them. I need you on the outside, okay? Come up with a plan. I know you can do it."

She looks like she might argue, before her shoulders slump. With a sigh, she nods. "I won't let you down."

"I know." I pull her to me, squeezing hard. Never in my life could I imagine having such an amazing friend, one who would put herself in such danger to protect me. So, not everything has been awful since the cabin. This thought gives me a thread of hope that I might survive the next destination as well.

When I release her, Sebastian takes my hand, weaving his fingers through mine. "I'm going to keep you with me as long as I can."

I look at our entwined fingers, for the first time wishing the flash of light would come. But it never does.

"Enough stalling," Frederick says. "I'm eager to leave this dirt camp and return to more *civilized* surroundings." He motions the other Mentis forward, and they exit the barn, carrying the King between them.

Several of the King's guards shift into crows, screaming as they follow them into the night.

Dread swells inside my body, threatening to anchor me to the ground. I feel anything but brave, and yet I manage to hold my head up as I follow the Mentis out the barn doors with Sebastian at my side.

"Remember," he says again. "I will find you."

I give his hand a squeeze. "Not if I find you first."

Chapter Twenty

The crows scream overhead as we walk the uneven trail to the Anima compound gates. Frederick whistles an upbeat tune that grates at my nerves.

Sebastian's hand is a vice on mine. His jaw flexes, eyes blazing with silver fire. I know him well enough now to recognize when his mind is spinning, searching for a solution for our predicament. Maybe because I've been doing the same. And if his silence is any indication, we're both coming up with nothing.

At least a dozen of Matteo's guards wait at the gate. Though their teeth are bared, they say nothing as we pass.

Frederick grins at them, giving a mock salute, which only makes them snarl. He laughs.

Ahead, two Mercedes SUVs wait.

"The girl and the King in one car," the main Mentis says. His lips curve into a wicked smile. "I want Sebastian with me."

"No." Sebastian jerks me toward him. "You will not separate us."

Frederick chuckles. "I hardly see how you're in a position to negotiate." He turns to the remaining woman vampire. "Collar him."

The woman slips on a pair of leather gloves and retrieves what looks like a silver dog chain out of her pocket. "Be a good boy," she says.

She reaches for him. Releasing me, Sebastian sidesteps her hand, grabs her arm and spins her around. Pulling the vampire to his chest, he places his arms around her neck and twists. The snaps that follows vibrates inside my bones.

The woman's eyes flutter wide, her head slumping at an awkward angle before she drops to the ground.

"You are not separating us," Sebastian says again.

Frederick huffs. "Now that's annoying. It's going to take her hours to recover." He kicks the discarded collar closer to Sebastian. "You are going to put this on, and go sit in the car like the good boy you are. If not, I can call the compound and make sure Rachel is made most *uncomfortable* while she waits for her family reunion."

Matteo's eyes narrow. "You will not touch her."

The Mentis shrugs. "That's up to Sebastian."

Sebastian turns to me, the tendons along his jaw flexing. Despite the fury radiating from his body, defeat is already written in his eyes. I know he'll do what I want without having to ask. "Remember what I said," he reminds me.

"Sebastian—"

He picks the collar up off the ground. It sizzles and blisters in his hand. He slips it over his head. Wincing, he grunts through clenched teeth.

"Now get in the car."

Hesitating, he meets my eyes. Already the collar has

begun to eat through his skin, exposing the muscle beneath. He stares at me long enough I get the feeling he's trying to tell me something, but for the life of me I can't figure out what.

"Now." The Mentis grabs him by the shoulder and gives him a hard shove to the car.

Sebastian snarls. He takes slow steps and climbs inside.

When the car door closes, Frederick turns to me. "I've got a little surprise for you. Something to make your trip a little more enjoyable."

My heart splits in half and sinks into my ankles. Whatever he's talking about, it can't be good.

The Mentis withdraws a syringe from his jacket pocket.

I can feel my eyes bulge as I take a step backward. From inside the car, I hear Sebastian roar in anger.

"What is that?" Matteo asks. His feeble struggles in the other Mentis's grip do nothing but make him wince. "You are not to hurt her."

"Aw, no need to worry, your highness." Frederick grins wide, exposing his long teeth. "This won't hurt…much."

My muscles coil, ready to dart.

This was a huge mistake. I'm an idiot for trusting my feelings, after all.

Before I get a chance to run, the Mentis pounces, snatching me by the arm. I scream as he plunges the syringe deep into my neck.

A burning wave washes over me as he empties the contents of the needle. I stumble away when he releases me, only to fall onto my knees. From far away, I hear Matteo and Sebastian shouting, but their words are muffled by the deafening roar filling my ears.

"Help." I say the word, or maybe I just think it. I never find out, because the entire world fades to black.

My brain is a rock, rolled around one of those stone smoothers I had when I was a kid. Round and round it tumbles, wearing down the sharp edges and leaving me wincing in pain when I'm finally able to open my eyes.

The cold, white marble floor beneath my body feels like laying on a slab of ice. I sit up and immediately regret it when the world around me spins. Wincing, I press a hand against my temple and groan. Whatever they injected in me, it wasn't fun.

"Charlie." Relief floods Matteo's voice. "Thank God you are okay."

"Sure," I croak. "We'll go with that." I look around the room, the size of a cell. The white floors, ceilings, and walls reflect the brilliant lights overhead, making me squint. A fourth wall is made entirely of glass, allowing me to see our cell is actually one in long row of cells. Two to three people reside in each. They are all ages, and all wearing white jumpsuits. Medical tags adorn their wrists, just like the one adorning mine.

A quick glance shows my name and age printed on it. I pull on it, but it won't break free. My pulse picks up speed. "Where the hell are we?"

I'm still in my original clothes, just like Matteo, who sits slumped against a wall, bleeding ribbons of blood down his chest. His skin color is noticeably paler, and dark circles color the skin beneath his eyes. He sighs.

"Welcome to the farm."

I can't tell if I'm still suffering from the injection, or if it's terror, but the floor shifts beneath me and I think I might fall over. I can feel the panic boiling beneath my skin, threatening to spill over. *Stay calm, Charlie. Think.* "How long?" I ask.

He shakes his head. "Easily twenty-four hours."

"And Aunt Rachel?"

Hanging his head, he points a finger at the glass. "Across the hall and one cell to the right."

I scramble to the glass, pressing my face against it. It's hard to see everything from this angle, but what I do makes my stomach lurch. Aunt Rachel is alone in a cell. Leather bands are looped around her wrists, keeping her strapped to the hospital bed she lays in. Her head is sunk deep into a pillow and her eyes closed. She's noticeably thinner, her skin almost the color of the walls around us. An IV draws blood from her wrists into a bag hanging just above her head.

I slam a fist against the wall so hard pain flashes like stars across my eyes. "What are they doing to her? Aunt Rachel! Aunt Rachel!"

She doesn't move, but an older man and woman across the hall look at me briefly before turning their attention back to the books in their hands.

"She's being harvested, Charlie," Matteo says.

"We have to help her." I slam my hand against the glass over and over, but it does no good. "We have to get out of here." My breath comes in quick gasps. "We have to do something."

"There's nothing we can do," he says, "except wait."

"Screw that," I shout. "Aunt Rachel! Aunt Rachel!" I continue to scream and slam against the glass until my voice is hoarse and my skin bruised.

And yet the blood continues to flow out of her. So much blood. It has to be the reason she looks so pale and sick. I slide onto the floor, head against the glass. As much as I'd tried to fight them, tears fall down my cheeks.

"It's too much. They're taking too much."

"I know. Make no mistake, Charlie, there's a reason they put us in this cell. They want us to watch her being drained. It's a message."

"Screw their message." I slam my fist against the glass one last time. My hand flashes with light and a jagged crack appears in the glass where I struck it.

With a gasp, I dash away from the glass, pulling my arms to my body.

Matteo's eyes widen. "What was that? What did you do?"

"I-I don't know." I turn my hand over, examining it. "It's this thing that happens sometimes and I don't know what it means." Dropping my hand, I look at him. "Do you?"

With his eyes still wide, he shakes his head. "Whatever you do," he hisses. "Don't let them know."

A Mentis in a dark suit appears in front of the glass. He has a shaved head, and wears a piece in his ear like a secret service agent. He examines the crack and frowns. "This is bullet-proof glass," he says, turning to us. "How did you do this?"

Matteo and I say nothing.

With a grunt, he shakes his head. "You can explain it to the Queen. She requests your presence."

My heart beats wildly. I move away from the door until my back meets the wall. Suddenly, the cell doesn't seem that bad.

He removes a keycard from his jacket and inserts it in a box beside the wall. A door in the glass I hadn't noticed before swings open.

"Charlie," Matteo whispers. "Look at me."

Licking my lips, I turn from the approaching Mentis.

"I didn't say anything before, but I have a plan. My people are coming. Don't panic, okay? I will get you and Rachel out of here. You have my word."

He winks.

"And Sebastian?"

He hesitates before nodding. "Yes. Just remember, whatever Seraphina asks, keep your answers short. The less she knows, the better. Got it?"

I nod, just as the Mentis twists a fist into my shirt and jerks me to my feet. He pushes me ahead of him, making me stumble several steps before I catch myself. He roughly grabs Matteo, making him cry out in pain, before hoisting the King's arm over his shoulder.

"Careful," I say. "He's got a stake in his heart, asshole."

"Oops." The Mentis grins. "Get moving, girl. Best not to keep the Queen waiting."

I raise my middle finger.

"Charlie," Matteo scolds.

The Mentis only laughs. "I can't wait to sample your blood. I bet it's spicy."

If it goes anything like last time, I can't wait for him to sample it either.

I drop my hand and exit the cell. I cross the hallway to

Aunt Rachel's cell. She looks even worse from this close. Pale blue veins stand out against her almost-gray skin. Her cheekbones are sunken, and her chest rises in short, shallow breaths. I'm not a doctor, but even I know she can't take much more of this.

I press a kiss against the cool glass. "We're going to get you out of here," I promise.

"Move." A hand slams against my back, shoving me forward.

I glare at the Mentis. We pass what feels like a never-ending tunnel of glass cells on either side of us. The humans are all ages, sexes, and nationalities. Most sit reading on their beds as we pass. It appears books are the only source of entertainment provided.

They glance at me with interest before quickly averting their gazes as the Mentis behind me comes into view.

A woman, who I guess to be in her sixties, sobs on her bed, her arms hugging her knees to her chest. Her gray hair has pulled from the braid at the nape of her neck, framing her face in wisps. She could easily be someone's grandma, the kind who bakes pies and mends stuffed animals.

"Silence," the Mentis roars as we pass.

She buries her head into her knees, muffling her cries.

I make a decision. If I get the chance, I'm going to kill this Mentis first.

After what feels like miles, we reach a pair of double doors. The vampire uses his keycard. The doors swing outward and we pass through. On either side of us are two large rooms, both the size of basketball courts, and both sealed off by a wall of glass. Like the cells, the rooms are brilliantly white. But that's where the comparison ends.

The room to the right is filled with gym equipment, from elliptical machines and treadmills to weight training machines and free weights. Each machine is occupied by a human. Several Mentis stand in each corner, observing. A young boy, maybe fourteen, steps off the treadmill. Clasping his knees, he pants hard.

A female Mentis is a navy suit strides over to him. "Back on."

He shakes his head. "I'm too tired."

"I said, back on." She removes a stun gun from her jacket and jabs it against the boy's neck. He cries out, falling onto his back.

I turn away, but the other side is even worse. Hundreds of hospital beds are occupied with humans cuffed to the bed in the same way my aunt was. They stare blankly at me as IVs pull the blood from their veins into bags hanging from metal hooks. The Mentis in this room wear white lab coats, scratching notes on clipboards as they pass by each bed.

Placing two fingers on my wrist, I feel for my pulse—just to be sure I haven't died and ended up in hell. The heartbeat I find proves that this is all-too real.

We reach another set of locked doors. After opening them with a keycard, we pass through what must be a cafeteria. Rows upon rows of white tables and chairs are filled with humans eating from white trays. Their menu appears to be a combination of salads and some sort of green smoothie.

A male Mentis stands over a girl, roughly my age, who has her eyes locked on her lap. "If you don't eat," he says, "we'll just feed you intravenously. Would you like that?"

Unmoving, she says nothing.

I don't realize I've stopped walking until I'm jabbed sharply in the back. I shoot a withering look over my shoulder and continue on. Somehow, someway, I'm going to burn this place to the ground, with every Mentis inside. I swear it.

We pass through another set of doors, this time traveling down a long white hallway. Two Mentis wait at the end, positioned on either side the doors. Unlike the white sliding ones we walked through before, molded golden tree branches embedded with glittering rubies decorate either side.

The vampires swing them open, revealing the room inside. A red velvet carpet stretches to a set of stairs leading to a golden throne, glittering with more rubies. At least a hundred Mentis turn as we step inside. But more terrifying than the hundreds of burning silver eyes and bared fangs is the woman lounging on the plush, velvet cushions of the glittering throne. Wearing a gold and ruby crown, along with a long, satin red dress, she is obviously the Queen.

And she only has eyes for me.

Chapter
Twenty-One

I'm going to die. The words play through my brain in an endless loop.

The only escape is the open, horizontal windows overhead. The problem is, they're at least twenty feet high.

The Queen eyes me the same way a cat watches a mouse struggle beneath its paw. Her crown balances atop her pinned, blond curls. Her blood-red painted nails are the same color as her lips.

Her eyes dart behind me, and her lips curve into a crooked smile. "Brother," she draws the word out, as if savoring it. "How long has it been?"

"Not nearly long enough," Matteo answers.

She laughs, a rich, bell-like sound that rings against the walls. She wags a finger at him, clicking her tongue. "I hear you've been most naughty, Matteo. The shadows talk, and they speak of your intent to go public with our existence to the humans. Such an action would disrupt my lifestyle, and I really can't have that."

"A lifestyle of torture and murder, you mean," Matteo spits.

She makes a face. "So dramatic. I believe you just toured our farm. As you can see, our humans are treated very well. They are exercised, fed, and kept clean."

"You're treating them like animals."

"They *are* animals," the Queen replies.

The Mentis surrounding us laugh.

She stands, the red silk of her dress rippling down her body like water. "Your ridiculous notion that we can coexist with humans would be our end. They are fearful and weak creatures, but they outnumber us by billions. If they found out about us, we would be hunted like we were all those years ago. I can't have that."

"They are not weak," Matteo replies. "You underestimate them."

She snorts. "You're a fool, as is our sister, Cordelia, and her disgusting Corpus. Their recklessness draws too much attention as well." She saunters down the stairs. "It seems I am the only one to care about the preservation and existence of the vampire. Pity, because we would have been so much stronger united."

At the bottom of the staircase, she holds out her hand. A nearby Mentis places a stake in it. She taps the wooden stake against her hand as she walks toward us. "You understand why I have to do this, brother. Once you and Cordelia are out of the picture, I will unite the vampire, ensuring our species' survival."

My muscles coil tighter with each step she takes.

The Queen stops in front of Matteo. She traces a line down his face with her fingernail. "Such a tragedy." She sighs. "Together, we would have been unstoppable—just like before."

Breathing fast, I search the room for a weapon, an escape, *anything* that might help me save Matteo. But there's nothing.

"You might kill me," Matteo says. "But you'll never kill my cause. The Anima are stronger than you think."

The Queen laughs, and the room joins her.

"Say hello to our mother for me." She raises the stake.

"You must release Rachel," Matteo says, eyes boring into Seraphina's. "You gave your word."

She rolls her eyes. "*Fine.* Someone put Matteo's pet outside by the dumpster. Maybe she'll find her way home before animal control picks her up."

The knots of anxiety twisted around my chest loosen a fraction. I *need* Aunt Rachel to get out of here. Now she might actually have a chance to survive. If only I knew of some way to save Matteo.

"Now," Seraphina raises the stake, "where were we?"

Matteo, still clutched in the arms of the Mentis, turns to me. "This isn't over."

I swallow hard. "What do you mean?"

A crow caws loudly from the open window. Looking over her shoulder, Seraphina misses the moment Matteo's skin begins to darken and shift. When she turns, it's already too late.

"No!" Dropping the stake, the Queen reaches for the necklace. She manages to tear it from Matteo's neck, only to have the golden snake hiss and strike her palm. With a yelp, she drops it on the ground at the same moment Matteo, now in crow form, flies for the open window.

"You won't get far!" she screams after him. "And you won't survive without your precious necklace." She points to the guards in the back of the room. "Go after him and return him to me by any means necessary."

Several—both male and female—run from the room.

I stare at the open window, wanting to breathe a sigh of relief, but I also know better than to attract attention to myself. *He made it. Thank God.*

My relief, small as it is, is short-lived when I look around and realize I'm surrounded by at least a hundred Mentis, all pissed, and all focused on me.

Awesome.

"So." The Queen grabs me by the chin, her nails digging into my skin hard enough to make me wince. "You're his new pet, I suppose."

I suppress a whimper. "I'm nobody's pet."

She laughs. "Care to guess how many humans have told me that before I broke them? All it takes, darling, is a little training, and I am a *skilled* animal handler." She releases my jaw and smacks me on the cheek. "It's a gift, really."

I open my jaw and work it side-to-side in an attempt to relieve the pain.

"Leave her alone."

The air squeezes from my lungs as I whirl around at the sound of Sebastian's voice. There's something wrong with it—different—almost broken. Still, as much as I search the crowd, I can't spot him.

The Queen arches an eyebrow. "Little pet, do you have two keepers?" She walks a slow circle around me, the train of her silk dress slithering behind her like a snake. "What makes you so special that you would catch the attention of a king and my favorite bodyguard? You're pretty enough." She frowns. "But not *spectacular*. So what is it?" Placing a fist beneath her chin, she tilts her head. "Maybe you just taste really good." She grabs my neck. "Let's have a sample, yes?"

"Don't touch her," Sebastian screams. There's movement in the crowd, followed by a grunt and the sound of bone against flesh. Several snarls turn into yelps and the crowd parts as a male Mentis falls forward, blood pooling from beneath him.

The Queen's eyes flash brighter. "How interesting."

Sebastian walks through the gap in the crowd and stands over the fallen Mentis. The sight of him makes me gasp. Silver chains crisscross around his body from his legs to his neck. Each link has eaten into his blistered skin, exposing the muscle and tendon beneath.

"What have you done?" I don't realize I've spoken the words until the Queen turns to me.

"My bad little boy wandered too far from home, so he had to be put in timeout."

"You're a monster."

She laughs. "My dear, my siblings and I killed the monsters. *You're welcome.*" She turns to Sebastian and snaps her fingers. "Come here."

He stands with a tight jaw, clenching and unclenching his fists, before finally moving forward.

He stops beside me. His skin is noticeably paler. The stench of blood and worse from his wounds makes my stomach twist. It takes all of my strength to keep from reaching out to him.

With viper-like speed, Seraphina grabs my arm and

spins me around, pinning my back to her chest. She digs the edge of the stake into my neck. A whimper escapes through my clenched teeth.

"Your disobedience needs to be punished," she says.

Sebastian goes still.

"Perhaps if I kill the girl, you will learn your lesson and never stray again."

An excited murmur goes through the crowd.

"That would be incredibly stupid," Sebastian says.

The Queen snarls, digging the wooden point deeper. White flashes of pain explode in my vision. A warm trickle of blood winds down my neck. The eyes of several Mentis go black as the smell triggers their bloodlust. "How dare you insult me."

"Not an insult." Sebastian's voice takes on a soothing edge. "A warning."

She eases the stake off my neck a fraction. "Explain yourself."

"The magical items you took from the Faerie Queen only work for the owner—this is why the necklace bit you when you tried to grab it."

The Queen glares down at the unmoving necklace on the floor. "As long as the owner is alive, yes. This is why I'm going to kill Matteo."

"That might take time, especially since he knows you're after him. My guess is that Matteo and the Anima clan are going to go into hiding. Rather than spend all that time and energy searching for him, wouldn't you rather wield the power of the necklace now?"

"Of course I would," she spits. "But that's impossible."

"Maybe not." Sebastian take another step closer. "The

necklace works for the one who possesses it, as well as their heirs. Charlie might be Matteo's daughter."

Barking out a laugh, the Queen lowers the stake from my neck. I gasp in relief. "I have a niece," she exclaims. "What a happy day, indeed."

Free from her grip, I bump into Sebastian. He takes my hand in his, pulling me behind him. My pulse beats so frantically in the back of my throat I can practically taste it.

"Now I understand Matteo's fascination with you," the Queen says. "How lucky to have found you before he could corrupt you further. Tell me, do you enjoy blood?"

"N-n-no." I shake my head.

She shrugs. "We'll change that." Her silver eyes flash brighter. "We'll change all of *that.*" She waves a hand at me. "But before we do, I need you to prove your worth." She pauses, licking her lips. "Pick up the necklace."

I glance at the golden snake on the ground, and my stomach sinks into my knees. Finding out who my father is, surrounded by hungry vampires in the Mentis court. This wasn't supposed to happen this way.

"Don't make me lose my patience, child." The Queen's words are heavy with an unspoken threat.

I ball my hands into fists, muscles tight as I walk toward the necklace. Kneeling, I hesitate before picking it up, certain it will come to life and sink its fangs into me the same way it did to the Queen. Sucking in a breath, I pick the necklace off the ground. I expect it to be cold, but instead, it's warm, and feels as if it's pulsing with a heartbeat.

"Hurry up," the Queen says, "put it on."

Unlike with Matteo, the snake never comes to life in

my hands. I carefully unclip the clasp that keeps the tail looped around the head and place it on my neck.

Holding my breath, I brace for—I'm not exactly sure what—*something?* But nothing happens.

Even though it confirms what I'd said all along, disappointment still squeezes my gut. I almost hoped I'd been wrong. I look to Sebastian for guidance on what to do next, but his brow is creased with worry.

"She is nothing," the Queen screeches. "Just another worthless human." She whirls on Sebastian. "You're going to pay for lying to me." She raises the stake.

"Don't touch him." As I scream, a light flashes, white hot, in front of my eyes. I'm not sure exactly where it's coming from until I see the horrified expressions of the Mentis around me as they dart away. I look down and gasp. The golden snake at my neck is ablaze with flames that somehow don't burn my skin.

The stake falls from the Queen's hands, clattering against the marble floor. "Impossible," she whispers, eyes wide. "What magic is this?"

With trembling fingers, I take the necklace off and drop it on the floor. The flames immediately burn out.

"What *are* you?" The Queen asks, stalking toward me.

"I-I-I'm nothing." Trembling violently, I hug my arms across my chest to keep from falling over.

"We'll see about that," she snarls. "Jameson." When she snaps her fingers, a tall vampire moves forward. His suit jacket appears to strain with the effort of keeping his muscles from bursting out. "Enjoy your dinner."

Crap. I scramble away, only to trip on my own feet and sprawl to the ground.

"No." Sebastian starts for me. The Queen snatches him by the neck and flings him backward. He lands against the wall with a grunt.

The large Mentis squeezes my arms to the point of bruising as he hoists me in the air. An inky blackness bleeds into his eyes, leaving them devoid of color. Curling a beefy arm around my neck, he pulls me toward him. I manage to kick him several times in the shins, but he doesn't even flinch.

He opens his mouth wide, teeth gleaming, and all I can picture are the hunters we left behind, bleeding onto the gymnasium from their torn-out throats. A whimper escapes my throat.

Snarling, Sebastian jumps to his feet and lunges for me. Again, he's struck by the Queen. He slides against the floor, his head cracking against the marble.

"No!" My heartbeat thrashes in my ears. No one can save me now.

The vampire sinks his fangs into my neck. Burning pain eats into my veins like acid, traveling the length of my body. I scream.

Another bright flash, this one a kaleidoscope of orange and red. My screaming grows louder, only I realize, a little late, that it's not my screaming. I'm dropped to the floor, knees colliding with marble, as the Mentis before me writhes inside the wall of fire consuming his body.

His dance of agony is hypnotizing. As much as my muscles are tight with the desire to flee, I find I'm unable to move from where I kneel on the floor. I can only watch him twist and scream, skin burning to muscle, and muscle burning to bone. His withering black form falls, first to his knees, and then on his face. The flames extinguish as black ash sweeps across the floor.

I'm barely breathing, gasping for breath when the Queen turns her horrified eyes on me. "You are no human, and you are no vampire." She points a trembling finger at me. "You are something much, much darker. Guards!" She whirls around. "Return her to the farm. Keep her quarantined from the other humans until we can figure out what to do with her." Her eyes narrow. "And we *will* figure that out."

Two Mentis—a male and female—step forward.

"No." I scuttle backward on my hands and knees. Tremors shake my hands. "Please. I can't go back there."

The Queen turns from me, focusing her attention on Sebastian.

I scream as I'm jerked to my feet. I thrash, kicking and punching, trying to free myself with no luck. "Sebastian!"

He shakes his head, a warning to be quiet. But I'm too far beyond the point of caring. "Sebastian." I reach for him, hand grasping through the air.

The two Mentis drag me down the red velvet carpet to the golden doors at the opposite end of the room. Before they pull them open, I see the Queen retrieve her fallen stake from the ground.

"Now," she says, her voice echoing against the walls, "what shall I do to punish a traitor?" Just as she moves toward him, the doors open and the Mentis carry me through, hiding Sebastian from view.

His screams follow me into the hall.

Chapter
Twenty-Two

This must be what it's like to go crazy. I'm on the cold marble ground in my cell. I trace circles on the stone—over and over—concentrating on the path of my finger in an attempt to keep the terror at bay.

I'm not sure how long I've been here. The lights never dim, so time passes in a loop, with no end and no beginning. If I were to guess, maybe a week has passed since I set fire to the Mentis in the Queen's throne room. I thought maybe they'd kill me. What I hadn't expected is they'd leave me alone to waste away.

Unlike my first time in the farm, the cells around me are empty. Sometimes I hear sobbing and other times screaming, but I'm never able to put a face to the voices. Other times I wonder if the voices I'm hearing are actually my own.

Food only comes when I'm asleep, and even then, it's inconsistent. Days pass between meals. Even if I can't measure the passing hours, I can weigh the intensity of the hunger pains that gnaw at my stomach.

If their plan is to keep me weak, they're succeeding. With no bed, and only a toilet in the corner of the room, my sanity has become a slippery thing, squeezing through my grasp no matter how tightly I try to hold on.

I crawl to the glass wall and breathe against it. I only have seconds to draw designs into the steam before it fades. If I don't keep busy, my thoughts inevitably go to Aunt Rachel, Matteo, and Sebastian, and whether any of them are still alive.

At least Matteo and Aunt Rachel made it out of here. If only I could have talked to her one last time. If only she could have given me some hint of who—*and what*—I am. I guess it doesn't matter as, at this rate, I'll be dead soon enough.

A tap on the glass startles me, and I look up. Outside the glass door stands a Mentis wearing a white lab coat. His gray hair sticks out from beneath his surgical cap. A face mask hangs loose around his neck. He wears latex gloves. The possibilities for what he might be prepped for twists my stomach into anxious cramps.

Beside him stands one female and one male Mentis in blue scrubs.

I scrabble away from the door until my back meets the wall. The female Mentis inserts a keycard, and the glass door slides open. She stands aside, allowing the Mentis in the lab coat to enter first.

"Are-are you a doctor?" I ask.

"I was, once. Now it is my duty to see that all humans on the farm remain in good health. And when they don't, it is up to me to put them down. Humanely, of course."

He studies me for several heartbeats, his face betraying no emotion.

Terror strangles me with icy fingers. "Is that what you're going to do with me?"

He tilts his head. "Possibly. We need to know what you are before we decide what to do with you."

I press myself against the far wall, as if by sheer force I might will myself to the other side. "How are you going to figure that out?"

He grins, revealing fangs still fresh with blood. "By opening you up, of course. Come along. It's time to prep you for surgery."

"No."

The two Mentis in scrubs enter the room and move toward me.

"No," I scream again, my breath coming in short, ragged gasps.

They each grab a shoulder and pull me up, letting my toes drag across the floor. I kick and scratch at them, but it doesn't take long before I've exhausted myself and can only hang limply in their grasp.

This can't be happening, I think as they carry me down the empty hallway. The doctor hums as he leads the way. We take several turns before we enter another room where a hospital gurney waits. This one, just like Aunt Rachel's, is equipped with leather cuffs, which they quickly fit over my wrists and ankles.

I scream, over and over. I scream until my throat is raw and my ears ring. "You can't do this," I plead. "You have to let me go."

They ignore my cries, busying themselves about the

room, collecting syringes and medical equipment.

"I want to go home," I say. And I do. Back to the cabin in the middle of nowhere. Back to my secluded, quiet life with my aunt and my dog. Back to a world where monsters are creatures only found in books. Back to a world where I'm still human.

The female Mentis rolls a tray with a needle and tubing to my bedside.

I pull at my binds. The leather bands rub against my skin until it's raw.

"This will hurt so much worse if you don't hold still."

In the corner, the doctor picks up a device that looks terrifyingly like a table saw.

Nope. Not going to stay still. Not today.

Something stabs into my arm, and I look up in time to see the nurse withdrawing a syringe. Instantly, I feel warm, the edges of my vision growing fuzzy.

Shit.

"There now," the nurse says, capping the syringe. "That should calm you down."

I slump against the bed. My muscles feel too heavy to move, but my heart continues to pound a frantic rhythm against my chest.

I can't quit. To stop fighting is to die.

Testing the saw, the doctor turns it on and off several times. The sound grinds against my bones. "Get the IV going," he says. "The sooner she's asleep, the sooner we can begin."

Nodding, the nurse grabs the needle from the tray. I barely feel the needle she slides into my wrist and tapes in place. The male nurse hands her another syringe.

Grinning, the nurse places the syringe in the tubing at my wrist. "Night night." She plunges the contents of the syringe into the needle.

No. Oh God, no. If I close my eyes, I have a horrible feeling I'll never ever open them again.

A wispy, floating feeling pulls at me, threatening to carry me away. I can't let it.

I'm not sure how to fight a battle inside my own body, I only know I can't lose. Clenching my fists, I grit my teeth as the waters that threaten to carry me away continue to rise. I feel for the uneven pressure of it—ever expanding— and push back.

Nothing happens. I'm overcome as wave after wave of exhaustion crashes over me, drowning me. I can't fight it. And maybe I shouldn't. Maybe I shouldn't even try. There's so much pain here, so much fear. Sleep is better. I can just close my eyes and drift into the darkness. At least then, it will all be over.

"Grab the scalpel," the doctor says from somewhere outside the darkness.

I lost, I think. And the fear I expect to follow is actually relief.

I'm prepared to fully let go of my grip on consciousness when I hear a gasp. I crack my eyes open. It takes several blinks before the scene in front of me falls into focus, and even then, it doesn't make sense.

The doctor and the two nurses stare at me with shared horrified expressions. I follow their line of sight to my wrist, where the vein in my arm glows as if on fire.

Suddenly, I'm wide awake.

"Impossible," the doctor says, as the syringe taped to my

wrist begins to melt. Both leather cuffs char black before crumbling to ash.

I peel off the tape and the melted mess that was the syringe and sit up. "People keep saying that to me, and yet, here I am." I lean forward and unbuckle the cuffs still attached to my ankles.

A hazy fog clouds my head. This might actually be a good thing, as I can't overthink what just happened. I swing my legs over the bed. "I'm going home now."

"No." The doctor, his eyes impossibly wide, shakes his head. "You're not going anywhere."

I rub my wrist, still sore from the needle. "No offense, but this place sucks."

The doctor turns to the male nurse. "Don't stand there. Grab her."

The nurse hesitates, a look of uncertainty on his face.

"Unless you want the Queen to know you are directly responsible for the girl's escape," the doctor adds.

Frowning, the nurse rushes toward me with outstretched hands.

A flash of panic courses through me. My back meets the wall. I didn't really think this through. Me against three Mentis isn't exactly fair odds. If only I had a weapon.

As the thought crosses my mind, my right hand grows warm and what look like flames encompass my fist. The vampire grabs me by the throat, fingers digging into my neck and cutting off my breath.

Sputtering, I raise my wrist just as a fiery blade grows from the flames, piercing the gut of the Mentis strangling me.

His eyes widen, and he releases me.

Coughing, I fall against the wall.

"What did you do?" the Mentis screams at me, throwing his arms wide. A fiery hole in his stomach burns outward, consuming his entire body. He screams as flames erupt. Seconds later, he's reduced to ash.

The other two Mentis look at the pile of ash on the floor, then back at me, before taking a collective step backward.

The blade of fire still burns in my outstretched fist.

The doctor pulls a keycard out of his pocket with shaking fingers. "We need reinforcements."

Licking my lips, I move toward them. I can't let them do that, which means I only have one chance.

With a yell, I charge.

"Stop her." The doctor shoves a nurse in front of me. With my pulse thundering inside my head, I slam the blade into her shoulder. It slides through her like butter, making my stomach lurch. But I can't allow myself to think about it. *Survive first, Charlie. Throw up later.*

Like the first Mentis, she gasps, falling to her knees before igniting in flames.

Holding out my free hand, I turn to the doctor. "Keycard."

With fumbling fingers, he places it in my hand. For a second, I consider leaving him locked in the room. But then I think of my aunt—pale, thin, and strapped to a bed as they drained the life from her body.

"This is for Aunt Rachel." I slam the blade into his chest. He grunts, falls to the ground, and erupts into flames. I watch the burning pile until there's nothing left but smoking ash.

The flaming blade retracts into my hand and disappears. I examine my hand for blisters or burns, but find none.

Balling my fist, I concentrate on willing the blade to come back. It doesn't.

I sigh and drop my hand. A vampire-killing blade of fire would be a lot more awesome if it wasn't completely random. "Kind of wish I didn't have to almost die to have superpowers," I mumble.

I jam the keycard into the door. It slides open and I dart outside. The empty hallway stretches to the left and the right. Having been dragged from my cell, I can't remember which way I came in from. I decide on the right. I take several steps, only to hear a groan in the other direction.

Might as well save as many people as I can. I trot past several empty cells until I find the one that's occupied. My blood turns to ice, and I gasp. Sebastian—or at least what remains of Sebastian—is strapped to the wall with so many chains covering his body only his blistered face is revealed. At least a half-dozen wooden stakes protrude through the chains from his arms and legs. His eyes are closed, his face pale and hollow.

If he's not already dead, he's close to it.

"Please be okay, Sebastian. *Please.*" With trembling fingers, I insert the keycard and open his door. He doesn't move when I enter. I pull the wooden stakes out first, dropping them to the ground, except for the last one, which I tuck into the band of my jeans. The chains are held together by hooks, which I unwrap and drop to the floor. Some of the silver has eaten so much into his skin that I have to yank it free from the muscle. Fresh blood wells from the wounds.

Sebastian groans, his eyes blinking.

"Hang on. I'll have you free in a second." I work frantically to unwind the metal links, some so deep his bones are exposed. A nauseous wave rolls through me as my gut clenches. The smell of blood and rot inside the room is overpowering. When I remove the last chain, Sebastian falls to the floor.

I drop beside him, stomach heaving as I throw up what little food I've eaten.

A hand touches my back, reaching for my hair and sweeping it away from my shoulders. I look over to see Sebastian staring at me, his skin already weaving together before my eyes. His clothes hang off of him in shredded ribbons. "Charlie, you're alive." He pulls me against him, holding my head to his chest. "I thought they'd taken you from me. I tried to escape." His voice quivers. "But I never anticipated this level of torture."

"I'm fine," I reply, voice strained. "I'm just glad you're not dead."

He pulls back, taking my face in his hands. "They will never hurt you again. Understand?"

Currently trapped in a vampire prison, the odds of a pain-free escape are not good. But the look in his eyes is so ferocious, I don't dare argue.

He runs his hands down my arms, his eyes running down the length of my body. "Are you okay? How did you escape?"

"Uh." I lick my lips. "I made a sword out of fire."

He frowns. "A what?"

I shrug. "I can't explain it any better than that. I don't understand it myself."

He stares at me a little longer. "I'm going to want that

entire story in detail," he says. "But it can wait until after we've escaped."

"*If* we escape. This place is crawling with Mentis—too many for us to fight."

Standing, he takes several unsteady steps across the room to a small fridge in the corner. "You let me worry about that," he says. "No one is taking you away from me again, understand?" Without waiting for a response, he opens the fridge and removes a bag of blood. He bites into it, tipping it back and draining it in matter of seconds.

A flush returns to his skin and the dark circles beneath his eyes disappear. He tosses the empty bag on the floor and grabs another, draining it as well. "They starved me." He tosses the second bag aside.

"They starved me, too."

His black eyes narrow, and he bares his teeth. "When I get you out of here, I promise to get you the greasiest, most disgusting human food we can find."

"Careful. Those words can make a girl fall in love." As soon as the words leave my mouth, I flinch. A sort of nervous energy crackles through the air between us. The black fades from his eyes, leaving them glowing silver. He looks like he might say something before apparently deciding against it.

Leave it to me to take a life-or-death situation and make it awkward.

A shout draws our attention. Outside the cell, a Mentis guard jams a keycard into the door, sliding it open.

"Get behind me," Sebastian growls.

I look down at my hand. Since a fiery sword has yet to materialize, I decide to do what I'm told.

Sebastian grabs the chain off the floor. It sizzles and smokes in his hand. He charges the incoming Mentis, wrapping the chain around his neck. Grimacing, Sebastian pulls tight. The chain eats through the Mentis's neck until the vampire's head falls to the floor.

I yelp, darting away as it rolls by my feet.

With his chest heaving, Sebastian drops the chain. "I told you I would kill every last one of them. Now," he holds a hand out to me, "let's get the hell out of here."

Swallowing hard, I take his hand. He pulls me through the open door. Together, we race down the hall past empty cell after empty cell.

With my hand in his, and the swiped keycard in the other, he winds around corners and through doors.

"I hope you know where you're going," I pant.

"I lived here, remember? If we're going to escape, we need to use one of the lesser-used exits through the kitchen."

He might have lived here, but I've learned a few things about this place myself. Mainly that it's filled with more Mentis than we could ever hope to fight off. If we're discovered, that's the end. "If something happens—"

"Not going to happen," Sebastian cuts me off.

"I'm serious. You have to promise me you'll make sure my aunt's okay."

"You can check on her yourself," he says, pulling me around another corner. "As soon as we get out of here." He slides to a stop and peers around the corner. He holds up a hand, motioning me to be silent. When he looks at me, he mouths the word, "Guards."

My heart plummets. This is it—the moment it all ends.

Sebastian reaches for me. At first I think it's so he can hold me in the last moments we have together. Instead, he plucks the stake from my waistband and charges around the corner.

"Sebastian," I yell, chasing him.

Three Mentis stare wide-eyed as we charge them. Sebastian reaches them first, plunging the stake into the heart of one, while grabbing another with his other hand. Withdrawing the stake from the fallen vampire, he twists the neck of the second. The crack of bone makes me flinch. Dropping the second, he stakes him in the chest.

The third Mentis snarls. "Betrayer! This is treason."

"This is a revolution," Sebastian answers. He swings the stake, but the third vampire blocks his arm and slashes a fist into Sebastian's face.

Grunting, Sebastian drops the stake.

I run after it, scooping it from the floor just as the Mentis's foot lands in my gut. I gasp, falling onto the ground, but somehow manage to keep hold of the weapon.

"You'll never escape," the Mentis says. "One weak Mentis and one human girl against an entire army?" He grabs a fistful of Sebastian's hair and brings his head down on his knee.

Sebastian collapses.

Snarling, the Mentis turns on me.

"You're wrong." I press the flat end of the stake against my chest with both hands. "I'm not human."

Sebastian is on his feet, standing behind the Mentis, who opens his mouth to reply. Sebastian shoves him before he gets a chance. The vampire's chest pierces the stake I hold. He snaps his teeth at my neck, close enough to make me gasp, before his eyes roll toward the back of his head. He falls to the ground.

Sebastian removes the stake, flinging the blood onto the floor. I try not to cringe. "The kitchen is there." He inclines his head toward a set of swinging doors. "We make it to the door in the back, and we're out."

"And then what?"

"I compel someone to give us their car, and we get the hell out of here."

It's not much of a plan, but it's better than what I have, so I nod.

I follow him to the double doors, and he pauses before opening them. "There will probably be at least five Mentis in here. Stay behind me, and I'll take care of them."

"I don't like those odds."

"I've had worse."

Frowning, I stare at my hand. If only I could make the fire-thing happen at will, then I wouldn't feel so helpless. Making a fist, I envision the flaming blade I conjured before. Nothing happens.

With a sigh, I drop my hand. Sebastian frowns at me.

"What were you just doing?" he asks.

"Apparently nothing."

He stares at me a bit longer, as if he might ask another question, before shaking his head. "Let's go." He stretches an arm behind him, touching my arm, and pushes the door open with the other.

The sharp tang of onions burns my nose. I hate onions, but that doesn't stop my stomach from grumbling. As hungry as I am, I'd probably eat one like an apple if I had the chance. The lights are on, revealing polished chrome shelves stacked with lunch trays. An industrial sink and dishwasher line one wall, three stoves line another.

"I thought you said there'd be vampires," I whisper.

"There normally are," he answers. "I don't have a good feeling about this."

Awesome.

I follow as closely as I can as we creep across the empty kitchen to a steel door in the back. Beside it, a keypad blinks on the wall.

Sebastian stops. "This door is always guarded. It's where food deliveries are accepted. It leads directly outside."

"Let's question it later, and escape now." I move past him to the door. I push on the handle. Without even using the keycard, the door swings outward.

"Charlie—" Sebastian warns.

A warm summer breeze grazes at my arms, beckoning me into the night. The invitation is too tempting to resist. After living in the compound with its artificial light and artificial air, I almost cry with relief when the wind pulls strands of my hair across my face. I never thought I'd feel the wind again, or see the way the moonlight turns my skin a ghostly pale. I turn to face Sebastian standing in the open doorway. "We did it."

Frowning, he walks into the alley, closing the door behind him. "It was too easy."

"We had to kill a half-dozen vampires. That wasn't easy."

"Half dozen?" He arches an eyebrow.

I wave the question away. "I'll tell you about the others later. Let's get that car." I start forward, but Sebastian snatches me by the arm, stopping me in my tracks. His eyes bleed black, and his lips curl in a snarl.

Before I can ask him what's wrong, from out of the corner of my eye, a flash of red draws my attention.

The Queen stands in the alleyway, flanked on either side by Frederick and another Mentis guard. The Queen wears a red pantsuit tailored to her curves. Her crown sits on top of her head, the rubies glowing red. Matteo's necklace is clasped at her neck, the stones dark.

"My dear guests." She pouts her strawberry-red lips. "Are you leaving so soon?"

Chapter
Twenty-Three

I reach blindly behind me. Sebastian finds my hand, pulling me to him. My chest aches from the force of my heart slamming against my ribs. "It was a trap."

"My darlings." She reaches a hand up to stroke the necklace. The snake hisses, but does not bite. Even it appears to know we've lost the battle. "After all the hospitality I've shown you, how could you think to leave without saying a proper goodbye?" She curls her lip, her eyes darkening to black pools. "Don't you know that's *rude.*"

"You don't have to do this, Seraphina," Sebastian says.

She snarls. "I am still your queen and you will address me as such."

"Are you?" he asks, pushing me behind him as he steps forward. "Or did you steal me from my Queen after you murdered her?"

Seraphina blinks, startled. "What *exactly* do you remember?" The two Mentis beside her shift uneasily.

"Enough."

She laughs. "Obviously not. If you remembered any of your time with the Faerie, you would know what torturous monsters there are."

"Unlike you," he says.

Clenching her fists, she says, "I'm a fucking Disney Princess compared to them, you ungrateful wretch."

"That's not what I remember."

"Really?" Her face relaxes as the muscles along her shoulders unwind. "Then tell me, *Sebastian,* if everything was so wonderful, why would the Fae wipe your memories just as we rescued you—unless they were hiding something."

Sebastian narrows his eyes, a frown pulling at his lips. "I don't know. There has to be a reason."

"Of course there's a reason," she snaps. "They didn't want you to remember the abuse, so you would return to them like the pathetic puppy you are. Only, now that we've killed them, there are none left to return to."

He shakes his head. "Just like you're going to kill the Anima and Corpus clans."

She laughs. "Obviously. Their elimination is the only way to ensure our existence. The Corpus and Anima would destroy us if they continue on their separate paths."

"No. You will *all* destroy us with this damned war."

She fans her mouth as she yawns. "I never realized how *boring* you are, little stray puppy. I was wrong to take you in. I thought you might make a guard dog, but turns out you're nothing more than a lap dog." She waves a hand. "Seize the girl."

The two Mentis start toward me.

"No." Sebastian lunges.

Seraphina is faster. She grabs him by the arm and wrenches it behind him, driving him to his knees. He hisses in pain. "Run," he screams.

I hesitate, rooted to the ground by the fear of never seeing him again.

"Goddamn it, Charlie. *Go.*"

It's the desperation in his eyes that springs me into action. Spinning on my heels, I only make it a couple of steps before the first Mentis clamps a hand around my shoulder. He spins me around as the second one joins him, grabbing my other arm, pinning me between them.

"Naughty, naughty puppy," the Queen says, pulling Sebastian's arm higher. He winces. "Maybe I'll rip your arm off and feed it to the rats? Or perhaps I'll stake you to the street and have you wait for the sun to melt your body onto the asphalt."

Tremors shake his body. "Do what you will, you bitch."

"*Or...*" She looks at me with a smile full of poison. "Maybe I'll just let you watch as I kill the girl."

"No!" He bucks his back, trying to fight her off. In return, she lifts her leg, stabbing the point of her high heel into his back, driving him to the ground. "These heels are made of wood, darling. I think you know what that means."

"Hurt Charlie and I'll kill you," he spits through clenched teeth. "I'll kill you all."

"Look at that." She cocks her head. "Puppy has some teeth after all. This should be fun. Boys, get on with it. Make sure she doesn't bleed."

Terror crushes my ribs, making it impossible to breathe. The Mentis to my right takes both of my wrists and pins them behind me, while the one on my left withdraws a clear plastic bag from his jacket pocket.

I don't know what they have in mind, but I know it's not good. My body trembles, knees knocking together. If it wasn't for the Mentis holding on to me, I'd be on the ground.

"Do it," the Queen orders.

I barely have time to scream before they place the bag over my head and pull tight. Reflexively I gasp, but I only manage to draw the plastic into my mouth. From over the sound of my pulse thrashing in my ears, I hear Sebastian shout. My lungs tighten as I struggle for air that never comes. Kicking and twisting, I fight to pull free, but the Mentis don't budge.

Black dots seep around the edges of my vision, warning of the unconsciousness to follow. I can't believe we escaped the Mentis compound only to die in the alley just outside the door.

My lungs feel as if they're filling with fire. I want to rip my fingers into my chest to force air in. I gasp, succeeding in only swallowing more plastic. The burning feeling travels from my lungs, over my shoulders, down my arms, until my fingers tingle.

I'm being consumed alive by fire.

Fire.

The darkness recedes from my vision. I know exactly what to do with fire.

With the Mentis's hands still on my wrists, I thrust myself into him, fists connecting with his gut. I don't have to look to know my blade is there, I can feel it in my grasp, flames pulsing against my skin.

The vampire screams, and I'm free.

The Mentis holding the bag over my head steps away, his lips parted in horror. Ripping the bag from my head with one hand, I slam the fiery dagger into his chest with the other. He makes a series of gurgling sounds before falling to the ground in a wash of flames. Seconds later he's nothing but ash.

My heart is a wild thing, throwing itself against my chest as I gasp for air. When I finally meet the Queen's gaze, her face is a mixture of horror and fascination.

"What *are* you?"

"I'm Charlie," I answer, taking a step toward her. "Now let Sebastian go."

She laughs, digging her heel farther into Sebastian's chest, making him grimace.

Invisible fingers curl into my chest. I freeze.

A ribbon of blood unfolds from the puncture. "My darling, I still have the upper hand. Here's how this is going to play out. Whatever you are, you are far too valuable to let walk away. You're going to come with me, Charlie, and be my weapon in the war against my siblings. Do as you're told, and I'll let him go."

"Charlie, no," Sebastian shouts. "Run."

With her lip curled into a sneer, she grinds her heel farther. Sebastian gasps, fingers curling into the asphalt.

"Stop!" I hold out my hand. It's as if she's driving the heel of her shoe into my own heart.

She hesitates, a grin unfolding on her lips. "Then we have a deal."

"Don't do it," Sebastian says, through clenched teeth. "You have to get out of here."

I swallow hard, my gaze flicking between his tortured

grimace and the Queen's smile. "You have to promise to let Sebastian go," I say.

"Of course, darling. You have my word as a queen."

I know the torture that waits for me inside her compound. But I also know she'll kill Sebastian if I run, and how could I live with myself after that? I escaped from her once, maybe I can do it again. Bowing my head, my shoulders fall. "I'll go with you."

"Excellent." She lowers her foot from the center of Sebastian's chest to his stomach, and slams it down. He cries out as blood spills from his stomach onto the concrete.

I scream.

The Queen rolls her eyes. "Don't be so dramatic. He'll live. But he won't be able to follow us." She pulls her heel out of his gut. She kicks her foot several times, shaking the excess blood from her shoe. The open wound gurgles blood like a spring. Sebastian closes his eyes and doesn't move.

"It's time to go." The Queen marches toward me, hooking an arm around mine and yanking me toward the door.

"But—" I reach a hand toward Sebastian, wanting to talk to him, touch him one more time. It might be my last.

"I said"—she jerks me hard—"time to go."

I nearly stumble to the ground, if not for her grip on my arm. I inhale deeply, trying to suck as much of the night air into my lungs that I can—who knows if I'll ever get to do it again.

The Queen places a hand on the door as the first cry of a crow pierces the silence. She drops her hand, lips pinched with amusement. "They wouldn't dare." She turns, pulling me with her. A crow lands on the building across the alley from us. Then another, then another. The flap of wings and cawing builds to a crescendo as what appears to be at least a hundred crows look down on us from the building overhead.

One crow stands out above the rest. With glowing green eyes and a patch of red feathers on the center of its chest, I know immediately it's Matteo.

The red-patched crow cries out, and the rest fall silent, watching us with their glittering eyes.

"You and your little birds can't scare me, Matteo," the Queen shouts. "You've lost this battle, and you're about to lose the war."

Matteo swoops from his perch, the others following at his wings.

With a gasp, Seraphina releases me, throwing me off balance. With a yelp, I reach out blindly, snagging her necklace and tearing it from her neck. It immediately begins to smoke in my hands.

The birds are a black tornado of wings and beaks, swirling around the Queen, pecking, biting, and scratching. Clutching her face, she screams. The crows fly faster, nearly obstructing her from view. Drops of blood pool on the ground by her feet.

"Charlie."

I tear my eyes away from the birds to find Sebastian standing, hunched over, with one hand pressed against the wound in his stomach. "We have to go. *Now.*"

Nodding, I run to him, tripping over a loose piece of gravel along the way. The necklace falls from my hands and lands at his feet.

He stoops to pick it up. The second his hands touch the

golden snake, its emerald eyes blaze green. With a sharp intake of breath, Sebastian drops the necklace onto the ground. The snake's eyes dim.

My blood turns to ice. "What the hell was that?" I ask, stopping beside him. "Does that mean—"

He shakes his head, stopping me. "We have to go. We can figure it out later."

"Okay." When it becomes apparent he isn't going to touch it, I grab the necklace and stuff it into my jeans pocket before it can ignite.

Sebastian takes me by the hand, and together, we run. We emerge from the alley to the blinding lights of car headlights. The engine revs, and we skid to a stop.

"Get in," a voice shouts.

Opal. I nearly laugh out loud as my eyes adjust, revealing Sebastian's silver Mercedes. The driver's door is open. Opal stands with one foot on the pavement, waving frantically for us to hurry. "Let's go. Let's go. Let's go."

Sebastian reaches the car first. He opens the back door, practically shoving me inside, before climbing in after me. "Drive," he shouts, slamming the door.

The tires screech, and we're thrown against the seats as Opal peels out. "Sunrise is just around the corner, so we have to get to the safe house, and fast."

I go rigid against the seat, my skin tingling. A large German Shepherd sits in the passenger seat beside Opal. He has the same red and black markings and red collar as my missing dog. "Jax?"

The dog tilts his head, tongue rolling out the side.

Opal laughs. "What did you call him? This is Turbo. He wandered into the Anima compound a couple days after you left and hasn't left my side."

Invisible bands squeeze my chest. "This is impossible."

"What?" Opal frowns.

"This is my dog. This is Jax."

Standing, he wags his tail as if to confirm what I've said.

"I don't understand," I continue. I lean forward, burying my head into his neck. Tears well in my eyes. "How did you do it, boy? You must have traveled two hundred miles." I look to Sebastian to see if he has any answers. He frowns.

Digging my hands deep into his fur, I continue to pet him, using my shoulders to wipe away my falling tears. "I'm so sorry I left you, boy. Will you please forgive me?"

"That is crazy." Opal peels around a corner, throwing us all to the right. "Come to think of it," she says, "Turbo, um, I mean Jax, did show up right after the Anima returned with your aunt."

I jerk upright as warm relief floods my body. "Oh, thank God. How is she?"

Opal's lips press into a grim line. "Those fuckers really did a number on her. She's awake and has been asking for you nonstop."

"When do I get to see her?"

"Soon." Opal twists her hands on the steering wheel. "The entire compound is scattering to a multitude of safe houses around the area. The clans were already at war, but the attack tonight is sure going to heat things up. The Anima compound is no longer safe, so everyone is laying low to regroup. Our particular safe house is a little farther out, but it should keep us hidden until Matteo comes for us."

Sighing, I lean back against the seat. "I'm so relieved he survived the transformation."

Opal's eyes meet mine in the rearview mirror. "Sort of."

Sebastian leans forward. "What do you mean?"

Averting her eyes, Opal licks her lips. "He can't transform."

"What?" I grab her headrest. "He's stuck as a bird?"

She nods. "It was so sad. Your aunt asked to see him, and he couldn't even talk to her."

After everything he went through to get her back, the thought hurts my heart. "Will my aunt be at our safe house?"

Opal shakes her head. "No. Matteo thought we would be more secure this way."

"But I need to see her."

She nods. "You will. As soon as the immediate danger has passed. That's what Matteo said. Or, at least what Delaney said he said."

"That's not good enough."

"Charlie." Sebastian places a hand on my arm. "It would be risky for you and your aunt to be together. As soon as the Queen recovers, she will be coming for you both."

"*Me* I understand. But why my aunt?"

"She will use her to control you. That's what Seraphina does."

I'm quiet for a moment, eyes traveling to his stomach. The skin has already woven back in place. The only sign that anything happened is the flaking lines of blood streaked across his skin. "Sebastian, what did she do to you?"

"Other than stake me, starve me, and bind me with silver chains?" He smiles tightly before looking out the window. "You don't want to know."

Maybe. But even more than that, I get the impression

he doesn't want to say. I drop it.

Jax stares out the window, ears twitching, as if he's listening for something. I still can't believe he's here. I mean, you hear about dogs traveling for miles to find their way home, but Jax didn't find me at home. How did he know where I'd be?

"What's the matter?" Sebastian asks.

"Nothing," I say, giving myself a little shake. "Why?"

His eyes narrow. "Your face. You're afraid."

"I'm just tired. And hungry."

He nods, but the expression on his face says he doesn't believe me.

I think back to the hidden photo he found of Aunt Rachel and Matteo, and the dog sitting between them that resembles Jax. A tremor jolts up my spine. There's something *wrong* about this in a way that it pulls the hairs on back of my neck on end. But for the life of me, I can't come up with an answer that makes sense — except for maybe one.

"Can Anima transform into anything but birds?" I blurt.

Opal and Sebastian frown.

"No," Sebastian answers. "At least, not that I've ever heard about."

Not at all helpful. But then again, Jax never had an aversion to sunlight, so he couldn't be a vampire.

You're being paranoid, Charlie, a voice whispers in my head. *You're dehydrated, hungry, and sleep deprived.*

"I'm going to close my eyes," I announce. The last thing I see before I do are the lines of concern etched across Sebastian's face. Even though I'm exhausted, after nearly dying several times tonight, I know there's no way I'm falling asleep anytime soon. Still, I'd rather sit here and fake it, then try to pretend everything is okay. I mean, these vampires have me so screwed up right now, for a second there I was actually afraid of my dog.

It's like the Queen said, tonight was just a battle — there's an entire war yet to come. And even though I'm free from her compound, I know, without a doubt, she's far from done with me.

Chapter
Twenty-Four

Nearly an hour later, miles after fleeing the city, the GPS on Opal's phone instructs her to make a right onto a barely visible gravel road.

The sky has lightened from black to inky blue, with streaks of lavender brushed across the horizon. Glancing out the window, Sebastian's brow furrows. "If I don't find shelter soon, the sun's going to fry me."

"Don't worry." Opal punches on the gas, kicking gravel behind us. "According to the map, the place is just ahead."

I know I should be relieved that we have somewhere to stay—at least for the day—but I'm unable to take my eyes off of Jax. I don't know what I'm expecting him to do—transform and kill us all? But if that was going to happen, wouldn't he have done it by now?

A thread of guilt winds through my ribs, pulling tight. What kind of terrible person suspects—even mentally—that their dog might kill them? I mean, I found him in a box when I was a kid. He's been my best friend ever since. Thanks to the vampires, am I now the kind of paranoid person who's going to suspect everyone of an ulterior motive? I mean, true, that kind of thinking might keep me alive, but it will also make me crazy.

The trees around us begin to thicken until they stretch over the car like a canopy. The road winds to the right, revealing a tiny, wooden cabin at the end. The sight of it tugs something inside me that makes me long for my own cabin. Several bird feeders sway from the branches of the surrounding trees. A small, rusted grill lays toppled on its side just beside the stone path leading to the door.

"This is it," Opal says, shutting the car off. "The Anima said the cabinets are stocked with canned goods, and there should be a couple bags of blood in the fridge for the bloodsucker." She wrinkles her nose.

"Wait here," Sebastian says, opening the door. "I'll go first and make sure it's clear. If I don't return, drive like hell."

Opal nods. Sebastian walks to the door and opens it. My muscles tighten when he disappears inside. When he reappears, waving us forward, I'm able to breathe again.

Jax jumps out the driver's side after Opal. He raises his nose in the air, sniffing a couple of times. He wanders to a tree and hikes his leg. When he's finished, he trots inside the cabin.

I almost laugh.

See, you paranoid freak? Your dog is a dog, after all.

Sebastian watches me from the doorway, the corners of his lips turned slightly down.

I shake my head to let him know nothing is wrong and follow them inside.

Sebastian shuts the door behind me and locks it. Next, he goes from window to window, drawing all the curtains closed. The cabin is set up much in the same way as my own. One large open room is a combination kitchen and living room. There are two doors on the right. One leads to a room with nothing but a set of bunk beds, and the other is a bathroom with a toilet seat so grimy you couldn't pay me to sit on it. A dust-caked bookshelf in the corner holds mostly yellow-paged books on bird and plant identification.

Opal climbs onto the kitchenette counter. Standing, she flings open the cabinets and roots inside. "Score." She withdraws a can and holds it above her head like a trophy. "Beefaroni."

"I will definitely take some of that," I say.

Sebastian makes a gagging noise.

When I turn to glare at him, he gives me a wink, warming the pit of my stomach. "You can get your own blood-aroni from the fridge there," I answer, pointing at the rust-pocked fridge humming in the corner. "Sorry this place didn't come equipped with a *Natalie* for you to suck on."

He arches an eyebrow, his grin amused. "Are you actually jealous I fed from that girl?"

"Of course not." I turn so he can't see the flush warming my cheeks. *Nope. No jealous, irrational, insecure girls here. Only a big fat liar.*

"Double score," Opal shouts, interrupting us. "There's a can opener." She looks at Jax, who sits on the floor, watching her with a tilted head. "Do dogs like SpaghettiOs?"

"He likes rabbit poop," I say. "SpaghettiOs will be like caviar to him."

"Cool." Opal jumps down to the floor. "Dinner—or

breakfast to normal people—is coming up."

A rattle at the window makes us all freeze.

Jax's hair lifts, as a low grumble emanates from his chest.

My breath catches in my throat. "Shit, not again."

Sebastian places a finger over his lips and moves soundlessly to the window, pulling the curtain back a fraction. His muscles visibly relax. In several quick strides, he walk to the door and opens it.

A crow flies inside, landing on the floor.

Jax stops growling.

The bird shakes, growing larger until Delaney stands before us. "Thank God, you are all right." She marches over to me, grabs me by the shoulders, and looks me over. "You're skinnier."

"They starved me."

Frowning, she nods. "Typical. Are you otherwise hurt?"

I shrug. "A little bruised, but nothing I can't recover from."

She pulls me to her, crushing me with a hug. I can feel my eyes bulge from their sockets. I mean, I knew Delaney was cool with me and all, but I had no idea we were at the hugging stage of our relationship.

Clearing her throat, she releases me. "Matteo will be pleased to hear it."

"How is he?" I ask. "And my aunt?"

"Your aunt is recovering well," she answers. "She is eating on her own, as well as moving a little. Like you, she was emaciated and drained of far too much blood. She still has a long road of recovery ahead of her. Normally Anima blood can heal minor wounds and illness, but Matteo was worried, with your aunt so unwell, that vampire blood might accidentally turn her. He decided to let her heal naturally."

My hands curl into fists. "I hate the Mentis," I say, my voice quivering.

Delaney presses her lips together. "She's asked for you. She refuses to answer our questions about your lineage until she speaks with you first—and that's not a safe option at the moment. Matteo won't leave her side. As you know," she says as pain pinches her face, "he cannot turn from his bird form."

I feel the blood drain from my face.

"Forever?" Opal asks.

Delaney shakes her head. "Nothing is certain. But it doesn't look good. Of course, the clan is just happy he is alive."

"How are they?" I ask.

"Scattered," she replies. "As expected, the Queen retaliated. An army of Mentis showed up at the compound last night and burned it to the ground."

I gasp, my chest tight with grief. I can't help but remember the laughing, singing humans who lived there, not to mention the Anima themselves.

"Not to worry," Delaney continues. "None of our clan or our human allies were injured. We'd moved everyone days ago. Which is why I'm here. Scattered the way we are, our people are hard to locate. This is by design, of course, as the Mentis have so far been unable to follow our trail. This is why I'm going to need you to stay put for a little while."

"Here? In this dump?" Opal groans. "How long?"

Delaney levels her with a gaze. "The Queen is on the

hunt. We all need to lay low until enough time has passed that we can regroup. I will visit you weekly to make sure you are safe and have provisions, as well as the latest news. Sebastian"—she turns to him—"the King is counting on you to keep the girls safe."

Sebastian turns to me. The intensity of his gaze brings heat to my cheeks. "You can trust me."

Delaney clasps a hand on his shoulder. "I was wrong about you. You've proved yourself a trustworthy and valuable ally."

He shakes his head. "You were right to be wary. This is a war, one I intend on making sure we all survive."

Delaney nods. "Me, too."

War. The word swells inside the cabin, until it rests heavy on my shoulders. My knees wobble. I sit on the couch, only to regret my decision when a cloud of dust billows up from the cushions. Fanning the dust from my face, I say, "I guess I was pretty dumb for thinking that, after we'd escaped from the Mentis compound, this would all be over."

Opal walks over to me and hands me an open can of pasta with a spoon sticking out of the top. She sits on the couch beside me with her own can.

"Not dumb," Delaney answers. Her lips twitch in an almost-smile. "That is why the Anima choose to ally themselves with humans. Your kind are so full of hope."

"Except humans aren't my kind, remember?" I say this as I shovel a bite of Beefaroni into my mouth. It's cold and easily the most delicious thing I've ever eaten. It takes almost all my willpower not to groan in relief.

"You're right." She nods. "It's easy to forget when you appear to be like any other young girl."

Taking another bite, I shrug. "I can't think of too many creatures that can survive off of Chef Boyardee."

"Speaking of creatures," Delaney says, shifting her gaze to Sebastian. "Is it true the necklace glowed when you held it?"

"Yes," he answers, his face expressionless. "But I'm sure it had to be a mistake—maybe a result of Seraphina wearing it."

Delaney shakes her head. "The necklace doesn't make mistakes. May I see you hold it?"

Sebastian hesitates, before finally nodding.

Setting my empty can on the armrest, I withdraw the necklace from my pocket. It smokes in my hand as a small flame runs along the tail. Frowning, I toss it to Sebastian. He catches it, the flames immediately going out as the snake's eyes glow green.

Delaney's own green eyes widen, blazing a little bit brighter. "I don't understand," she whispers.

"I don't either." He tosses the necklace to me, but I'm not ready. It hits the tip of my finger and falls onto Opal's lap. The golden snake lifts its head and stares at her, tongue flicking from its mouth.

"Okay," Opal says. "It's warm. Why is it warm? Please take the creepy jewelry away." She picks the necklace up by the tail, and the snake's emerald eyes blaze green. "Holy crap," she yelps, dropping the necklace on the floor. "It glowed. Why did it glow?"

"Does it glow for *everyone* but me?" I ask.

Frowning, Delaney scoops the necklace off the floor. The snake flicks its tongue at her, but the eyes remain dim. "Impossible... A human hunter and a Mentis..." Pocketing the necklace, she shakes her head. "King Matteo will need to know about this immediately. I'm afraid at dusk I must leave you. Stay safe, all of you."

"I will make sure of it," Sebastian says.

Delaney nods. "I know you will. Now," she turns her gaze back to Opal and me, "there are clean clothes in a suitcase in the closet. I cannot guarantee how well they fit. Remember, the Queen is looking for you. Do not leave the cabin unless absolutely necessary. I will return as soon as I can."

"How long do you expect us to wait here?" Opal asks.

"As long as it takes," Delaney replies.

"That's all well and good, but I kind of need to know what the glowing necklace thing means. It's really freaking me out."

"We will figure it out," Delaney says. Turning from us, she strides over to the window beside the door. Pulling back the curtain, she peers out into the waning night. "The answers we seek might be the only things that can save us now."

Chapter Twenty-Five

I'm not sure how long I drift in the depths of dreamless sleep before a frantic tapping sound startles me awake. Opal snores beside me on the couch, her head back against the cushion at an uncomfortable angle. Sebastian and Delaney sit at the table, both frozen and watching the door.

The tapping continues.

Jax uncurls himself from my side and runs to the door. He lets out a low growl.

The two vampires are on their feet in an instant. Delaney reaches the window first and peers outside. "It's a messenger. Let her in."

Sebastian opens the door, and a crow swoops inside, transforming into a light-skinned woman with blond hair before her feet even touch the ground.

"What news do you have?" Delaney asks.

The woman smiles, exposing her fangs. "The Mentis have followed our false leads. They've completely lost the trail."

Delaney grins. "This is excellent news."

She turns to us. "I must leave you now while I have the chance. I will return as soon as I'm able. Remember, stay hidden."

"Wait." Opal stands. "You're leaving *now*?"

"I'm afraid so," she answers. "With the Mentis chasing their tails, there is no better time to travel undetected." Her face softens when Opal scowls. "Do not worry. I will return soon." She turns to Sebastian. "Be on guard."

"You can count on it," he says.

Delaney nods. "See you soon." She follows the other vampire out of the cabin, shutting the door behind her.

Sighing, Opal opens a closet and rummages through boxes. "So we're just stuck here?"

"For now." Sebastian pulls back the window curtain and peers outside. His eyes narrow as he stares into the night. I have no doubt he can hear every cricket chirp in a ten-mile radius.

"It's like we're in prison," Opal mutters.

The irony of being trapped in another cabin is not lost on me, and I chuckle.

Quirking an eyebrow, Sebastian looks at me.

I shrug. "It's not so bad. I mean, it's no Mentis Farm, but at least we have each other, right?" If only Aunt Rachel were here to fill the house with her soap making, I'd never criticize our boring life ever again. Just thinking about her squeezes my heart.

"We have Life," Opal cries, holding the board game above her head. "Now it's a party. I get to be the green car." She eyes Sebastian. "Prepare to have your ass handed to you, bloodsucker. I mean, you're dead, so really you've already lost."

He snatches the box from her hands and frowns at the picture. "As much as I've already saved your life, I'm pretty sure winning this game will be no challenge at all."

She grabs the box back. "Then it's on. I'll set the board."

I chew on my lips as I watch Opal sort the money and game pieces. The memory of the snake's blazing green eyes replays in my mind. If Rachel and Matteo are not my parents, does that mean—? I shake my head, to free the question before it can form. *Ridiculous, Charlie.*

A hand touches my arm, dislodging me from my thoughts. Sebastian stares at me, brows furrowed in concern. "Charlie, are you all right?"

"I will be," I say, hugging myself. "When this is over."

"That's if it will ever *be* over," Opal says, shuffling cards.

"Even if it never ends," Sebastian says, "we've survived." He tugs me to him, folding me against his chest. He rests his chin on the top of my head. "And I mean to keep you safe."

My heart flutters like a bird against the cage of my ribs. I don't want him to let go. "Because I can give you answers."

"No," he says, chin tickling the top of my head. "Because I care about you. *Both* of you. We're in this together. It doesn't matter who our parents are or aren't. *We* are family now. We have been brought together for a reason."

And just like that, I feel it in my gut—the familiar weight that lets me know what he says is true. "Wait? This from the guy who doesn't believe in feelings or love?"

He shrugs. "Stranger things have happened. I don't think anything is impossible now."

"Family." Opal snorts. "A vampire, a hunter, and a whatever-the-hell Charlie is. Who would have thought?"

"Not me," I mutter, entwining my fingers around

Sebastian's neck. I want to stay safe within his arms forever, where no monsters can ever touch me. It's funny to think several weeks ago I had no idea vampires existed. And I never considered the possibility that I was anything but human. I wonder if I'll ever know what it is I am—or if it even matters.

Opal makes a gagging noise. "Gross. If you keep this touchy-feely stuff up, I'm going to leave and take my chances with the Mentis." She pats the board game. "Are you two ready to taste defeat?"

Reluctantly, I ease out of Sebastian's arms and take a seat at the table.

Sebastian sits beside me. He picks up a plastic car and eyes it with a grimace. "What is the objective of this game?"

"To have the best life possible," Opal answers, spinning the dial in the center of the board. "Whoever has the biggest house, the best job, and the most money wins."

He sets his car on the Start square. "And what stands in our way?"

She shrugs. "Fate, I guess. It's all the luck of the roll."

"No vampires?" he asks.

Opal makes a face. "No."

"Monsters?"

"No," she repeats.

"War?"

She huffs. "No."

Grinning, he leans back, stretching his long legs in front of him. "I think I'm going to like Life."

BONUS
CONTENT

from risen

Death and the Farm

I do not know much about laundry, but I can only guess how much trouble the human slaves will have getting all this blood out of my suit. Though as much as I bleed, it's not like they don't have experience. My tie is nothing more than a shredded piece of fabric around my neck. My shirt collar, once white, is crimson. Several buttons are missing, revealing my chest.

The silver chains around my neck eat through my skin, digging into my shoulders. The agony of it burns through me like fire, not that I dare let it show. To display weakness in front of the Queen only guarantees more punishment. And my days spent in chains greatly outnumber my days spent without them.

A leash is attached to the restraint around my neck. Frederick, the Queen's favorite, holds the end of the leash and walks me into the throne room.

A handful of vampires lounge inside the room, but I only have eyes for one. Sitting on her golden throne, Queen Seraphina smirks when I enter. The glittering ruby crown sits on her golden curls. A red silk dress leaves nothing to the imagination. She strokes a fluffy white dog perched on her lap. The creature growls at me as I draw closer.

God, I hate that dog. I fight the urge to growl back. Instead, I jam my hands in my pants pockets and raise my chin to meet the gaze of my Queen, doing my best to appear bored. After all, it's not like I haven't been here before.

Seraphina chuckles, flashing her fangs, nearly twice the size of my own. "Well," she says, tickling her fingers beneath the dog's chin, "if it isn't my naughtiest pet."

I dip my head. "Your Highness."

She drums her long, manicured fingernails on the golden arm of her throne. The clicking sound makes me clench my jaw. "Frederick tells me you've been neglecting your disposal duties."

"Frederick would tell you anything to remain your favorite. I think he's only jealous because he knows how much you favor me." I flash Frederick a smile.

Scowling, he snaps the leash hard enough to make me stumble.

"Hmm." Grinning, the Queen sets aside the dog and stands. The silk dress ripples along her body. With the creature scurrying after her, she saunters toward me, raising a slender finger and running it down my cheek. "It's true you are one of my most beautiful pets. But I can't afford to have a pretty dog who won't obey his master." She gives me a light slap.

Reflexively, my hands ball into fists. "My allegiance is to only you, my Queen. I am now, and will forever be, your humble servant."

"As you should." The humor drains from her face. "Don't forget for a moment it was I who rescued you from a life of slavery with those wretched Fae."

Standing before her with chains wrapped around my neck, it almost makes me laugh that she doesn't recognize the irony of her words. "And for that I am eternally devoted to you." The Queen always reminds me of how much luckier I am now that I'm with her, but with no memory of my life before a year ago, I wonder if that's actually true. How do I know with any certainty that every glimpse into my past that she's given hasn't been a lie? It means I have to trust her. Except I can't.

She presses her red lips into a pout. "Then why have you been so disobedient, my pet?" She holds out a hand, snapping her fingers.

Frederick opens his jacket and removes a wooden stake from the interior pocket. He places it into her waiting palm. She takes the sharpened end and traces it down my neck, hard enough to draw blood.

I inhale but am careful not to make a sound.

"Might I remind you of what happens to those who refuse to do their disposal duties?" She rests the stake in the hollow of my throat.

"And what proof is there to back up these claims?" I ask through clenched teeth.

"Bring in the girl," she calls out.

Seconds later, the throne room doors bang open. Two vampires drag a young girl, who can't be more than thirteen, into the room by the arms. Her dark hair hangs in tangles around her red face. Her chest heaves with sobs as tears trail down her swollen cheeks.

Damn it. My shoulders slump. *So much for saving her. Not sure why I thought I could when I can't even save myself.*

"Tell me something, my pet," the Queen demands, digging the stake's point into my neck. "Did I or did I not ask you to dispose of this human?"

It's true. While vampire blood cures all illnesses, the Queen refuses to harvest from a sick human. She finds tainted blood beneath her. Instead of curing them with her own blood or waiting for them to heal, she orders them killed. And while I might be a vampire, I still don't understand the reasoning behind killing without a purpose. Maybe it's a hint of the humanity I've forgotten. Maybe it means I'm not as lost as I think.

It's times like these I wonder why I can't be like the rest of Seraphina's pets and merely do what I'm told without question. Without conscience. Continuing down this path will only lead to my true death, so why can't I stop myself from defying her?

"I beg your forgiveness, my Queen, but I did as you asked," I say, wincing. "I released her."

The Queen's silver eyes flash with fury, and for some reason, this makes me happy. I guess I really do have a death wish. At least if I die I will finally escape this miserable existence.

"Wrong. I did not ask you to *release* her." Snarling, she jabs the stake farther. "I asked you to dispose of her."

"But we have doctors to handle that for us."

"I didn't ask a doctor to dispose of the girl, Sebastian. I asked you. To make it plain, it was a test of your loyalty. And you failed miserably." Pushing farther still, she penetrates my windpipe with the tip of the stake. My lungs burn, desperate for air that doesn't come. Black spots appear around the edges of my vision, and I gasp for breath. A warm ribbon of blood flows from the wound. She's killing me. And while it might not be my true death, it doesn't make it any less painful.

"F-foolish of me," I rasp. "Miscommunication—not disobedience."

The Queen gives the stake a final push, piercing through my throat. I fall to my knees. She releases the weapon, but the damage is already done—I'll be dead soon. Tilting her head, she grins, and I can see the pleasure in her eyes. She thoroughly enjoys watching me die. "You're very lucky I am a patient queen. You see, Sebastian, I use moments like these as learning opportunities. And you *will* learn not to disobey me."

She walks to the girl and smooths her hair.

The child whimpers.

Seraphina *tsk*s. "Poor thing. Your death could have been fast and easy. Now I must set an example." She turns. Despite my blurred eyesight, I can feel the heat of her gaze on me. "Feed her to the dogs."

The girl screams as my vision fades to black. I open my mouth to protest, only to fall forward on the cold concrete. As I drift away on icy waves of death, Seraphina's voice echoes in the darkness.

"You will not fail me again."

• • •

Screaming, I open my eyes. That's how it is, every time I die. I'm not sure if it's the memory of my death or what's on the other side that causes me to wake in terror. I jerk upright on the leather couch inside my room. I take several deeps breaths before I'm able to calm the tremors shaking my body. Reflexively, my hands go to my neck, only to find smooth skin where, only hours before, a stake had protruded.

Chest heaving, I swing my legs over the couch's cushions, my feet pressing to the marble floor, and hang my head beneath my knees until the flood of nausea passes. The Queen says, as superior creatures, we are blessed to be vampires. But this existence of torture and servitude feels far more like a curse. Beads of sweat prickle along my scalp. Sometimes I wonder if I wouldn't be better off staying dead.

"Ah, good. You're awake."

I jerk upright to find Frederick leaning against the brick wall. There is no light, but my enhanced vision makes it easy to see the smug look on his face. "Screw you," I mutter.

He smirks, one hand buried in his pocket, the other holding a shirt. He throws it at me, and I snatch out of the air mid-toss. "Get yourself cleaned up. We have a mission."

I rake my fingers through my sweat-damp hair. "What kind of mission?"

"A retrieval. Should we encounter any problems, the Queen wants you to resolve them." Frederick grins, exposing his fangs.

Of course she does. I fight to say as much as I whip off my jacket and unbutton my torn, bloody shirt. "Is that all?"

His smile dissolves. "This is an important mission, one that could be the deciding factor in the war."

My fingers fumble with a button. The war. I try to look nonchalant. "How so?"

"We may have a lead on King Matteo's lost human *love*." He spits the last word as if it leaves a bad taste on his tongue. For good reason, too. Love is a human weakness, which is exactly why Matteo is an unfit King.

"And you want me to kill her?"

"No. The Queen wants Rachel alive. We don't know, however, if she's alone. If we find anyone with her—a new family, perhaps—you'll do what I tell you to do."

"Of course." Standing, I withdraw a folded tie from my dresser and drape it around my neck. As much as I hate the Queen's missions, I hate dying even more. This most recent death, it was a bad one. Swallowing, I can still feel the frantic pull in my chest when I struggled for my last breath.

Seraphina finally won. I will do what I'm told.

When I finish tying the knot at my neck, I leave it looser than normal. My throat already feels tight enough.

"The Queen also wants you to search Rachel's residence for any proof that her son with Matteo survived." Frederic folds his arms. "I told the Queen this mission is too important for you to botch, but she demands you be given the chance to redeem yourself." His lips peel back in a snarl. "I don't have to remind you how unfortunate it would be for you to let Her Highness down again. I doubt she would be so forgiving a second time."

I bow my head in acknowledgment. The memory of the girl screaming as they dragged her away echoes inside my mind. I suppose if I had the sentimentalities of a human, I might be upset. Instead, I push the memory away and focus on the task at hand. I'm more committed than ever to staying in line. I do not wish to die again.

"Good." Frederick turns for the door, only to pause. "I'm glad to see you finally coming around, Sebastian. Fail again and—"

"I know," I cut in. "The Queen will give me my true death."

Frederick barks out a laugh. "Death? Oh no, naive boy. If you disappoint the Queen one more time, what she has in store for you would be infinitely worse."

A Cabin in the Woods

I park the Mercedes behind Frederick's black Porsche Cayenne. I know I'm late, but I couldn't help but take my time. I've never been so far from St. Louis before—at least not that I remember. It's so rare I'm given the opportunity to leave the Mentis compound, I want to drag out every second of my freedom.

I open the car door with a sigh, hating to end my solitude. And if I am to be completely honest, I'm not looking forward to whatever it is Frederick wants me to do.

The smell of pine and dirt is a welcome change from the garbage and exhaust smell of the city. The Queen forbids us from dressing casually. What I wouldn't give for a pair of boots right now—and maybe a pair of jeans. Given my limited memory, I'm not sure if I've ever owned a pair, but they do look comfortable.

My dress shoes crunch against the gravel. That and the screams from the cabin ahead are the only sounds to puncture the silence. The door is nothing more than wooden splinters. Frederick and Marcus stand in the flood of light, their backs to me. I can't see who they're talking to, but from the whimpers I assume the cabin's occupants are female.

God, I hate when they cry. Not that I can blame them. Two small humans against three vampires? They don't stand a chance.

Doesn't matter. I give myself a shake, pushing the troubled feeling deep inside me. Fulfilling my duties to the Queen is my only objective. I will not die again.

Frederick waves a hand over his shoulder, cutting through my thoughts. "Sebastian, come."

With a sigh, I step into the small cabin. "Yes, Frederick?"

The vampire holds a compelled woman by the arm. She's a frail thing, thin with sharp joints. She sways in his grip, her unfocused eyes staring into the night. With long blond dreadlocks hanging to her waist, this must be the famous Rachel—the human who destroyed a King. It doesn't make sense. Why risk a throne, and your very existence, for something so pathetic?

"We're taking Rachel to the Queen," Frederick says. "I want you to stay behind and search the cabin. Rachel claims the boy is dead. See if you can find evidence to prove or disprove the claim."

A whimper draws my attention. Huddled against the wall is a girl. She shrinks when I look at her, her large eyes glassy with fear. Wisps of black hair have escaped the bun on top of her head and frame her narrow face. There's something about her—a familiarity I can't quite place. Arching an eyebrow, I ask, "What about the girl?"

Frederick shrugs. "She has no value. Eat her. Kill her. I don't care. Just make sure she's disposed of."

"I didn't agree to a disposal."

"You don't have to. Consider it an order." Frederick slides his glasses back into place. "Meet us in St. Louis when you are through." There's no mistaking the warning in his tone. *This* is the mission I've been assigned, the one I cannot fail.

The frightened girl can't be more than seventeen. Even as terrified as she is, I can't help but notice she's beautiful. With glossy black hair, flushed cheeks, and red lips, she exudes health, making her a prime candidate for farming. To kill her is a complete waste. Still, I know this order has nothing to do with blood and everything to do with my loyalty. I frown. "I'll take care of it."

Frederick and Marcus exit the cabin with Rachel in tow. Minutes later, car doors slam and an engine roars to life.

The girl makes a strangled sound that pulls at my chest. This won't be as easy as I want it to be. Then again, nothing ever is in this existence. Still, there's no reason the girl has to die right away. I have to search the cabin and find proof of Rachel's surviving son. To do that, I could use her help.

I take off my jacket and drape it across the couch. Turning to the girl, I ask, "What's your name?"

Glaring at me, she presses her lips into a thin line.

"All right." Again, nothing is ever easy. With a sigh, I sit on the edge of the couch. "Maybe I can guess. Sarah? Michelle? Olivia? Am I getting warmer?"

"Screw you."

Her response startles me, making me chuckle. I've never met a human brave enough to insult me to my face, and I can't help but admire her a bit for it. "Interesting name. Is that German?"

Ignoring me, she faces the pile of wood that used to

be the cabin door. "My dog." Her small fingers clench into trembling fists. "What the hell did you do with my dog?"

Like I would do anything with a dog. Given Seraphina's fondness for the creatures, I'd be happy to never see one again. I shrug. "What would I want with a disgusting animal? Your dog ran off."

"No. I don't believe you. Jax would never go anywhere without me." She starts for the door.

I snatch her arm and whirl her around. She swallows hard. "It doesn't matter what you believe. You're not leaving this cabin unless I say so." My patience has a limit. Even if she could help lead us to Rachel's son, I'm not about to let this girl jeopardize my life by escaping.

"I'd like to see you stop me." She slams her fist against my chest, immediately wincing.

Stupid girl. I sigh. "It's almost cute how you think you stand a chance, but you're only wasting my time." She needs a reminder who is stronger. With my hand clamped around her arm, I drag her across the room and thrust her onto the sofa with more force than needed. I might feel bad if she wasn't such a pain in the ass. "Sit."

She stands. "No."

Flames of anger burn to life inside my gut. *Really, really stupid girl.* My eyes narrow. "You're starting to annoy me."

"I don't see how that's my problem."

Maybe disposing of her won't be so hard after all. "I'm happy to show you." Looking around, I snag a handkerchief off the top of a nearby laundry basket. "Hands behind your back."

"Screw you," she says again, even as her face contorts with fear.

I grab her wrist and wrench it behind her back. If I don't do this, I'll be killed again. Her pathetic attempts to struggle do nothing to slow me down as I take her other arm and tie them together. Pushing her onto the couch, I grab another scarf and wind it around her feet, securing the ends in a knot.

"Now," I say, standing, "let's try this again. *Sit*."

She struggles for a couple of minutes until her shoulders fall slack. Tears well in her eyes. "So how are you going to do it? Stab me? Shoot me?" She shudders.

If only she knew how lucky she is, that her first death will be her only death—a final escape from this existence. "You are all so afraid to die. You spend your entire lives dreading it—fighting it. If only you would learn to embrace death for the gift it is, you would have nothing to fear."

"Easy to say when you're not the one tied up."

"Maybe." I incline my head. "Can I be honest with you?"

She glares back.

"Thank you." I chuckle. I can't help it, there's something about her defiance that makes me like her. "I don't really enjoy killing like the others. It's messy and I just don't understand the thrill the others get."

She blinks several times before speaking. "Is that what those men are going to do to my aunt?" Her voice trembles.

So Rachel is her aunt. The girl is family, then, just not important enough to be of value in Seraphina's eyes. "Truthfully?" I rake my fingers through my hair. "I don't know. I try to avoid court politics."

"Court?"

I shake my head. "Nothing you need to worry about." No point in getting her bogged down with information if she only has hours to live. The image of the young girl I failed to save, of her staring back at me with lifeless eyes, twists my stomach . I quickly push it away. When the time comes, I hope she fights back. At least that will make it easier.

Unless I find verification of the existence or death of Rachel's son, as he would be crown heir to the Anima throne.

The thought makes me pause. Rachel's son is the real prize here. I'm sure if I brought the Queen the evidence she wants, she wouldn't give a care to whether I let some pathetic yet surprisingly spirited girl live.

I turn a small circle, taking in everything from the sun-faded curtains to the threadbare furniture. While my life may be one of servitude, at least the Mentis have modern furnishings. "What I do need from you is the proof the Queen is looking for—proof that your aunt's son is dead."

She snorts. "If she had a living son, don't you think I would know about it? There is no *proof* of anything here."

"Maybe. Maybe not." I pull open a nearby closet, wrinkling my nose at the musty smell of dust and mothballs. Yanking coats off their hangers, I throw them onto the floor. Next, I run my fingers along the top shelf, searching for a death certificate, an address—anything. "If you did know something, I'd be willing to make a deal with you in exchange."

She shifts on the sofa. "What kind of deal?"

I stop rummaging. "Your life in exchange for information about your cousin's whereabouts."

"I already told you, there is no information. My cousin died when he was a baby. End of story."

"We'll see." I lift a cardboard box off the shelf and dump

wool hats and gloves onto the floor. Grunting, I kick them aside. The cabin may not be big, but it's crammed with junk. "This is going to take a while."

"Great," she mutters. Settling back against the couch, she squeezes her eyes shut.

I open the bifold pantry doors and grab a bag of something called sour cream and onion chips. Sniffing, I nearly gag. *How can humans eat such garbage?* I set the bag aside and continue my search.

Behind me, the girl begins to hum. The familiarity of the sorrowful tune makes me jerk upright. It's not a tune I recognize from this existence, which means it can only be from the one I can no longer remember. A slight tremor spirals down my spine. It's the first solid clue from a hidden past I've been desperate to uncover. I whirl around. "What is that?"

She stops humming, and just like that, the connection to my past is severed.

"No." Fighting to steady my hand, I return a jar of tomato sauce to the shelf and move toward her. "That song—it's familiar. What is it?"

"I don't know." She shakes her head. "It's a song my aunt used to hum when I was little."

"Interesting." Anticipation coils through my chest, making me struggle not to appear too eager. I'm certain if this girl knows I'm desperate for something, she won't give it to me. "I don't remember anything of *before*. But this song—I know it. I'm just not sure how. Do you know the name?"

"No. Aunt Rachel never said. It was just something she did when I was upset."

Like she is now—because of me. Exhaling loudly, I sit in the chair across from her, resting my elbows on my knees. She squirms away from me, which does nothing to ease my guilt. "Scaring you was never my intention."

"Yeah, well, you're not really great at making friends."

This makes me crack a smile. "I have no desire to make friends."

"That's good, because you suck at it. I've only known you for a short while, and I hate you."

I laugh. "Fair enough. But I'm afraid you're stuck with me until I find something. The Queen won't like it if I return empty-handed."

"Sucks for you, because there's nothing here."

"No. That would suck for *both* of us." Which is exactly why I need to forget about my missing memories and focus on the task at hand.

She shifts uncomfortably beneath the weight of my words.

"Where would someone hide something of value in this hovel?" I stand, my gaze sweeping the room before settling on the bookcase. What I see there tickles another memory buried deep inside my brain. As if swept in by a breeze, the notes of a stringed instrument waft through my head. "Is that your violin?"

"Yes."

The violin and the song—they're connected. The certainty of it propels me forward. I retrieve the case and flick open the latches. Withdrawing the instrument by the neck, I turn it over in my hands. The wood feels like glass. I guess there's only one way to know for sure. "You know how to play?"

"No. It's for decoration."

Always with the sarcasm, this one. I scowl.

In turn, she rolls her eyes. "I've taken lessons through the homeschool co-op since I was four. I can play."

A thread of hope winds around my chest and pulls tight. "The violin—that song you were humming—could you play it? Maybe then I could remember where I've heard it."

She looks like she might argue but shrugs instead. "Sure. You have to untie me."

I hesitate. "I will, but you have to promise not to run. I *will* catch you, and it won't be pretty."

"Fine."

Setting aside the violin, I untie her restraints. She rolls her shoulders several times, making no secret of how uncomfortable she is. If she's trying to make me feel bad for tying her up, it works.

I grab her violin and hold it out to her. "Remember, do not run."

Scowling, she snatches the instrument. "This is a waste of time."

"Maybe."

With a huff, she places the violin beneath her chin, then runs the bow across the strings and makes minor adjustments to the pegs. Swallowing hard, she closes her eyes and begins to play.

Just like before, the familiarity of the tune tugs at something buried inside me, only it's stronger this time. Because I know with a certainty deep within my bones that when I heard this song before, it was played on a violin.

My hands ache from their white-knuckled grip on the couch cushion. Muscles tense, I brace myself for whatever will rise to the surface—a voice, an image, a memory. Only it never comes. All that I have is the certainty this is rooted in my past—and while it's barely a clue at all, it's more than I had before.

And it's because of the dark-haired girl before me. I open my eyes. She sways to the music, her brow creased in concentration. What is it about this small, large-eyed human girl that she's able to bring to the surface the very things I've spent my existence trying to dig out? And why do I get the uneasy feeling our meeting is more than a coincidence?

She keeps her eyes closed after drawing the last note. The only sound filling the cabin comes from her labored breath. When she finally does open her eyes, she levels my gaze with her own.

We stay like that for several heartbeats, staring into each other's eyes. For a moment, I fully expect to fall into the depths of her dark-brown irises and drown. This girl is unlike any human I've ever encountered—and that makes her extremely dangerous.

It takes me several tries before I'm able to speak. "You play beautifully."

Shrugging, she zips the violin back into the case.

"That was *exactly* how I remember the song—played on a violin."

"So?"

"*So.*" I stand. "It's the only memory I have from before." She doesn't know it, but she's given me a gift, one I can't possibly repay.

She shakes her head. "I don't understand."

"When I was human," I explain. "And you don't know

the name of the song?"

"I already told you I don't. It's just something my aunt used to hum." She hesitates. "*Hums.* It's something she hums and will continue humming." She locks eyes with me, daring me to argue. "Because I will save her."

Poor stupid girl. The only person she should be concerned about saving is herself. "You know that's not going to happen, right? The most you can hope for is your own survival—and that's provided you help me."

Her hands ball into fists. "You're wrong."

There's that defiance again. While adorable, it's going to get her killed. "If that's true, what is your plan?"

She opens her mouth to answer, but the words don't come.

I feel for her, watching her struggle to form a plan. I've been there myself, desperate for a way to break free of Seraphina's grip, only to be killed for it over and over again. Now I know there is no beating the Queen. "You can't fight them," I say. "No one can."

Outside the cabin, off in the distance, a dog barks. I turn toward the sound.

As I do, she pushes off the wall and launches through the open door. Before I can shout, the blood in my veins heats to a boil. My vision sharpens, my lips peel back into an involuntary snarl, and a pulsing ache throbs inside my chest.

I *need* blood.

God help that stupid girl. As much as I wanted to save her, there will be no stopping myself from drinking her dry now. It's the last rational thought I have before primal instinct takes over. The desire to feed is a relentless beast I must sate. Running from the cabin, I'm careful to not chase her down too fast. I want to savor the hunt. I want to enjoy every second of her warm blood trickling down my throat.

This could have been avoided, but she did the one thing she wasn't supposed to do. She ran. And by doing so, she awoke the bloodlust.

Blood and Thorns

The girl tears recklessly through the pine trees. Thorns and branches pierce her skin. The coppery-sweet scent of her blood drives me into a ravenous frenzy. Hunger consumes every inch of my body, driving me forward as I stalk her from the shadows. Her frantic heart beats erratically, giving me an easy trail to follow. Every so often, she whimpers like a wounded animal, making me desperate for every last drop of her blood. I won't be satisfied until I bleed her dry.

She pauses in a small clearing. Fragments of moonlight patch the forest floor around her feet like broken shards of glass. Chest heaving, her breath a loud whir as she gasps for air. I'm almost disappointed the chase is over. *Almost.*

But at least now I can eat.

I slam into her back, knocking her onto the ground.

She screams in fear. It only makes me want her blood more.

I open my jaws, bringing my fangs an inch from her neck.

Don't do this. A voice — my own — breaks through the haze clouding my mind.

I shake my head, confused and so goddamn hungry. But then there's the girl beneath me, terrified, and I know I have to fight the bloodlust for her sake.

"Don't yell," I say. I can almost taste the pulse throbbing in her neck. I bet her blood is sweet, like cherries.

She opens her mouth, and I lock my hand over it. I'm barely hanging on as it is. Another scream would push me over the edge. Even now, my lips curl back, exposing my fangs. Closing my mouth, I swallow hard. "I'm trying really hard not to kill you right now. But when you run and, even worse, scream, I lose control. Can't be helped."

She sniffles. Moonlight reflects off her eyes. The monster within wants to watch them dim as I drink the life from her body. Removing my hand from her mouth, I curl my fingers into her hair and jerk her head back, exposing the jugular. The artery quivers beneath her skin.

Maybe just a taste.

I bring my face to her neck. Even through my hunger I can tell something isn't right. A foul sap-like odor brings me back to my senses. My muscles strain against my will, wanting to defy the weak hold my brain has on my body. *Very clever, Rachel.* "She made you wear that disgusting oil. Even it can't help you if you don't stop making those noises. It's taking every ounce of strength I have not to eat you."

"No," she whispers.

Her fear is intoxicating. A shudder ripples down my back. I don't know how long I can hold off.

"No," she repeats and places a hand against my cheek. A blaze of light spills from her fingers the moment our skin connects. An invisible force slams into me, knocking me onto my back.

As I writhe on the forest floor, the force suffocates me while a series of images flashes through my mind. A throne made of branches. A crown of flowers. People dancing. Laughing. And a beautiful woman with long golden hair extending a hand toward me.

I open my eyes with a gasp.

Several yards away, the girl sits in the mud, eyes unfocused and swaying to a breeze that isn't there.

I push myself from the ground to sit. "What did you do?"

She shakes her head, her gaze falling into focus. "What did *you* do?"

"That wasn't me." Climbing to my feet, I move away. She's definitely not human, so what the hell is she? "I'm going to ask again, what did you do?"

She stands, knees wobbling. "Nothing."

"Not nothing. First the song and now this. I saw things— flashes—memories?" I sweep a hand through my hair. "I don't know."

She takes a step backward.

"Don't do that." The last thing I need is her drawing out the monster again. "If you run, it triggers the bloodlust. Besides, you're not going anywhere until you tell me what the hell is going on."

"I don't know." Her face crumples like she might cry.

Too many thoughts tangle inside my head. Who I am, where I came from—somehow this girl is the key to remembering my existence before death, before torture, before *vampires*. Maybe she's even my way out of servitude to the Queen. I stride toward her. "You have to do it again."

"What?" Trembling, she clambers away until her spin bumps the tree behind her. She curls her fingers into the bark.

"Who *are* you?" I stop inches in front of her, still struggling to control the hunger instinct within me. If she continues to let fear rule her, I'll give in and she'll die. "How do you know these things?"

"I've already told you, I don't know *anything.*"

"Do it again." I grab her hands and place them on my face. Her fingers are cool against my skin. "I'm sorry for scaring you earlier. I mean, it's actually your fault because you ran, but none of that matters because you did something just now and I need you to do it again."

"I'm sorry," she says with a quiver in her voice. "I don't know what I did or how I did it."

I touch her wrist. "Maybe if you just concentrate." Of course she doesn't want to help; she's terrified of me. But maybe I can show her I'm more than the obedient monster Seraphina wants me to be. "Please."

Emotions war across her face. "Let go of me." She jerks her hand out of my grip. "I can't do...whatever it is you want me to do."

I stare at her, my hands empty and at my sides. "What *are* you?"

"Not a monster like you," she snaps.

Her words hit me like a slap, especially since I'd just been thinking the same thing. I'm quiet for several heartbeats before replying. "I'm not a monster—I'm a vampire. And I wasn't always. I think—I almost remembered—" I'm not sure. My home? My family? There's no way to know unless this strange girl unveils more. Whatever it was, it wasn't the Mentis, and that's enough.

Her bottom lips trembles. "Are you—are you going to eat me?"

There's the question of the hour. "Honestly?" Folding my arms, I lean against a nearby oak tree. "I have no idea what to do with you. I don't even know what *you* are."

"Stop saying that. I'm human."

I laugh. "If you're human, then I'm Santa Claus."

"Screw you." She raises her middle finger.

At least I know she's feeling better. "Why make this more difficult? Why not just tell me what you are?"

"I already told you, I'm *human*. Even if I wasn't, why the hell would I tell you anything? You think I owe you answers?" She snorts, and it's the most adorable sound I've ever heard. "I'm the one who doesn't know what's going on. You're one of the monsters, remember? You helped them kidnap my aunt, you made my dog run away, and you tied me up. I hate you, and I don't owe you a damn thing."

I can tell already, she's going to make me regret not eating her. "You can hate me all you want, but I'd strongly advise against running. You have a choice here. You can run, trigger my bloodlust, and I'll probably end up killing you and ruining a perfectly good suit. Just so you know, I'll only be upset about the suit. Option number two, you can come back with me to your cabin, and maybe we can find a clue about what you are and how you were able to do that…thing."

"Have you not been listening?" She pinches the bridge of her nose. "Spoiler alert. I'm human. And I can't do any *things*."

I narrow my eyes and she shivers. "Then we go back to the cabin and prove it."

"What about my aunt?"

"There's nothing we can do now." My jaw is sore from clenching. I work it side to side to loosen the muscle. I don't have much experience with humans, but if they ask as many questions as this one, then I'm slowly coming around to the idea of disposal. "She's well on her way to the farm."

"What the hell is the farm?"

"Every question you ask brings us closer to daylight." I lace my words with warning. "And time is something we can't waste. If you want me to help you, you need to help me."

She licks her lips. "Why the hell would you help me? You're one of the monsters."

I fight to keep from flinching. If she had any idea how much that word stabbed like a knife, she'd never stop using it. "I have no memories of my human life. I'm the only vampire I know who can't remember my past." I look away. "But then you hummed that song and it stirred something inside me—a sense of familiarity I've never experienced. When you touched me I saw something—just for a second. A woman with golden hair. And all I could feel was her love. I wonder—I wonder if she is my mother. I always assumed my mother was dead—but now I'm not so sure." I search her face, knowing I won't find the answers there but looking nonetheless.

Her expression softens. "I'm sorry. Whatever it is you think I can do, I can't."

Her apology is surprisingly genuine.

"Would you be willing to try?" I ask. "My Queen plans

to use your aunt as a pawn in a centuries-old war. I cannot help you myself, but I could take you to someone who might be able to."

"You would do that?"

"Yes." Even though it means risking my life and more torture than I can imagine. That is the price of hope. And I have to believe the Mentis aren't all I have.

"Fine." She raises her chin in defiance, as if I can't see the rest of her trembling. "I'm going back to the cabin to look for nothing—because that's what we'll find."

She takes several steps the wrong way, forcing me to clear my throat.

"What?"

I point in the opposite direction. "Your cabin is that way."

A flush burns up her neck, igniting her cheeks. Spinning on her heels, she trudges through the woods.

Even if I wasn't a vampire with heightened speed and agility, catching up to her short-legged strides would be easy. I lift several branches and vines out of her way as we walk.

"I'm not helpless," she snaps.

"Maybe not, but you're not exactly graceful. The way you're scratching yourself up—I might have some restraint, but I'm still a vampire. You keep slicing open your skin and I might as well be walking beside an all-you-can-eat buffet."

She says nothing, only casts me a sideways glance. Still, I note she maneuvers more carefully around branches and sticker bushes.

We walk the rest of the way in silence. Occasionally I'll grab her arm when she drifts in the wrong direction or pull her to the side before she tumbles into a hole. I tell myself it's because I don't want her triggering the bloodlust. Deep inside, though, a part of me—the weak part, Seraphina would say—doesn't want to see her get hurt.

It's that part that's going to get me killed—for good.

Before long, the light from the cabin spills through the trees. The girl goes ahead, entering the cabin first. "Jax?" she says, spinning a small circle. "Here, boy."

The dog doesn't answer. Because of my abilities, I already know nothing else breathes inside these walls and there is no musky scent of fur nearby. I don't want to tell her this, though. She looks disappointed enough.

She whirls around, her eyes accusing. "Did the other vampires do something to my dog?"

"If your dog isn't here, then he ran off. Animals have a natural aversion to vampires. They're smart, unlike humans."

She glares at me. "You don't understand. Jax won't let me take a shower alone. There's no way he wouldn't be here if he was okay."

"My kind do not eat dogs." I make a face. "We're not disgusting Anima."

"A what?"

"You really don't know anything, do you?" I'm almost envious. For her entire life, she lived with no knowledge of vampires, clans, or the war raging in the shadows, threatening the existence of vampires and humans alike. What I wouldn't give to forget, just for a day.

Grunting, she snatches a piece of splintered wood from the floor. The scent of Rachel's struggle against Frederick and Marcus still hangs in the air. "Then tell me something. I read books, so are the stories true? Can I kill you with this?" She raises the stake in the air.

"You?" I smirk. It's cute, really, how fearless she can be—even if it makes her incredibly stupid. "Never. A more skilled hunter, maybe. And only if he or she caught me off guard. Care to guess how many times that's happened? Now put that down before you hurt yourself."

She throws it at me. I easily bat it off to the side. "The sooner you quit wasting time, the sooner we can find what I'm looking for."

With a sigh, she flops onto the couch. "There's nothing to find here. I know, because I've already searched."

I arch an eyebrow.

She shrugs. "I was curious about my parents. Aunt Rachel doesn't talk about them unless she's had more than three glasses of wine. I thought maybe I could find a photo or something. There's nothing."

"We'll see." After what she did to me in the woods, I'm willing to believe in the unlikely. The question is, where would Rachel hide something of extreme value in this dingy shack? I stride to the bookshelf in the corner and pull out a book. I flip through every page before replacing it and grabbing another.

"This is dumb," she mutters. Standing, she walks into the kitchen, pulls open a drawer, and sorts through the contents. "We should be going after my aunt. What are we even looking for?"

"Evidence." I take another book and shake it open. "I was ordered to find proof your aunt's son is really dead. But I'm more interested in anything that explains *what* you are." I meet her eyes with my own.

I hear her pulse skip a beat. "Of course he's dead. He'd

be here if he wasn't, right?" She slams the drawer shut. "And why do you keep calling me a *what*? I'm human. What else could I be?"

Now that's a dangerous question. I shrug. "Vampires aren't the only creatures to look human."

"I don't believe you," she says, her voice pinched.

I don't blame her for not trusting me. I *did* try to eat her. Instead of arguing, I replace the book and lean against the shelf. "What is your name?"

She licks her lips. "Charlize. But nobody calls me that."

"Then what do they call you?"

She hesitates. I can tell it's costing her something to reveal this little bit. "Charlie."

"Charlie." I test it out, liking the way her name feels rolling off my tongue. "I don't remember my human life, but I do remember where I was when the Mentis clan found me. I was being held captive, and it wasn't by humans."

Her eyes widen. "Who was holding you captive?"

"Not a *who*. A *what*." I hold her gaze long enough to see her fear flash through them. And I'm glad for it. Fear makes you cautious. And we'll both need to be careful now that we're pawns in Seraphina's war.

Dusk

Sleep — another human weakness. At least it is according to Queen Seraphina. Just another reason vampires are superior and destined to rule mankind, she'd say.

Standing in the doorway by the bookshelf, I can't help but feel a little envious watching Charlie's chest rise and fall in a steady rhythm from the couch where she's sprawled. What must that be like, to drift away from the present to a world unknown? To escape everything without truly leaving?

Death is the closest I come to sleep. But where I wake up screaming in terror, Charlie's relaxed face and easy breathing exude peace.

Maybe that's why, with time running out, I'm hesitant to wake her. I don't want to be responsible for dragging her from her dreams back to this hellish nightmare — especially after what I found searching the cabin while she slept.

Or it could be something else. Purple twilight filters through the window, giving her already pale skin the illusion of glowing. She sighs through parted rose-colored lips. Tendrils of black hair, free from her hair band, curl around her ivory neck. I can't remember the last time I've noticed such things about a human.

Maybe I don't wake her because she reminds me, in a world of horrors, that beauty still exists.

Still, as much as I want this moment to linger, time is our enemy. "Charlie."

Her eyes flutter. "Aunt Rachel?" she murmurs. "What time is it? The sun's not even up yet." She rubs her eyes with the heels of her hands.

"Actually, the sun is just setting."

Gasping, she whips her head around. Her large eyes meet mine. I can almost feel the heat of her gaze as it travels down my neck to open buttons of my shirt, revealing my chest.

Her cheeks blaze crimson. "Dang it." She yanks the hair band free from the limp bun at her neck. "I didn't mean to fall asleep." She combs her fingers through the tangled knots, re-winds her hair, and secures the band around the bun at the top of her head.

Her grooming habits are just one of many things about her that fascinate me. "I decided to let you be," I say. "It is my understanding that humans need rest. My kind do not sleep. While the sun kept me confined to the bedroom, I was able to search every inch."

"That's my room." Standing, she stretches her arms above her head. "There's nothing to find in there."

"Actually—that's not true." I watch her for any sign that she already knows what I'm about to show her, but she genuinely appears confused. What I found will change everything she thinks she knows about her aunt, her world, even herself. I almost can't bring myself to share it with her. At the same time, what I found might also save her life. "Come see."

She snorts. "Impossible. You think I don't know what's in my own room?"

"Then there's nothing to be afraid of."

Pushing her shoulders back, she follows me into the bedroom. "Fine. Show me this *thing* you think you found."

Unlike my room, useless clutter takes up most of the space. Aside from the bed, the stuffed animals and ceramic horses have no practical purpose that I can decipher. This is something else I will never understand about humans— their love of impractical junk. How would you kill an enemy with a plastic cat? Ridiculous.

I lead her to the nightstand beside the bed and pick up the framed picture. A very young Charlie and Rachel laugh from a riverbank. They both look so happy, which leaves no doubt as to why Rachel hid the truth. I only hope Charlie is strong enough to take it. I lower the frame. "Rachel is very cunning."

She makes a face. "This is your big clue?"

I tap the photo. "Sometimes the best way to hide something is in plain sight."

"Are you kidding me?" Anger laces her words. "That photo doesn't prove anything. And now we've wasted an entire day looking for nothing while Aunt Rachel is God knows where with monsters."

I cringe. *That word again.* As if I need any reminding. "Vampires," I correct her. "And you're right, *this* photo doesn't prove anything. But the one behind it does." I turn the frame over and unclip the back, tossing it aside. From there, I tilt the frame toward her and reveal another photo behind the first.

She inhales sharply. "What is that?"

I remove it from the frame and hand it over to her. "I was hoping you could tell me."

Eyes wide, she stares at it. The edges are slightly bent, but the color is still glossy and sharp. The photo was taken at night, dimming the colors. Even so, there's no mistaking Rachel, though she appears much younger than when Frederick took her away, recognizable with her dreadlocked hair, beaded necklaces, and long skirt. She sits on a park bench beside a man. He wears flip-flops, and his jeans have holes in the knees. His long, dark hair is braided and falls over his shoulder. His rich skin tone, sloped nose, and dark eyes hint at a Hispanic heritage.

While I've never seen the King of the Anima in person, I've heard enough about him to know he's the man in the photo. He has his arm wrapped around Rachel's shoulder. Her head rests in the crook of his neck. Matteo's other arm holds a baby dressed in a blue onesie. Rachel holds an identical baby dressed in pink. On the ground, resting between their feet, is a large black and tan dog.

"I don't understand," she says, voice nearly a whisper. Goosebumps ripple across her skin. The photo slips from her shaking fingers and lands on the floor. "I've never seen this man before in my life."

I want to touch her, to give her some comfort, but I know I don't dare. As terrified as she is of me, I don't want to upset her even more. "I'm afraid this photo is the proof the Queen was looking for."

"What proof?" she spits. "It's just a photo of my aunt and some guy I don't know."

Holding her gaze, I pluck the photo off the floor. I know how she feels. I was there last night, struggling to make sense of my own memories and past. Now it's her turn to decipher the truth. Only, unlike me, the evidence makes things abundantly clear. "Charlie, you know exactly what it means."

Hugging her arms to her chest, she drops onto the bed. "You think Aunt Rachel is really my mother?"

I let my silence be my answer.

Her head falls into her hands. She takes several deep breaths before answering. "I don't believe it. She would have told me."

I tuck the photo inside my shirt pocket. "Not if she thought she was protecting you—because of who your father is."

She looks up. "My father is dead."

"Your father is *undead*. His name is Matteo, and he is King of the Anima Clan."

She bursts out laughing, startling me. "Of all the things I have heard and seen these last twenty-four hours, that is the most insane."

"Sometimes the truth isn't what you expect."

She stands. "My father can't be a vampire. That's crazy. What would that even mean for me? I'm human, aren't I?" She holds her arms in front of her, as if to examine the blood beneath the skin.

I glance at my own arms, my skin not much darker than hers. "It would make you a dhampir," I reply. "It's nothing to worry about. Dhampirs are rarely gifted with anything more than heightened sight and smell. Though I've never heard of a dhampir doing what you did to me last night."

"I didn't do anything," she says, her words laced with venom.

"Denying it won't make it less true."

She swallows hard. "Even if what you say is true—and it isn't—why does your queen care about Aunt Rachel or me?"

"Because of who your father is. War is brewing, Charlie, and you both are leverage in a very deadly game."

"What does that mean?"

I sigh. As much as I would love to protect her from the darkness of my world, if she stands any chance of surviving, I can't hide the truth from her. "It *means* she is going to use your aunt as bait to lure Matteo into an unfair fight. She will do the same to you if she knows your connection."

She swallows several times before speaking. "What do I do?"

"You?" While imagining Charlie flipping Seraphina the bird makes me chuckle, I know the Queen would enjoy nothing more than to torture the determined spirit out of Charlie until only a husk remains. "Nothing. When I return to the Queen, I will tell her I found nothing and killed you to save her the trouble."

Pushing her shoulders back, she lifts her chin. "Then what? I just sit here in the cabin and pray your freaky buddies don't kill Aunt Rachel?"

I make a face. "No. You can't stay here; it's not safe. If *my freaky buddies* found you, others can, too."

She folds her arms. "Maybe I should take my chances with the others."

Glaring at her, I lower my voice. She has no idea. "You called my kind monsters. There are others who make us look like kittens."

This causes her to pause. "You got a better idea? It's not exactly as if I'm flooded with options."

"I told you I would take you to someone." Even if I have to risk everything to do it. "Matteo. He can protect you. And he's the only one who might be able to rescue Rachel." I walk to the open doorway and peer out into the darkness. Nothing moves, but then again, the animals can sense vampires from miles away, just as we can them. "The Anima Clan would kill me on sight, but I can get you as close as I can. Grab your things. We have to leave before others arrive."

"Are you kidding? Your entire plan is to drop me off with another vampire? As in, another one of the monsters that *eats* people? What could possibly go wrong?"

I turn from the door, leveling her gaze with my own. "Like you said, you don't have a lot of choices. You want to call the police and explain all of this to them? You go right ahead and see how fast they place you in a mental institution. I offered you a solution that will save your life—and possibly your aunt's. It's the best I can do, so if you're going with me, you need to hurry."

With a huff, she moves, stuffing a backpack full of clothes, a phone charger, and various other belongings. Lastly, she takes a vial from the kitchen and tucks it into her pocket.

I can smell the stench of the garlic from where I stand. Raising an eyebrow, I say, "I already told you that stuff won't actually keep me from biting you."

Shrugging, she zips everything in place and hoists the bag over her shoulder. "It doesn't matter. I would smother myself in garlic if I thought it would piss you off."

"While that would be amusing, we're running out of night." Especially since garlic does nothing to ward off vampires. We only have our speed to help us get ahead. "Are you ready to go?"

She licks her lips. "Why are you helping me?"

The question unsettles me, particularly since it's the same one that's been running through my mind from the moment I chased her in the woods. "I don't want you to think what I'm doing is some sort of noble undertaking. I need you alive, Charlie, for selfish reasons only. That thing you did in the woods—I need you to do it again. This gap in my memory, it's haunted me my entire existence. Not knowing is its own type of prison. And I think you might be the one to set me free."

And while that might be the truth, there's something else that draws me to her. What it is is undefinable, and that frustrates the hell out of me. Seraphina would call it weakness, which is exactly why I need to bury whatever feeling Charlie gives me deep inside. I want to protect her, but how can I do that when I can't even protect myself? In a world of war, blood, and vampires, a weakness of any kind will only get you one thing—dead.

ACKNOWLEDGMENTS

First and foremost, I want to thank Rianne, who continues to inspire me with her creativity and imagination. Bub learned pretty early in life she has to share me with the laptop, but I'm so grateful she always knows when to pull me away for some Yoshi's Woolly World. I know I've said this before, but no matter how many books I write, you will always be my most amazing creation.

This book wouldn't exist if not for my amazing agent, Nicole Resciniti. Thanks for being not only the most amazing advocate on the planet, but also my friend.

Special thanks also go to Liz Pelletier for giving me the chance to bring my undead vampires to life. Thank you to Candace Havens for your brilliant editorial insight. Heather Riccio, thanks as always for making me feel like family. And last, but not least, thank you to Hannah Lindsey, Curtis Svehlak, Melissa Montovani, and the rest of the amazing Entangled Staff who supported me during all stages of this book.

And to my sisters from another mister, much love to Shawntelle Madison and Sarah Jude for always having my back.

Thank you as always to my amazing critique partners, Brad Cook, T.W. Fendley, and Jennifer Lynn. You always provide the perfect amount of coffee, critique, and crazy. Love to you all.

Grab the Entangled Teen releases readers are talking about!

Assassin of Truths
by Brenda Drake

The gateways linking the great libraries of the world don't require a library card, but they do harbor incredible dangers.

And it's not your normal bump-in-the- night kind. The threats Gia Kearns faces are the kind with sharp teeth and knifelike claws. The kind that include an evil wizard hell-bent on taking her down.

Gia can end his devious plan, but only if she recovers seven keys hidden throughout the world's most beautiful libraries. And then figures out exactly what to do with them.

The last thing she needs is a distraction in the form of falling in love. But when an impossible evil is unleashed, love might be the only thing left to help Gia save the world.

Haven
by Mary Lindsey

Rain Ryland has always been on the outside, looking in, and he's fine with that. Until he meets Friederike Burkhart. She's not like normal teen girls. And someone wants her dead for it. Freddie warns he'd better stay far away if he wants to stay alive, but for the first time, Rain has something worth fighting for, worth living for. Worth dying for.

By a Charm and a Curse
By Jaime Questell

Le Grand's Carnival Fantastic isn't like other traveling circuses. It's bound by a charm, held together by a centuries-old curse, that protects its members from ever growing older or getting hurt. Emmaline King is drawn to the circus like a moth to a flame… and unwittingly recruited into its folds by a mysterious teen boy whose kiss is as cold as ice.

Forced to travel through Texas as the new Girl in the Box, Emmaline is completely trapped. Breaking the curse seems like her only chance at freedom, but with no curse, there's no charm, either—dooming everyone who calls the Carnival Fantastic home. Including the boy she's afraid she's falling for.

Everything—including his life—could end with just one kiss.

Zombie Abbey
By Lauren Baratz-Logsted

1920, England

And the three teenage Clarke sisters thought what they'd wear to dinner was their biggest problem…

Lady Kate, the entitled eldest.

Lady Grace, lost in the middle and wishing she were braver.

Lady Lizzy, so endlessly sunny, it's easy to underestimate her.

Then there's Will Harvey, the proud, to-die-for—and possibly die with!—stable boy; Daniel Murray, the resourceful second footman with a secret; Raymond Allen, the unfortunate-looking young duke; and Fanny Rogers, the unsinkable kitchen maid.

Upstairs! Downstairs! Toss in some farmers and villagers! None of them ever expected to work together for any reason.

But none of them had ever seen anything like this.

entangled teen

an imprint of Entangled Publishing LLC